To my dream sisters

who believed in me

when I didn't believe in myself.

AUTHOR'S NOTE

Susan Sexton is the maiden name of Susan Court who works in an independent school in London. She has published a number of academic works, particularly on English Language, under the name of Susan Court. This is her first novel.

PREAMBLE

Sometimes we feel an affinity with a certain place on this earth which is beyond rational explanation. That is the way it has been with me and Simon's Town. I first visited it as a student over forty years ago and loved it then. I returned to it as an adult in 1989 and felt a surge of passion for the place. It was not only the beauty of the locality on the western shores of False Bay, but also a sense of timelessness, of reaching back into the past which captivated me.

In 1990 I returned to Simon's town with my family and I felt particularly drawn to Admiralty House, a gracious building, the oldest in Simon's Town, at the northern end of the town near where the old tollgate used to be. I was fortunate to be able to visit the house and as I strolled through the commodious rooms I felt the stirrings of a story within me. The following pages tell the tale.

The choice of L'Ourmarin for the setting of the remainder of the story belongs to the realm of fiction itself. I had decided that Charlotte would fall in love with a son of a Huguenot from the Franschhoek Valley. I imagined the house with a lake in front of it, flanked by oak trees with towering mountains behind it. While I was researching background material for the book I came across an illustrated volume on Cape Dutch houses and there was a picture of the house I had imagined but never visited! The original seventeenth-century name was L'Ourmarin, after a village in France which was staunchly loyal to the Protestant faith and this is the name which I have chosen for the home of the le Rouxs. Nowadays the farm is called L'Ormarins and is the home of Johann and Gaynor Rupert who have turned it into a thriving wine estate.

Water's Edge, which is the locale for much of the action of the novel, and in a sense, features as a character in the story, is a small cove between Seaforth Beach and Boulders Beach on the outskirts of Simon's Town. It was here that our family holidayed in the early nineteen-nineties in a cottage belonging to Mike and Anne Munnik. Our family is now spread all over the world but whenever we go to Cape Town we always make a point of visiting Water's Edge which is a reminder of special family times. It has recently taken on a significant resonance as it is the place where my son proposed to his wife Danni in September 2009.

I have done a good deal of research into the history of the Cape Colony in an attempt to reconstruct life in general and Simon's Town in particular as it was in the Cape 1815, and some of the characters who form part of the background tapestry like John Osmond, Dr James Barry and Lord Charles Somerset are authentic. Lieutenant Henry Keppel did ride a tandem down the Trappe between Kalk Bay and Fish Hoek but this event took place some years after my story. Rear Admiral Sir Jaheel Brenton who was Naval Commissioner of the Cape of Good Hope in 1815 was responsible for building the Mast House and Sail Loft. I have allowed Admiral Lacey this achievement although the Sail Loft was used as a church after St George's church was washed away in a storm in 1822 and it is still used as a church today.

The first owner of L'Ourmarin was the Huguenot Jean Roi who by 1694 had already planted more than 4000 vines on the slopes of the Groot Drakenstein Mountains. The le Roux family are my invention.

I wish to emphasise that the characters of the novel are entirely fictitious. Any resemblance to any known persons is entirely coincidental.

Susan Sexton
Ryde
Isle of Wight
August 2010

CONTENTS

TITLE PAGE i
DEDICATION iii
AUTHOR'S NOTE iv
PREAMBLE v
ACKNOWLEDGEMENTS ix
GLOSSARY xi
PROLOGUE 3
1. Simon's Bay January 1815 7
2. The Promise 13
3. The Lovers 20
4. To Cape Point February 1815 24
5. The Two Oceans 28
6. The Engagement 34
7. The Ball 38
8. Disgrace 44
9. Escape 50
10. Respite 56
11. Discovery 62
12. Revelations 67
13. The Confession 70
14. Recovery 74
15. A Truce 80
16. The Plot 85
17. L'Ourmarin 88
18. Paul 92
19. The Waters of the Bay 101
20. Sam 105
21. The Funeral 113

22.	Samuel Joseph	115
23.	Drama at Home and Abroad	120
24.	Reunion	128
25.	The End of the Beginning	133
26.	Conflict at Water's Edge	138
27.	A Significant Journey	143
28.	An Unforeseen Conflict	148
29.	Decisions	154
30.	From Franschhoek to Cape Town	158
31.	An Unexpected Meeting	163
32.	The Homecoming	167
33.	The Wedding	171
34.	Confrontation	174
35.	Reflections	178
36.	Caroline	181
37.	Finding a Purpose	184
38.	Restoration	189
39.	A Visit to Water's Edge	193
40.	A Strange Meeting	197
41.	A New Direction	200
42.	Another Farewell	204
43.	An Eventful Return	209
44.	The Shadow of Death	213
45.	A Promise to Help	218
46.	The Slave Auction	221
47.	A Proposal	227
48.	The Slave Ship	233
49.	A New Strand in the Tapestry	239
50.	Father and Daughter	244
	EPILOGUE	247
	BIBLIOGRAPHY	249

ACKNOWLEDGEMENTS

This novel would not have come about without the assistance of a number of people who have supported me in this project over twenty years and I would like to express my sincere gratitude to the following.

The late Professor Pryce-Lewis walked me through the village of Simon's Town in 1991, pointing out the original Simon's Town buildings and the Dockyard Wall and checked my description of the bridle path to Cape Point. I owe particular thanks to the staff of the Simon's Town Museum, especially the curator, Cathy Salter Johnson, who, not only answered my many questions, but also made available the resources of the museum for my research.

My friend Tessa Scheppening has been unfailingly enthusiastic from the beginning to the end. In the early days she gave me two books to sustain my interest – on Lady Anne Barnard and Cape Dutch houses – both of which have been valuable in my research. Debbie James hosted me on my research trip to Cape Town in August 2008, ferried me back and forth between Simon's Town and Cape Town and around the Constantia Valley in the search for the original site of Wittebomen. Megan and Roger Bagshaw provided accommodation in Simon's Town and also facilitated my return visit to Admiralty House.

At L'Ormarins (L'Ourmarin in the book), I was entertained by Gaynor Rupert, wife of the present owner Johann Rupert, who graciously approved the project. Jo-Anne Mettler, public relations officer, arranged a delightful day when I was able to view the estate especially the wine cellar where the cellar manager Neil Patterson explained the method of wine-making in 1815.

Jackie Loots was an invaluable support with not only her own book *Echoes of Slavery* but several of the articles that she has written and her prompt, informative replies to my many questions.

Boet Dommisse clarified my understanding of the history of the Royal Navy in Simon's Town through his books and his responses to my questions.

The Cape Wine Academy supplied essential information on the wine cultivars grown in the Cape in 1815.

The Royal Geographical Society in London provided early nineteenth-century maps of Cape Town, Table Bay and the Cape of Good Hope.

Sophia Kingshill who proof-read the manuscript made useful observations about the anachronisms, particularly in the dialogue.

Felicity Fair Thompson, who in the writers' course which I attended on the Isle of Wight in August 2006, helped me to see the strands that hold the book together.

My cousin, Christine Lacey, read the first manuscript, and encouraged me to continue.

Christopher Reps and my cousin Jerry Lacey contributed their information technology skills, with particular regard to the photograph of the house in Portland Place and the map of Simon's Town.

The books and other sources which I have consulted I have included in the bibliography.

My children, Misty, Richard and Penny have supported me in many ways and have understood how important this project has been to me.

GLOSSARY

Dutch or Nederlands was the official language of the Cape until the British Occupation in 1806 and continued to be used for official purposes until the twentieth century.

During the period of my novel Afrikaans would have been developing as a language out of Cape Dutch borrowing vocabulary from other languages including Malay, Portuguese and indigenous African languages and developing its own grammar, morphology and spelling.

I have used Dutch for forms of address but elsewhere have used Afrikaans vocabulary and spelling as it probably would have been used by the ordinary folk.

Ag – interjection – Ah! Oh! Alas!
Agterkamer – back-room of a house
Baas – master; 'boss'
Baba – baby
Ballasmandjie – bushel basket – for carrying grapes
Burger – citizen
Fynbos – natural shrub occurring in the Western Cape of South Africa
Goeie More – Good Morning
Ja – yes
Jonkershuis – young man's house on the estate where the eldest son of an estate owner would set up home
Juffrouw – lady; miss

Kêrel – fellow
Kleintjie – little one; baby
Klomp – crowd; number; lot
Kom – come
Lekker – nice
Mantoor – man in charge of slaves, usually a slave himself
Meisie – girl
Mijnheer – Mister; gentleman; sir
Mevrouw – Mrs; lady; madam
Moeder – mother
Mooi – pretty
Nee – no
Nooi – mistress; lady of the house
Ouma – grandmother
Perlemoen – abalone; mother-of-pearl
Rix dollar – unit of currency in the Cape at the time
Skelm – rogue, rascal
Tot siens – au revoir; good-bye
Voorkamer – front room in the house; a drawing room
Vrouw – woman; wife
Walvis – whale

HEIRS OF WIND AND WATER

Home of Lord and Lady Granville in Portland Place, London.

PROLOGUE

London
August 1814

'I won't marry him!' Charlotte exclaimed, her cheeks flushed, her blue eyes flashing and her chest heaving with pent-up emotion.

'Yes you will!' said her father in his Royal Naval officer's voice, which in the world of men commanded instant obedience. Edward Lacey had the upright bearing of his ancestors and piercing blue eyes which were accustomed to scanning the horizon. On this summer evening he stood with his back to the marble Adam fireplace in much the same position as he had over many years at sea at the helm of a ship. He had to admit to himself that he found a crew of sailors easier to manage than his spirited daughter. The languid summer air which wafted in through the huge sash windows was at odds with the drama being played out in the elegant drawing room of Lord and Lady Granville. His daughter turned her back to him to look out onto the carriages below which were clip-clopping along Portland Place to Regent's Park.

'Papa, I can't believe that you are speaking to me like this when you've brought me up to have opinions of my own and have listened to what I have to say.'

'Because I'm also a realist and you need to get married. You will have no position in society unless you do.'

'But why do I have to marry Lord Lascelles? He doesn't appeal to me at all!'

'Because he's the most eligible man in England.'

'In what way is he eligible for me?'

'Apart from his title, he's got a huge estate in the north of England, a townhouse in Grosvenor Square and a sugar plantation in Jamaica!'

'That doesn't make him attractive to me! He's proud and self-opinionated as far as I'm concerned! And he can't talk about anything other than horses!'

'You're being romantic and silly, Charlotte. You've done the season for two years now and you haven't liked anyone to whom Sophie has introduced you. Who on earth do you think is going to marry you if you turn him down?'

'I don't care if I get married or not!' said Charlotte. 'And I'm certainly not going to marry some arrogant bore who owns half of England and the West Indies.'

Sophie Granville, Edward's sister-in-law, the sister of his deceased wife, who had been relaxing on a chaise longue in the opposite corner of the room, chose this moment to stir herself and glide into the conversation. The feathers atop her ornately dressed hair quivered as she spoke.

'You see now, Edward, the results of your laissez faire upbringing of Charlotte. You've been far too indulgent with her. She's spent too much time reading inappropriate literature like Mary Wollstonecraft.'

Charlotte turned from the window and challenged her aunt. 'Mary Wollstonecraft had some very sensible ideas about the education of women. Why should women be educated any differently from men?'

'Because, child, they have very different roles to play in society. And a woman's role, your role, is to be a wife and mother.'

'Mary Wollstonecraft was a wife and mother!'

'Eventually, yes, but you obviously haven't read her biography written by her husband, Godwin. The woman had no morals at all. She had affairs, children out of wedlock, and probably an affair with another woman. She even tried to commit suicide by throwing herself into the Thames, but some well-meaning passer-by pulled her out, unfortunately. I was a young woman when all this became public knowledge and nobody could take her seriously after that.'

Charlotte shook her head. 'I'd rather jump into the Thames than marry Lord Lascelles or any of his ilk!'

'Don't be ridiculous, Charlotte,' Edward said, with a shade of alarm in his voice.

'Papa, please don't make me marry someone I dislike,' Charlotte said, running over to her father and grasping his tanned, capable hands in her small, white ones. 'Life would be intolerable!'

'I think that you will find life even more intolerable if you remain a spinster all of your life,' said Edward in softened tones. 'There will be no future for you here in London. You'll languish back in Everhurst.'

'Well, then, I'll come to the Cape with you!'

'Don't be absurd, Charlotte! I can't possibly allow you to do that! There's a war on, you know – that's why I've been called out to the Cape Colony to take charge of the fleet. And even though Napoleon's exiled to Elba, it's not over yet. He still has a lot of popular support and the Cape is of considerable strategic importance.'

'Oh Papa, please!' Charlotte pulled her father round so that he couldn't look at Sophie. 'It would be so exciting. No-one knows us in the Cape, so I wouldn't have a social reputation, and Ellen could come as well to keep me company.'

Admiral Lacey considered carefully. He loved his daughter dearly, and the truth was that he hated leaving her alone when he was away at sea. 'I'll think about it,' he said.

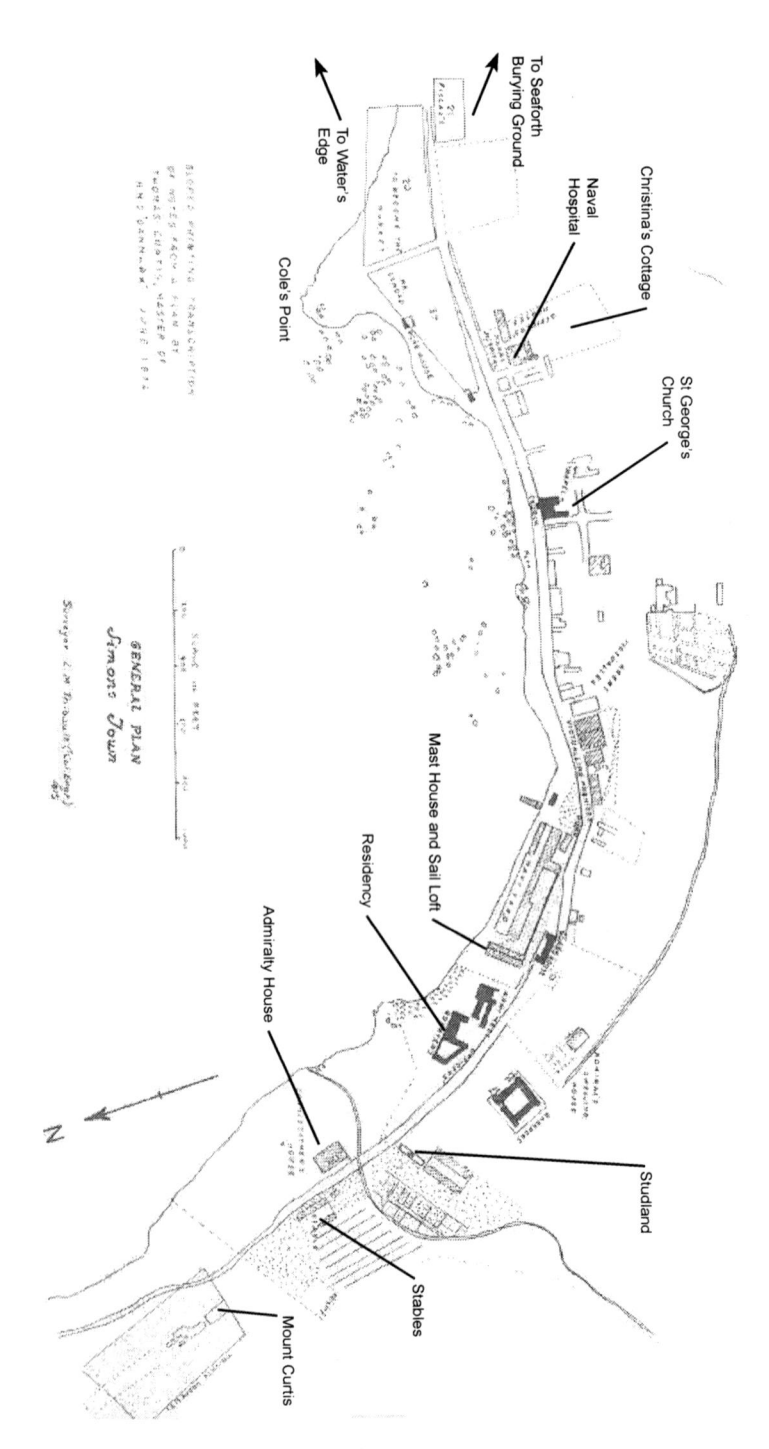

Map of Simon's Town in 1815 based on Thibault's map of the same year. Reproduced with kind permission of the Simon's Town Museum.

CHAPTER ONE

Simon's Bay
January 1815

It was the nineteenth of January 1815 and Charlotte woke up early with a delicious tremor of anticipation. It was her twentieth birthday, and her cousin John du Rand was expected on the fleet which was due to arrive in Simon's Bay. She climbed out of the four-poster bed and ran through to the room that led off her bedroom in Admiralty House. It faced east and from here she had an uninterrupted view of Simon's Bay and the further reaches of False Bay. The tall ships, which had come in during the night, rested on the water like gigantic gulls. Somewhere among them was the *Argonaut* which had her cousin on board. The light had a luminous quality like the perlemoen shells that she and Ellen had collected on the beach at Water's Edge. It was all so different from the lowering skies and drizzle of England. She could hardly believe that she was here in Simon's Bay in the Cape Colony. She felt as though a whole new chapter in her life was beginning. Her reflections were interrupted by a tap on the door.

'Ellen? Come in.'

Ellen, Charlotte's maid, burst in like an energetic puppy. Tendrils of glistening chestnut hair had escaped from her mob-cap. She carried a pitcher of hot water to the washstand.

'Mornin', ma'am.' Her voice had the warm tones of the

Hampshire countryside where she had been born. 'Happy birthday,' she said as she fumbled in the folds of her pinafore for a small parcel which she handed to Charlotte. Charlotte opened the wrapping to reveal a mother-of-pearl pendant which shone with the colours of the morning.

'It's beautiful, Ellen! Thank you.'

'I thought you'd like it, ma'am. I made it myself.'

'That makes it very special, Ellen,' Charlotte said as she hung the pendant around her neck. 'A special beginning to a special day. The fleet's in!'

'Yes, I know, ma'am. Sam told me this morning while I was getting your hot water in the scullery. He saw the ships when he was out exercising Champion on Seaforth Beach. The Admiral has told him to get him ready for Sir John when he arrives later today. He said there's fifteen sail out there.'

'Fifteen? I thought that I had counted twelve.'

'There's another three just entered the mouth of False Bay, ma'am. You probably couldn't see them from your window,' said Ellen, walking over towards the deep-set window where the drapes rustled in the breeze. 'Look! There they come!'

Charlotte followed Ellen's outstretched hand to see the three frigates sailing across False Bay. The south-easter filled their sails, which bulged like proud peacocks as their prows cut cleanly through the waters.

'You're right, Ellen,' Charlotte said, picking up a telescope from a table near the window. 'I've borrowed this from Papa,' she said as she scanned the water. 'I think that's the *Argonaut*!' she cried. 'Yes, it is! I can see the figurehead. That's John's ship. He's here, Ellen, he's here!'

Charlotte's eyes met Ellen's in undisguised excitement. Her cousin John, a lieutenant in the Royal Navy, had been a midshipman under Lord Nelson. He spent most of his life at sea and she had not seen him for five years. In her mind he was the medieval knight, the embodiment of all the heroic virtues – honour, loyalty, bravery and physical prowess – and he was handsome as well.

The three ships joined the others of the fleet and dropped

anchor in Simon's Bay. The sails were furled and the shouts of the crewmen rang across to the land. It would take a little while for the disembarkation to take place and for the first of the rowing boats to move away from the giant hulls of the mother ships to bring the new arrivals onto dry land.

'Oh Ellen, how I'd love to run down to the jetty to meet him when he arrives!'

'Well ma'am, you know that you can't. It's just not done, and the Admiral would be very vexed, I'm sure,' Ellen said primly.

'I get so exasperated with all this protocol – how one is expected to behave,' Charlotte said, turning away from the window with an impatient swirl. 'This is why I left England. Sometimes I feel like jumping onto my horse and riding away as far and as fast as I can.'

'I understand, ma'am. Sometimes I feel like doing that myself. But we women don't have any choice. In the meanwhile let's get you ready for the day. What would you like to wear?' Ellen asked, opening the doors of a highly polished mahogany wardrobe.

'The blue and white sprigged muslin. Papa bought it for me especially to wear on my birthday.'

'A good choice, ma'am, it suits you well,' Ellen said as she helped Charlotte to slip into the dress.

It was true. The blue matched Charlotte's eyes and the soft material accentuated the youthfulness of her frame.

'You know, Ellen, I haven't seen John since I was fifteen.'

'Yes, I know, ma'am,' Ellen said. She took out the silver hairbrushes and Charlotte sat at the dressing table. Ellen gathered up the golden strands with a blue ribbon so that the curls cascaded down into the nape of Charlotte's neck.

'His arrival is the best birthday present that I could imagine. It's going to make such a difference to my life. I'll be able to really explore now he's here. Papa never has the time. He's too busy to go gallivanting, as he says. Any trip that he makes has to have a purpose, like official business in Cape Town.'

'Well, we haven't been here long really, have we, ma'am – six weeks, is it?'

'Almost exactly, because we arrived on the eighth of December last year, and there was all the bother of settling in and preparing for Christmas, let alone recovering from that gruelling voyage. I wouldn't like to go through that again.'

'Neither would I. I don't know which is worse – being becalmed as we were two months out of Portsmouth or being caught in that storm off Cape Point. I thought then that we'd never see dry land again.'

'I'll never forget those huge seas when all you could see was a wall of water rising above you.' Charlotte shuddered. 'I still don't know how it was that we didn't capsize.'

'Fortunately we didn't,' Ellen said pragmatically. 'The Good Lord must have been watching out for us. But you have been out and about a bit, ma'am, with Sam. Only yesterday you went riding to the whaling station at Miller's Point.'

'I know, Ellen, but it's not the same. Sam is a groom and I can't really talk to him. He's a servant and I have to keep my distance.'

Ellen paused in her ministrations. Her expression was inscrutable.

'Oh, Ellen, I'm sorry if I've offended you. It's different with you. I know Papa employs you, but you're a friend and a woman and we're the same age. We played together as children. You understand. I can talk to you in a way that I can't possibly talk to Sam. Also he's – black…'

Ellen caught Charlotte's eyes in the reflection in the mirror. 'He's not really black, you know. He's coffee-coloured. His mother was a Malay slave and his father was a Dutch burger. That's where he gets those green eyes from. But in any case, does it matter what colour he is? Does it make a difference to you?'

'Well, I suppose it does, Ellen. I'd only mixed with white people until I came here to the Cape. And all of the black people I meet are slaves or former slaves. The Xhosa on the eastern frontier are black savages by all accounts.'

'I don't know about the Xhosa but I do know that Sam is one of the gentlest men that you could meet. He has an amazing way with horses. Even the friskiest colt or the most spirited young stallion will calm under his hand,' Ellen said with feeling.

Charlotte turned from the mirror to look directly into Ellen's eyes. 'Why, Ellen, it seems that you know him rather well?'

Ellen flushed. 'I chat to him often in the kitchen when he comes in for his meals. He's distantly related to Elsie who's very fond of him and keeps little treats for him.'

'You wouldn't be feeling something special for him, would you, Ellen? He's an attractive fellow, I have to say, although I find it difficult to understand his speech, which sounds guttural to me. It wouldn't do, you know, to get involved with someone across the colour line. Papa wouldn't tolerate it and he'd probably send you back to England.'

Ellen did not reply. She busied herself with putting the hairbrushes back into their leather case.

'But I do understand that you want someone special. We all do, don't we? I mean here I am, desperate that John, who's been a big brother to me all of my life, should see me a little differently.'

'I think he will, ma'am,' Ellen said, standing back as Charlotte rose from her seat in front of the dressing table. Charlotte had a presence, a natural dignity, which was even more powerful because she was unaware of it. The two women returned to the window. There was an eerie silence about the *Argonaut* which they could sense even from the distance of their vantage point.

'Why aren't they coming to shore? They should be here by now,' Ellen said.

'Yes, they should. Something's not right. There's no sign of the boats being lowered.' Charlotte's voice was anxious.

'The whole crew is gathering on the deck,' Ellen said. 'What do you think is going on?'

'I don't know,' Charlotte replied, picking up the telescope again, 'but I can see the captain and the officers in the front. I can pick them out in their royal blue jackets. John must be among them.'

'But what are they doing now?' Ellen insisted.

Suddenly a piercing whistle penetrated the early morning

quiet. This was followed by the sound of marching feet as the entire complement of the ship lined up in rows on the deck. Two marines in their scarlet uniforms, holding fast to a crewman who was manacled between them, marched forward to the base of the main mast. Another sailor was shinning up the ratlines of the mast to attach a rope to the yardarm. He threw the end of the rope down, and from where they stood Charlotte and Ellen could clearly see the noose swinging like an empty frame. The manacled sailor stood on a wooden box in order for his head to be placed in the noose. He was strangely quiescent. The voice of the captain carried across the water in the still morning air. Even though they couldn't distinguish the words, the intonation carried an unmistakable meaning.

'It's a funeral service,' Charlotte whispered.

There was silence. A thundering roll of drums echoed around the bay. The box was kicked away. The body struggled and writhed in an agony of death. At last a final jerk and a shudder and it was motionless and hung limp with its head on one side.

'Oh, Miss Charlotte!' Ellen cried. 'What is all that about?'

'I don't know,' Charlotte replied. 'Whatever the particular reason, the man must have been insubordinate. The Navy depends on strict discipline.'

'But surely the death sentence isn't necessary,' Ellen said. 'A stern warning or a severe punishment would be enough.'

'There's no time for that in war, and especially at sea,' said Charlotte, who, growing up in a naval family, had learned about the necessity for discipline and the constant struggle to find crew to man the ships. She had heard stories of how men were lured into taking the King's shilling by unwittingly accepting a tankard of ale, only to find the coin mocking them at the bottom of the vessel. She knew too about the press gangs which roamed the port towns of England in search of crew. It was one thing to hear the stories: it was quite another to come face to face with the brutality of life at sea. A cold hand seemed to have passed over the glory of the morning.

CHAPTER TWO

The Promise

When Charlotte saw that the landing craft with the officers on board was making its way towards the Admiral's jetty, she ran to the top of the stairs to wait for John to arrive. The staircase curved round as it led down into the inner hall so that she could hear without being seen. Soon she heard the quick march of feet and voices at the main door of the house. She knew that he would be taken in immediately to meet her father who at this hour would be in his study. She also knew that in a very short time her father would call her down to meet John again. It seemed like hours before she heard Ellen's voice.

'Miss Charlotte! Miss Charlotte! Your father's called for you!' Ellen came running down the passage from the study and up the stairs, calling as she ran. She was every bit as excited as Charlotte. They were close friends, although separated by the great divide of the English class system. Charlotte skipped down the stairs into the inner hall of the house and paused briefly before she knocked on the heavy panelled door of the study. Edward's tanned face was creased in smiles as he opened the door to her. A tall man, he had to bow his head to kiss his daughter on the cheek. He was in his late forties, his hair now silvered at the temples. He put his arm around Charlotte.

'I'm sure I don't have to tell you why I've called you,' he said, and put his other arm around the shoulders of his young nephew whom he regarded as the son that he had never had. John was his sister Cassandra's son and the only surviving member of his family. His older brother, Charles, had been killed in action at Trafalgar when John was a young midshipman. Edward and Charlotte Lacey were thus all his family. He was very close to both of them. He had in fact lived at Everhurst, their country home near Petersfield in Hampshire, for most of his life. After his parents' untimely death during the Reign of Terror he and his brother had been smuggled across to England. Both boys had followed their uncle Edward into the Navy, starting as midshipmen at the age of fourteen.

John du Rand was exceptionally tall, with wide shoulders and long shapely legs which were displayed to advantage by the white naval breeches that he wore. He had the face, thought Charlotte, of a Greek god: even features, a clean-cut jaw and a well-shaped mouth. His eyes were arresting – hazel with a golden light to them.

'John! It's wonderful to see you!' Charlotte flung her arms around his neck. Behind the closed door of the study they could relax, away from the prying eyes of servants.

'Well, little Charlie. How are you?' John grabbed her round the waist and wheeled her round and off her feet. 'It's your birthday, I do believe. Twenty years old! You're quite a young woman now,' he said as he set her down on the floor again. 'And you've grown,' he added. 'You're no longer the scrawny schoolroom miss in her pinafore. The Cape seems to agree with you.'

'What do you mean "scrawny"? That's hardly a respectful way to greet me after all this time!' laughed Charlotte, straightening the folds of her dress. 'But yes, the Cape is wonderful – it's wild and exciting... Do you know I saw baboons when I went out riding yesterday? But I miss England too. How is everything at home?'

'Just the same as when you left it five months ago. Everhurst sleeps on in the Hampshire countryside. Nothing changes there except the weather, which will be miserable now – winter gales, sleet and short daylight hours. Nothing like this marvellous climate here. What have you been doing?'

'Nothing much. A little exploring with Sam, Papa's groom. But now you are here we can go on all sorts of adventures.'

'I think I've had enough of adventures for a while,' John said, catching Edward's eye. 'I was hoping for some quiet pleasures on land.'

Charlotte drew back a little. She felt a mixture of emotions – joy in seeing John again, and yet the horror of the incident which she and Ellen had witnessed earlier in the day was still with her. The image of the helpless rag doll of an anonymous man hanging from the yardarm was etched in her brain.

'I saw the hanging.'

John and Edward looked at each other.

'I'm sorry that you did,' Edward ventured. 'It was not meant for your eyes.'

'Papa, you can't protect me all my life!'

'It's not a question of protection.'

'Yes, it is. I think you forget how old I am.'

'I could never forget that,' Edward said quietly.

'When you've been away at sea, I've virtually run Everhurst by myself. I've had to be grown up.'

'There are some things which are not appropriate for women to see.'

'Papa, that's an old-fashioned thing to say. Women have to take responsibility just as much as men. Look at what happened to Cassandra.'

There was a sudden silence as they all remembered lovely, laughing Cassandra, John's mother, who had made a love match and had married Pierre du Rand, a young French nobleman. Their fate in the guillotine at the hands of the mob didn't bear thinking about.

'She was loyal to her husband,' Edward said. 'That's the spirit of the Revolution for you. All these ideas about liberty, equality and fraternity lead to the destruction of civilised values. And that's what led to that execution on the *Argonaut* today.'

'No, Papa, that's prejudiced. We all want to be valued for who we are. Women's voices need to be heard. We are not just chattels to be bartered in marriage.'

'Well, you've certainly shown your views on that score, Charlotte. I suppose you haven't heard,' said Edward, turning to John, 'that Lord Lascelles offered for Charlotte and she, with all the foolhardiness and impetuosity of youth, turned him down!'

'Oh, Charlotte, did you indeed!' laughed John. 'You always were headstrong! I remember how you insisted on riding from Everhurst to Portsmouth to see me off five years ago when the squadron was leaving, even though it was far more fitting for you to travel by carriage, which is what we wanted you to do.'

'Don't patronise me,' said Charlotte with a touch of impatience. 'I don't want to be cosseted. I want to experience all that life has to offer me. I want to understand. Why did that man have to be executed? What had he done?'

'Mutiny.' John spoke tersely and his facial expression hardened in a way that Charlotte hadn't seen before. 'There had been rumblings among the crew when we were at sea. Before we came in sight of Table Bay there was an attempt to take over the ship. It was thwarted. That man was the ringleader. We waited until we were in the safety of the waters of our naval headquarters in Simon's Bay before executing the sentence. We wanted to keep it as quiet as possible. There was no point in putting on a show for the inhabitants of Cape Town.'

'But was this violence really necessary? Maybe the men had a legitimate grievance.'

'That's irrelevant Charlotte,' Edward intervened. 'You don't understand. The Navy runs on discipline. Any hint of uprising must be crushed from the beginning. We can't afford to be lenient. There are larger issues at stake.'

Charlotte remembered her own words to Ellen earlier in the day when she had parroted the attitude that she had learned from the men in her family, but she didn't really understand their reasoning. And she knew that her father and John didn't understand her either. There was a huge gulf between them which could not be traversed. They were a product of their age and upbringing, and there was no point in pursuing the matter any further at the moment.

'Oh well, 'she said with forced gaiety, 'shall we have some coffee? I'll go and tell Elsie to bring us some.' And she swept from the room.

'It's a bad business this, John.'

'Yes, I know, Uncle Edward. The morale of the men has never been so low.'

'I suppose now that the war with France is over and Napoleon has abdicated and has the little island of Elba as his kingdom, there isn't a common enemy any more.'

'It's more than that, Uncle. Ships have been paid off, and men who have spent their lives at sea and have known nothing else have been discharged with no prospects. There is little faith in the government or the Navy. Mutiny is contagious. We can't allow it to contaminate the fleet.'

'Especially while we're still trying to establish ourselves here in the Cape. There are many problems to deal with. But we'll talk about this some other time,' Edward said, as he heard the light step of Charlotte returning.

John moved towards Charlotte as she re-entered the room and took her hand. He was eager to remove any shadow in their relationship at this moment of meeting after such a long parting.

'You were talking about some adventure that you were planning for us?' he smiled.

Charlotte's face brightened perceptibly. She too was keen to return to untroubled waters. 'Yes! I want to go on an expedition to Cape Point. That's where the two oceans meet – the Atlantic and the Indian. I want to see if there actually is a line which divides the waters!'

'Oh, Charlotte,' John laughed,' I can tell you before we even get there that that is not the case. Nevertheless, I'm as eager to explore as you are. I've been thinking that this might be the place for a young man to settle down. I hear that the new governor, Lord Charles Somerset, is keen to encourage the settlement of Englishmen here. There is even talk of offering grants of land.'

'It's not quite as generous as it might seem on the surface,' Edward intervened dryly. 'The major problem facing the

Colonial Government here is the frontier situation. The Xhosa on the eastern frontier of the Colony are continually marauding and creating havoc. Somerset's idea is to establish a European settlement near the border. It's not the first time our illustrious government has used its loyal citizens as cannon fodder!'

'Well, I certainly don't relish that idea. But for the moment all I want to do is to get my land legs again. To tell the truth I've been looking forward immensely to being with you both again. Especially here in this most beautiful corner of the earth.'

'I know what you mean,' Edward responded. 'I've seen many parts of the world during my years at sea ... the Mediterranean, the West Indies... India. But there's nothing to equal this Cape.'

John nodded in agreement. 'As you know, Uncle, we anchored in Table Bay for a day or two to pick up some supplies to bring round to the Dockyard here. I don't think that I will ever forget my first view of Table Mountain. You can see it long before you actually sail into the harbour. That summer evening there was a slight breeze, just enough to keep us moving at a steady pace and there before us rose this splendid natural monument. It looked to me like a sculpture of God. As we moored ship, the sun sank and the mountain changed colour through shades of purple until it was a silhouette against the glow of the sky.'

'You're revealing an artistic sensitivity that I didn't know you possessed,' Edward said with a smile. 'But what you say is quite true. The Cape has had a profound effect on European sailors since they landed in this part of the world. The King of Portugal is said to have given the Cape the name of "The Cape of Good Hope", although it may well be that Bartholomew Dias, who discovered it, may have done so. Francis Drake called it "The Fairest Cape in all the Circumference of the Earth" and he had seen a thing or two.'

'It's also called "The Cape of Storms",' Charlotte said, 'and after our voyage I can quite understand why. I suspect that its beauty hides a great deal of tragedy.'

'That's true,' Edward said. 'That's why we've moved the headquarters of our naval establishment to Simon's Bay. Like the

Dutch East India Company before us, we lost too many ships in the wild winter weather in Table Bay.'

'I've never seen Table Mountain,' Charlotte said. 'I haven't been to Cape Town. I've not yet been further than the outskirts of Simon's Town.'

'Well, I can make you a promise, Charlotte,' John said. 'You have a great deal to look forward to.'

CHAPTER THREE

The Lovers

Ellen's heart was thudding as she ran along the causeway to Seaforth Beach. The distance from Admiralty House to Seaforth normally took forty minutes at a brisk walk. She had been delayed by domestic duties and had to run most of the way in order to keep her appointment. The wind was much stronger now, a real south-easter, which whipped up her cloak behind her as she ran and raised flurries of sand which stung her bare ankles.

A broad expanse of sand extended to her right as she skirted the sea, zigzagging to avoid the eddies of water as she ran across the beach. Her path led her under the lee of a towering rock formation and through a field of boulders to a second beach where she knew Sam would be waiting for her.

It was a small cove, bordered on either side by rocks. From the Seaforth side the rocks were flattish with an occasional outcrop of granite boulders with pockets of sand in between. On the far side a larger line of rocks, made smooth by the constant battering of the elements, stretched out into the sea. Within these two rocky boundaries the grass grew down to meet the sand. Behind the grassy perimeter the land which sloped gradually upwards was covered in a profusion of green fynbos which rippled and rustled in the wind. Behind this again was a high sandstone ridge. Evergreen scrub clung to the hillside, growing most densely in the valleys and depressions which caught the winter rains. At the summit the green gave way to a craggy battlement of the sandstone mountain, the Simonsberg. Here in this natural, protected haven was their trysting place. It was known as 'Water's Edge'.

The sun was hovering over the western rim of the Simonsberg, bathing the landscape in peachy hues. She looked for Sam and suddenly caught sight of his athletic frame silhouetted against the mountain. Her heart leapt as she saw him. She pushed Charlotte's words of warning from her mind as she ran across the remaining stretch of beach and flung herself into his arms. Together the thrill of the closeness of their being overwhelmed them. Gently he put his hand under her chin and lifted up her head. Sam was a powerful man, yet capable of infinite tenderness. It was this combination of strength and gentleness which Ellen found so alluring. She had known strength in her brothers and their friends back home but never moderated by this gentleness. The thought of her brothers brought vivid images of her parents to mind: Agnes and Gabriel, back at Everhurst. Gabriel was sixty-five now, but still in charge of the Admiral's stables on the estate. They had been heart-broken when the Admiral had told them that he wanted Ellen to accompany Charlotte to the Cape. They thought, with good reason, that they might never see her again. What would they think of her having a relationship with a coloured man? But she couldn't think about that for the moment.

'Sam! I'm sorry I'm late.'

'I was starting to get worried. The sailors are in town from the ships which came in this morning. They're rough at the best of times but today they're angry about the execution of one of their mates.'

'I know. Charlotte and I saw the hanging.'

'But how? It took place on board ship.'

'We were looking at Sir John's ship through the Admiral's telescope and saw it all.'

Sam grimaced. 'Not a pretty sight,' he said. 'But Ellen, it's best to keep as far away from the sailors as you can. Don't walk alone in the town, especially at night.'

'You're right, I know, Sam, but I had to help Charlotte get

dressed for this evening and she couldn't decide what to wear. It's her first dinner with Sir John and her father and she's happy that he's here at last. She's always loved him, you know, since she was a little girl. He was her hero, especially after Sir Charles, his brother, was shot at Trafalgar. He's become very precious indeed.'

'I suppose it's going to be more difficult for us to meet now. Do you think that Miss Charlotte suspects us?'

Ellen thought back on her conversation with Charlotte that morning. 'No, I don't. She knows that I like you, but she doesn't think that there could be anything serious between us. She's warned me about the dangers of getting involved with someone of …'

'A different colour,' Sam finished for her as Ellen hesitated, groping for the right words. 'Though she pretends to be so independent, Miss Charlotte is still caught up in English prejudices.'

Ellen was silent, torn between her loyalty to her friend and her lover. 'And how do you feel?' Sam continued.

Ellen looked up into his liquid-green eyes, and said, 'I feel as though I've known you all my life. I don't have to explain things. You are like the other side of me.'

Sam smiled.

'I've never known anyone like you before. You are so different from the women in the Cape – the way you talk, the way you move and the way you think – and now, since I've known you, I want nobody else. I'll never forget seeing you as you stepped from the rowing boat onto the Admiral's jetty, so pretty with your beautiful hair – the same colour as the Admiral's hunter, Sultan.'

'I'm not sure that I like to be compared with a horse,' laughed Ellen, 'but I suppose that is high praise coming from you.'

'Come,' said Sam, grasping her small, firm hand in his strong muscular one, leading the way across the beach towards the line of boulders where a rough-hewn natural path led to a small headland. They had to climb down a steep boulder and wait for the withdrawal of the waves before they could crawl through a narrow aperture which gave access to a track which led to a small sandy valley where wild heather and hardy fynbos grew. They climbed a dune and from the top they paused to view their surroundings. Across the water a large, flat-topped rock called Noah's Ark rose starkly above the waves. Its surface, whitened by guano, bleached by the Cape summers, reflected the dying rays of the afternoon sun. Far beyond Noah's Ark, on the other side of False Bay the chain of the Hottentots Holland mountain range shimmered in deep mauves and purples.

'I'm so pleased that you're safe,' whispered Sam, drawing Ellen towards him. 'I don't know what I'd do if anything happened to you. I love you Ellen.'

'Yes, Sam, I feel the same but what are we going to do? We can't carry on meeting in secret. Simon's Town is too small, and people talk. We may be watched even now.'

'I don't think so,' said Sam, looking up towards the Simonsberg and over towards Seaforth Beach where there was no sign of any human being. A cormorant on a nearby rock ignored them in his solitary vigilance for food. 'Anyway, no-one would think of looking for us here. It's too desolate.'

They descended once more to the sandy valley floor which led them into another cove hidden from view by the rocks on both sides, and a bush-covered hillside behind. As they jumped down onto the sand they moved out of the wind into a sheltered space, a space removed in time where each existed only for the other.

CHAPTER FOUR

To Cape Point
February 1815

It was one of those beautiful summer mornings in the Cape when the whole landscape looks as though it has just been freshly washed. Everything had a radiance which reflected Charlotte's spirits as she looked out across the dancing waters of the bay. Today she and John were going on the planned expedition to Cape Point. She had told Ellen that she wouldn't need her, so she dressed herself in her riding habit, fastening the ribbons of her bonnet under her chin as she ran down the stairs to the study where she knew that she would find her father reading his mail. She tapped lightly on the door and opened it as soon as she heard his welcoming voice.

'Good morning, Papa. I've just come to say good-bye. I've arranged to meet John at the stables. We shall be back before nightfall.'

'Take care, my dear.' Edward looked up from the sheaf of papers on his desk. 'I only wish I could come with you as well. But, as you know, I have a great deal to see to here.'

'Don't worry, Papa, John will take good care of me.'

'I know he will, and I think that perhaps you would rather be by yourselves in any event,' smiled Edward. 'I told Sam to saddle up Amber before he left for Cape Town this morning.'

'Why has he gone to Cape Town?'

'Some family business, he said. His cousin has asked him to fetch some equipment for his boat. Anyway, let me walk you across to the stables. I could do with some fresh air.'

Admiral Lacey rose as he spoke and walked over towards his daughter. She was looking particularly lovely: her eyes shone and her cheeks were flushed. She reminded him, with a sharp pang, of her beautiful mother Elizabeth. She had the same laughing blue eyes and thick blonde hair. He felt the old stirring of youthful enthusiasm. It seemed aeons ago that he himself had been able to look on the world with such verve and optimism. At times his chosen path in life seemed a lonely and weary one. At this point it seemed especially burdensome. The weight and responsibility of the naval establishment in Simon's Bay lay heavily on his shoulders. The latest despatches from England were not particularly encouraging. The Allies were still thrashing out the spoils after Napoleon's abdication. Only a fool would under-estimate the power of the little Corsican who was holding court on the island of Elba and exerting considerable influence, so it was said, despite his physical isolation. His activities had reverberated throughout Europe and the British Empire in the last two decades. The Cape had enjoyed considerable strategic importance since the seventeenth century because of its location on the sea route to India. So although it was many thousands of miles away from Europe, Edward could not afford to be complacent in his position of Commander-in-Chief of the Cape of Good Hope and Africa Station.

Added to all of this, there were problems in the interior affairs of the Colony which impinged on his situation and responsibilities. Not everything was harmonious between the British colonial administration and the Dutch burgers in the Cape. The Dutch valued their religion, traditions and way of life, and suspected Lord Charles Somerset, the newly appointed governor of the Cape Colony, of wanting to anglicise them. There was also a good deal of bitterness towards the British because of their liberal attitude towards the slaves and the native population – the Hottentots as the Boers called them. Although the British had abolished the slave trade in 1807, slavery was still practised in the Cape, and the Boers relied on the slaves for their farm labour as the local indigenous population generally refused to submit to the working conditions. Further, there were constant problems on the border with the Kaffir Wars. Edward was more directly involved with this because the troops fighting the Xhosa tribe on the border had to be supplied with victuals, arms and equipment from Simon's Town.

So there was much to think of. But in the meanwhile he could share in the happiness of the two people whom he loved most. He pulled his daughter's arm through the crook of his elbow as they walked from the study across the highly polished floor of the entrance hall, through the great arched double door of Admiralty House and out into the glorious sunshine. As they walked across the dusty road to the stables the keeper of the turnpike saluted them, but otherwise there was little traffic about.

'You couldn't have chosen a better day for your trip to Cape Point,' Edward said. 'You'll be able to see for miles.'

'I've brought my sketch book and pencils to capture the view if I have a chance,' said Charlotte, holding up a bag.

'I haven't seen Ellen this morning, Charlotte. Where is she?' Edward enquired.

Charlotte hesitated. 'I've given her the day off, Papa. I just couldn't bear to think of her working when I am feeling so full of holiday spirits.'

'You need to be a little careful, you know, Charlotte,' said Edward, with a slight touch of reproof in his voice. 'You won't be doing Ellen a favour if you make the other servants jealous of the privileges which she enjoys. In fact, her life could be quite intolerable below stairs. And you wouldn't want that, would you?'

Charlotte was slightly taken aback. 'I hadn't even thought of that, Papa,' she said. 'I'm sorry. I'll be more careful in future.'

As father and daughter approached the stables they saw John waiting at the door, handsome and very English-looking in his riding gear. He was holding the reins of Amber, Charlotte's mare. Just behind him was James, the head groom, with Champion.

'Good morning, Uncle. Are you ready, Charlotte?'

'I certainly am. Did Elsie bring you our lunch?'

'It's already in the saddlebag on Champion.'

Charlotte stood on the mounting block and climbed into the saddle while John held Amber steady. Then, taking Champion's reins from James, he leapt into the saddle himself. They made a handsome pair as they waved goodbye to Edward and trotted down the main street of Simon's Town, past the Residency and the Naval storehouses. On their left the bay sparkled in unending blue.

CHAPTER FIVE

The Two Oceans

As Charlotte and John rode out of the settled area of Simon's Town, the road became little more than a rough track, hugging the shoreline, with a chain of mountains towering up on their right. They passed several small coves each of which was different from the one before, with varying configurations of boulders, translucent water and shimmering sand. They paused to watch a bevy of seals sunning themselves on a large flat rock, slipping off every now and then to gambol in the water.

'Look at those seals, John. They're enjoying themselves immensely, basking in the sun and then gliding into the water.'

'They're so clumsy on the land on those awkward flippers,' laughed John, 'but in the water they're as graceful as ballet dancers.'

'They've got such appealing, soulful eyes,' commented Charlotte.

'Yes, you can understand why early mariners who had been confined to the company of men at sea for months on end mistook them for beautiful women like the Sirens or the Lorelei. But talking of women, who's that white woman down there on the beach?' said John, leaning forward on his saddle so that he could get a better view.

Charlotte looked carefully. Even from that distance she recognised Ellen's figure and long, flowing locks. But who was she with? A young man of athletic build and dark burnished skin. Was it? Yes, it must be – Sam. Charlotte's heart sank in dismay. It would be better for no-one to know that Ellen was consorting with a man of mixed blood.

'I don't know,' she said absently.

'I think it's Ellen,' said John. 'In fact I'm sure it is. There aren't many women with hair like that wandering around Simon's Town. Who's she with?'

Charlotte said nothing.

'Good God!' exclaimed John. 'She's holding hands with a nigger! It's the one who works in the stables – your father's groom. What's his name? Sam!'

'I'm sure that you are mistaken,' said Charlotte, startled by John's language, but also shocked despite herself at the implications of what they had seen.

'Come, John. We want to get to Cape Point before the sun is too high in the sky and it gets too hot,' she said, turning her horse's head into the road.

The track on which they rode was designed for wagons and was no more than twelve foot wide. It brought them eventually to Miller's Point, the whaling station where Charlotte had ridden with Sam, where the road became a meandering bridle path which was washed away in places and where they had to rely on the horses' good sense to guide them. As they travelled this precipitous path, the cerulean waters of False Bay stretched out on their left while on their right soared high sandstone ramparts, covered with green low-growing scrub. The shrill call of the gulls echoed across the water. They circled around a deep bay after which the path wound inland and they found themselves travelling down the centre of the peninsula. The land levelled out into a plain, carpeted in vivid low-growing vegetation interspersed with splashes of blazing white.

'This reminds me of Land's End in Cornwall! It's the space and the light and lack of trees. And even the gorse – those vivid yellow and purple colours!' exclaimed Charlotte. 'Do you remember when Papa took us to visit his old aunt in Penzance?

It was before you went into the Navy as a midshipman. It must have been about twelve years ago.'

'Yes, I remember it well. It was the last holiday that we had before I joined the Fleet. It was a brilliant summer just like this one and I was due to go into the Navy after my fourteenth birthday, the following February. Charles was with us as well. It was the first leave he had had after joining up and he thrilled us with his exciting stories of his adventures at sea but that was before...'

A shadow passed over them as they remembered Charles, young, tousle-haired, energetic, confident, with a great future ahead of him, snuffed out like a candle at Trafalgar. He had been shot on the same day as Nelson. They carried on riding in silence. There was nothing to be said in the face of the loss which they both felt so deeply.

As they continued, they were aware of the line of the coast on either side converging to a point with the sea glinting on both right and left. The land rose before them but they followed a track which wound down to sea level where there was a rough pebbly beach leading round to a headland. The open ocean yawned wide in front of them. They dismounted and tethered their horses to some sturdy shrubs.

'I wouldn't like to bring a ship in here with all those rocks. I wager they've had some nasty shipwrecks around here,' John remarked. 'Just the same as at home. There have been hundreds of wrecks along the Cornish coast. This splendid beauty can be deceptive.'

'This must be the Atlantic Ocean and the Cape of Good Hope,' said Charlotte, 'and that point up there is Cape Point.' She gestured to a promontory high above them.

'There's a rough track leading up there,' John observed. 'What a pity that we can't climb up to the top.'

'Why can't we?'

'I could, of course, because I'm used to heights and running up rope ladders and masts on ships. But you'd never be able to clamber up there in your long skirts!'

Charlotte turned round to face him indignantly. 'If that's what you think, then you're very wrong. I haven't come all this way to play the genteel damsel. I'll get there before you!'

With these words she gathered up her skirts on either side and started to walk briskly up the uneven path with John behind her, smiling and a little breathless in his surprise and the exertion of keeping up with her. The way was rough but not precipitous and thirty minutes later they found themselves at the crest of the promontory.

They stood, silent and awe-struck for a timeless moment. The ground fell away steeply below their feet, a sheer drop as if chopped off by a giant axe. On the south side the rock, which bore the brunt of the gales, was bare of all vegetation. On the leeward side plants and greenery clung to the rocks. In front the ocean swept away to infinity. Far down on their right was a cove with a small beach and cliffs rising above it. Black-winged gulls floated on the air below them. On their left they could see the great arc of False Bay, miles of undulating blue. Across the waters was Hangklip, mistaken for Cape Point by early explorers who had given it the name 'Cape Falso' because they had sailed into the wide bay between the points thinking that it was Table Bay. The water near the base of the promontory was a light green, merging to a darker blue as the water deepened out to the Atlantic rollers. Looking back over the route which they had travelled on their horses they could see the sweep of the shoreline with its cliffs, coves and inlets. Buttresses of rock challenged the sea and behind there was a further ridge of mountains.

The young couple stood together on the top of Cape Point, neither wanting to break the silence. After the strenuous activity of the ride and climb they were still and reverent in the face of the natural majesty before them. At last John spoke. 'Well, Charlie, here we are at last! What do you think?'

'It's better than I imagined. Everyone said that the view is good but it's breathtaking. You can see for miles.'

'Yes, but it's the sense of openness and liberation that overwhelms me. Can you imagine how this feels after months of being at sea in cramped, confined living conditions, even as an officer? It's like being released from a cage!'

'Language is inadequate, isn't it?' responded Charlotte. 'How do you begin to express these things that you feel so deeply?'

'You can't, and you don't have to. It's enough to have someone special to share it with,' said John as he took her hand and they stood in quiet communion.

At that moment their attention was distracted by a scurrying noise and they glanced down to see a rock rabbit looking up at them with bright inquisitive eyes. They burst out laughing at the incongruity of the intrusion, at which the rabbit scampered away and the solemn mood was broken.

'Papa says that this is not the southernmost tip of Africa,' Charlotte said.

'No, that's true. Cape Agulhas is actually further south, but this appears to be the tip of Africa on the map.'

John spread his arms out wide and embraced the scene. 'I feel as though I've got the world at my feet, that I could conquer anything!'

'In a sense you have got the world at your feet, or rather the world has you at its feet,' teased Charlotte. 'But seriously, John, I'm sure you could achieve anything you want to. You have everything in your favour – youth, intelligence, confidence and courage.'

'You flatter me, Charlotte,' laughed John, 'but you know I think that this is where I want to be. I have been here a very short time but already I feel an affinity with this land. I love England but it's a tired country just now. There are many problems. Thousands of soldiers and sailors returning from the Napoleonic Wars, sick in mind and body and no employment for them at home. It's not the place for a young man keen to start a new life.'

'What about your naval career?' asked Charlotte. 'You have done so well, you're a lieutenant already, and you know how proud Papa is of you. He thinks of you as his son and, especially now Charles is gone, imagines that you will follow in his footsteps and end up an admiral one day.'

'Yes, I love the sea,' admitted John, 'and I'd always want to live close to it. But I've had enough of war and strife. I've seen too much suffering and destruction. I want to start building now, something with the land, something tangible. I want to create rather than destroy. And I think that this is the place where I would like to do it.'

'It would be wonderful if you were close by,' said Charlotte. 'I feel as though I have been saying good-bye to you all of my life.'

John took both of Charlotte's hands and turned her round so that they were facing each other. Charlotte, looking up at him, saw the golden lights around the pupils of his hazel eyes. He said in softened tones. 'We don't always have to be saying good-bye, Charlie. You know that I've always loved you since you were a little girl, and you've grown so beautiful. You're a woman now and I love you more than ever. I'd like to think that you would be at my side always.' His words started to stumble. 'Do you think, I mean, would you ... will you ... do me the honour of marrying me?'

Charlotte had often dreamed of this moment and could hardly believe that it was happening, that her hero whom she had loved and worshipped all of her life was asking her to be his wife. She felt the sun warm on her skin, smelt the sea and heard the waves crashing far below. There was only one answer. She smiled and whispered, 'Yes, of course I will.'

He pulled her towards him and there at the top of the world it seemed, at the tip of Africa, he took her in his arms and kissed her gently and with growing warmth and passion.

CHAPTER SIX

The Engagement

Admiral Lacey, Charlotte and John were having dinner in the small dining room which they used whenever the family was dining alone. The large dining room was reserved for more formal entertaining. Although not large, the room was exquisitely proportioned. In one corner stood an Adam fireplace above which hung a large oval mirror in an ornate gilt frame which reflected the glow of the candles on the table. Heavy velvet drapes were drawn over the deep window recesses. The little party around the table was comfortable and relaxed.

'That was a splendid dinner, Uncle Edward. The beef was as good as anything I've ever tasted in England.'

'Well, I should think anything would taste good after months of salt beef rations at sea,' laughed Edward. 'But it's true that we do get extraordinarily good beef here. The cattle are watered at Groendam near Miller's Point which offers excellent pasturage. There's a slaughterhouse between Miller's Point and Simon's Town so we have a regular supply of fresh meat.'

'You should give Elsie some credit as well!' exclaimed Charlotte. 'The finest beef in the world can be ruined in the hands of a fumbling cook. Elsie has a natural talent for good cooking and she knows some marvellous traditional Malay dishes. She can make the most ordinary food taste exotic. I wish we could take her back to England when we return eventually.'

'Talking of England, John, when do you rejoin the fleet?'

'That's a matter to which I have given a great deal of thought.' John paused. He realised that his words would fall heavily on the ears of his uncle. 'I don't know if I will rejoin the fleet.'

Edward placed his knife and fork on the table, stopped eating and looked steadily at his nephew.

'I don't know if I'm going to go back to England at all. I'm seriously considering buying myself out of the Navy. I've quite set my mind on settling here. I was discussing the matter with Charlotte when we went on our trip to Cape Point. I intend to approach Governor Somerset to apply for a tract of land on the eastern border.'

John realised that he was delivering a monologue. But somehow he couldn't stop. Once he had started he had to have it all out and the words tumbled over each other.

'Well, I hardly need say that this is a shock. It's been a family tradition for generations for a son to join the Royal Navy. And you know well that I've always regarded you as a son. Don't you think that you owe something to the family name? Think of your brother who was killed at Trafalgar.'

There was an edge to Edward's voice and John could feel a resistant spirit rising in him as well.

'I think, Uncle Edward, that I want to lead my own life, make my own decisions. I'm tired of jumping to somebody else's orders.'

'That's discipline, young man. That's what life is all about. It's not a self-indulgent ride.'

'I resent your implications, Uncle …'

'In any case, you don't know anything about farming!' Edward cut him short. 'It's a vastly different life from that of the sea. Do you honestly think that you could settle permanently on the land?'

'That's the whole point, Uncle. I'm tired of being constantly on the move. As I said to Charlotte, I want to put roots down. I want to build. And I have fallen in love with this magnificent country. It fills me with excitement. I have never felt so passionate about any place before.'

Edward sipped his wine and looked away.

'I suppose I can understand your passion,' he said. 'That's how I've always felt about the sea, and I thought you felt the same.' He sighed. 'Nevertheless, you're certainly old enough to know your own mind now, but I'm not sure that the eastern border is the place to go. As I indicated before, this is not a philanthropic move on the part of the Government. Somerset's plan is to offer land in exchange for a defence force. It's a hard life on the eastern Cape border. The Xhosa are renowned for their savage ways and there will be many difficulties which you could not possibly foresee.'

'I'm not afraid, Uncle. Think how many times I have come within a hair's breadth of losing my life at sea, whether in storm or in battle. I'm tired of that life now. I don't see any purpose in it. I'm sure that farming will be full of hazards, but it's the potential which excites me. I've had enough of fighting battles for a government which at times seems to care little about its children. I want to fight for myself and my own family.'

'Remember that it's the same government that sends its children, as you call them, to fight in Africa as well as at sea.'

John caught Charlotte's eyes across the dinner table. She rose diplomatically. 'Please excuse me,' she said. 'I must speak to Elsie about domestic matters. I'll leave you gentlemen to enjoy your port. I'll meet you a little later in the drawing room.'

As she glided out of the room both men, each of whom loved her dearly, rose from their seats. Edward moved across to the liquor cabinet and removed a bottle of port.

'Serious conversations need good wine,' he said. 'This is not from Portugal but from right here in the Cape, from Groot Constantia, the wine estate founded by Simon van der Stel. Try it.'

John took the glass from Edward, sniffed the bouquet and took a tentative sip. His eyes widened in surprise.

'Very good,' he said. 'I think I'd like to try to grow some grapes and make some wine myself when I have my own land.'

'There's more to it than you think,' Edward said. 'The Dutch have a long history of wine-making in this country that goes back to the seventeenth century. It's not something that the English have invested in.'

'Perhaps I'll break the mould,' laughed John, 'but, seriously, there's another matter that I must speak to you about, although this is not perhaps the best moment.'

Edward raised his eyebrow and gestured to his nephew to continue.

'It's about Charlotte. And, and me…' stumbled John thinking how his finely prepared speech seemed to have dissipated into nothingness and how surprisingly difficult it was to speak of something so dear to his heart to someone who had been so close to him for so long.

'The fact is, sir, I would like to ask you for the very great favour of Charlotte's hand in marriage.'

'Indeed?' Edward choked on his wine. 'I thought that you two regarded each other as brother and sister. I know that you've always been good friends although I must admit when I saw you riding off to Cape Point the other day I thought that you looked well together.'

A slow smile spread over Edward's face. Here was the solution to the problem of finding a suitable husband for Charlotte being handed to him on a plate. But the warm pleasure had a chill undercurrent. His beloved Charlotte going to that wild unprotected border? Never. But that matter could be sorted out later and he consciously pushed the fearful, anxious thoughts away. In the meanwhile this was an occasion for rejoicing. He rose from his chair and walked round the table. John stood, out of both respect and uncertainty. The two men stood facing each other. Edward put his hands on John's shoulders.

'Come, my son, let us walk on the terrace. There is much for us to discuss.' In those first three words, never spoken by him before, Edward had in fact given his blessing on the match between the two people whom he loved most in the world.

CHAPTER SEVEN

The Ball

Admiralty House was in a fever of activity. Admiral Lacey was giving a ball to celebrate the engagement of his daughter Charlotte to Sir John du Rand, Lieutenant of the Royal Navy. It was the first occasion of this kind to be held at Admiralty House since it had become the official residence of the Commander-in-Chief of the Cape of Good Hope and Africa Station in Simon's Town.

All the families of note in Simon's Town had been invited and there were many naval officers with their wives from visiting ships and a few who had made the journey from Cape Town. The ball was being held in the inner hall of the house. Edward had invited John to join him in his study before the festivity began.

'Thank you, Uncle,' said John, accepting a glass of white muscatel. 'Is everything going to your satisfaction?'

'Yes,' said Edward, 'sitting down in a chair next to his nephew. 'Most people have accepted the invitation so we should have an amusing evening.'

'Anyone I know?'

'You'll probably know the naval officers: Captain Devenish and his wife; Lord Clarendon and his wife and Lieutenant Lamplough. Otherwise there are my old friends, the Lansdownes, from Cape Town.'

'Any local families?'

'There are only six permanent families in Simon's Town, you know.'

John registered surprise.

'Yes, most of the population are itinerant workers who have come to work in the Dockyard. John Osmond and his wife are coming though. He's the richest man in Simon's Town. I don't like him much – he's an upstart, but he does business with the Navy and I can't leave him out.'

'We won't let him spoil the evening. I must say, Uncle, that the house looks splendid. I like the house anyway but it's certainly showing to advantage tonight.'

'Yes, I like it too. It's not as grand as Everhurst but it's big enough to host a number of guests and yet small enough to feel to feel comfortable.'

'Was it built by the Navy?'

'No, it was built in the last century by a Dutch soldier, Antoni Visser, who bought the land in 1743. Subsequently another Dutchman, Willem Hurter, acquired it and amassed a considerable fortune providing victuals for passing ships and accommodation for captains and officers. Accommodation in Simon's Town has always been scarce.'

'It's ironic that the home of a man who profiteered at the expense of the Royal Navy has now become the official residence of the Commander-in-Chief of that same Navy,' John said.

'Indeed, but now,' said Edward, glancing at the clock on the mantelpiece, 'I had better go and await my guests in the entrance hall.'

The carriages rolled up and halted at the imposing entrance to the house. The massive double doors were opened wide to reveal a forest of candles which transformed the inner hall into an Aladdin's cave. The guests alighted and stepped onto the highly polished floor of the entrance hall where they were greeted by Admiral Lacey in full dress uniform. The men in naval uniform or civilian dress provided a perfect foil to the women in their ball gowns like a flock of tropical birds. At one end of the hall the members of small orchestra were tuning their instruments for the dancing.

* * *

Meanwhile upstairs, Ellen had been helping Charlotte to dress. She had chosen a gown of white silk, fashionably low cut with a simple blue sash. As Ellen dressed her hair Charlotte looked out of the window. It was a tranquil night. The moon shone in a cloudless sky and silvered the waters of the bay. Against the sheen the ships with their tall masts were silhouetted in inky blackness.

'You do look lovely, ma'am!' whispered Ellen. 'The Admiral and Sir John will be very proud of you.'

'Why, thank you, Ellen. I must admit that I'm feeling very excited, but a little frightened too. It's a big step to take, this public promise to be married.'

'But you'll be so happy, ma'am. Sir John loves you so much. You can see it in his eyes. I only wish ...' Ellen's voice trailed off.

'Wish what, Ellen?'

'Oh, never mind, ma'am. I've got a careless tongue.'

'No Ellen, tell me. There's something on your mind, I know,' said Charlotte, turning to face her.

Ellen's colour heightened and tears started to brim in her large brown eyes.

'I was only wishing, ma'am, that I could be married too.'

'I'm sure you will one day, Ellen, when you meet someone suitable.'

'Well...the truth is that I have met someone, ma'am.'

'Have you?' Charlotte was surprised and turned to look into Ellen's eyes. 'And may I ask who he is?'

Ellen paused and bit her lip. She and Sam had sworn to keep their relationship secret. They knew that people wouldn't understand. Even Charlotte with whom she shared so much. Charlotte looked intently at her. Suddenly the picture came into her mind of the two lone figures walking on the beach that she and John had seen when they had been on their excursion to Cape Point.

'It's Sam, isn't it?'

Ellen nodded, unable to speak.

'You're not seriously involved, Ellen?'

Ellen nodded again as the tears spilled over onto her cheeks.

'You're surely not thinking that you want to marry him?'

'But I do, ma'am!'

'No, Ellen. You're not thinking straight. This is a passing fancy. You know that it wouldn't be right. He comes from a different background and you could never take him back to England. He wouldn't fit in.'

'But ma'am, I don't want to go back to England. I want to stay here with Sam forever. He's part of me just as I'm part of him. It doesn't matter that we're of a different race. We belong together. Besides…besides…'

'Besides what, Ellen?'

By now the tears were coursing over Ellen's face. 'Oh, Miss Charlotte…ma'am, I'm….I'm with child.'

'Oh no, Ellen!' Charlotte was aghast. The implications of this announcement swirled around in her mind. What could Ellen do? Where could she go? Marriage was surely out of the question, yet the alternative was too awful to contemplate. She could not remain in Admiralty House and have the baby. Charlotte's father would be outraged. And Simon's Town was such a small community that the news would soon be out. Ellen's life would be a misery. But could she go back to England? Even if she could get a passage home what would her parents say? What would they think of Charlotte and her father to whom they had entrusted their daughter? Charlotte's own happiness was temporarily forgotten as she realised the enormity of the problem facing her handmaid and friend. But she must not make things worse for Ellen by conveying her own misgivings.

'I'm not ashamed, ma'am, because I love him true,' said Ellen, mopping her eyes with the corner of her pinafore, 'but I don't know what to do!'

'Does Sam know?'

Ellen shook her head.

'Well, let's not worry about it now,' said Charlotte with a

heartiness which belied her inner anxiety. 'We'll find a solution. Papa will know what to do.'

'Oh no, ma'am, you can't tell the Admiral! He'll kill me or leastways throw me out.'

'Never, Ellen. He may have an abrupt manner but underneath he's kind and understanding. He's the wisest man I know. This problem is nothing compared to the difficulties of running a ship or a fleet or managing a naval establishment of several hundred men!'

However Charlotte knew that these were issues of a very different order and that this kind of domestic problem was a vexed one. But she would not allow Ellen to see her disquiet.

'Now come, help me with my shawl. I can hear the music starting up and I have to go downstairs to greet our guests. You go and get some sleep now. Don't wait up for me. We'll talk again tomorrow.'

Charlotte gave Ellen an affectionate hug before she stepped lightly out of the room to join the party below.

* * *

John, resplendent in his naval dress uniform, was waiting for her at the bottom of the stairs. His eyes shone and his wide smile made Charlotte's heart turn over in delight.

'You look more beautiful than I could ever have imagined,' he whispered in her ear as he took her by the hand.

'Beauty is in the eye of the beholder,' Charlotte laughed. 'It's still the same Charlie you've known all her life. Where's Papa? I expect he's wondering where I am.'

'He's in the entrance hall welcoming the guests who have started to arrive. He wants us to go and join him.'

Charlotte rested her hand lightly on John's arm as he escorted her to where Admiral Lacey was in conversation with some new arrivals. Charlotte walked up and kissed her father on the cheek. 'The room looks splendid, Papa. Thank you.'

'May I introduce John Osmond and his wife?' said Edward.

'Oh Mr Osmond, how do you do. You're a neighbour of ours, aren't you, at Mount Curtis just up on the hill?'

'Delighted to meet you, Miss Lacey,' said Osmond, bowing low over her hand.

'And you too, sir,' he said to John. 'This is just the kind of occasion to bring some elegance to Simon's Town society.' And he moved on.

Charlotte suppressed a giggle at these social pretensions and caught John's eye. 'I think that it's time that we started the dancing,' she said and led him back into the ballroom. As John took Charlotte's hand for the first dance she wondered whether she should share Ellen's secret with him. As she looked up into his smiling hazel eyes she knew intuitively that she could not. She remembered his outburst when he saw Ellen and Sam on Seaforth Beach. 'She's holding hands with a nigger!' What would his response be if he knew that Ellen was carrying the nigger's baby? John was a fine, decent man, but he came from a male-dominated world regulated by harsh discipline. This kind of problem would be beyond his understanding. The rules he lived by could not bring a satisfactory solution. She realised that there were parts of herself that she would not be able to share with him. However, she must not let dismal thoughts spoil this wonderful evening and she determined to cast the problem aside for the time being as she gave herself over to the rhythms of the dance.

CHAPTER EIGHT

Disgrace

Charlotte's inner world was thrown off balance. On one level she was still revelling in the excitement of the engagement ball which had been a huge success: all of their friends and acquaintances were delighted with this very suitable match. On another level she was deeply perturbed over Ellen's predicament. After the last guest had left she kissed her father and John and went upstairs to bed. But sleep evaded her. She spent the whole night tossing and turning, trying to arrive at some solution to Ellen's problem. Whichever way she tried to disentangle it another complication seemed to present itself. As the first fingers of light made their way through her bedroom window she arose and dressed. Throughout all the maze of trouble, one thing was clear: Ellen needed protection, love and support. She realised her own helplessness in dealing with the situation. She needed the assistance of someone in a position of authority, but also someone of kindness, compassion and wisdom. The only person she knew who fitted this description was her father. She determined to lose no time in discussing the problem with him.

It was the Admiral's habit to rise early and deal with his correspondence before breakfast and he would allow nothing to disturb this routine. Charlotte's heart was thumping as she ran down the stairs to her father's study. She had to persuade her father to support Ellen. He must understand. He would. When had he ever refused her anything she genuinely wanted? Even though he had wanted her to marry Lord Lascelles, he had given way to her wishes. She was aware of the problems which might ensue, but she had to convince him that he should protect Ellen. It was unthinkable that she could be thrown out into the world, friendless and alone. She would never survive.

Charlotte knocked on the heavy oak door of the study. She traced the brass escutcheon plates of sailing ships with her finger as she waited. It seemed an age before her father called out, 'Who is it?'

'It's me, Papa!'

'Come in, my dear.'

She opened the door and paused on the threshold. Her father sat at the mahogany desk, writing. He looked up at her and smiled, and saw immediately the agitation in her young face.

'Whatever is the matter, Charlotte?'

'Oh Papa, you've got to help. It's desperate. I ... I ... just don't know what to do ...we've got to help her ... there's nobody else...'

'Hush child ...now, now.'

Admiral Lacey rose, walked over to his daughter and put his arm around her, attempting to still her heaving shoulders.

'What is it?' he repeated. 'Tell me.' He led her to a chaise longue and sat down beside her.

'It's Ellen, Papa ... she's in terrible trouble and we have to help her.'

'What kind of trouble? Is it money?'

'No, Papa, she ... she's ... in love!'

Admiral Lacey laughed out loud at this.

'Well, that's hardly an uncommon malady for a young person of that age. You seem to have caught it yourself, and, if I may say, do not appear to be suffering under the affliction.'

'Oh, Papa, don't be facetious. It's not a laughing matter. Ellen is in a desperate plight and we've got to support her. She's all alone here. There's nobody but us to stand by her.'

The smile faded from the Admiral's rugged features.

'Well, if we're going to help, you had better tell me what the problem is. I can hardly see that the state of being in love is a cause for concern. Who is the lucky man who is the object of Ellen's affection?'

Charlotte was silent. Her clear blue eyes gazed directly into those of her father.

'It's Sam.'

'Sam! It can't be! Sam's a half-caste, the son of a slave girl and a Dutch burger. His own father doesn't acknowledge him!'

'So does that mean that you don't either?'

'Of course not, Charlotte! Sam, along with several other freed slaves, works for me as well as apprentices from the slave ships that the Navy has intercepted. Employing these people is one thing, but we don't consort with them, just as we don't consort with our servants at home.'

Charlotte got up from the chaise longue and walked over to the French windows which faced the garden while her father was talking. Would she never be able to escape these social prejudices? She thought of her own words to Ellen last night: 'He comes from a different background. He wouldn't fit in.'

'It's impossible to accept him as a potential match for Ellen. You know that, Charlotte. I'm surprised that you should even see fit to bring the situation to my notice. Ellen will soon find someone else.'

'She won't, Papa. She loves him too much, and besides …'

'Besides what?'

'She's with child!' burst out Charlotte, sobbing.

'Foolish girl!' exclaimed Edward, getting up and walking across to the window which faced the road into Simon's Town. 'Why did she allow herself to get into such a predicament?'

'Because she loves him, Papa!' repeated Charlotte. But even as she said it, she looked at her father and knew that he would never understand how passion could overcome reason. She realised that Edward's marriage to Elizabeth had been a considered decision. She was of good family, well endowed financially, and a perfectly acceptable marriage partner. The fact that she was also beautiful and had a lovely serene nature had been an added blessing. Since Elizabeth's death his sexual passions had been sublimated and found expression in his work and duty. He lived a celibate life. His love for his men was a lofty emotion, grounded in genuine regard for them. The softer side of love was reserved for his daughter. That she could support this illicit love relationship was something he was unable to comprehend.

Edward gazed through the window with unseeing eyes. A wagon laden with wine barrels was creaking its way down from the turnpike to the Studland wine house across the road from Admiralty House. Without meeting Charlotte's eyes he walked back into the room and across to the fireplace. He put his elegantly shod foot on the brass fender of the hearth and rested his elbow on the mantelpiece. It was a habitual pose for reflection.

'Poor Gabriel,' he said with feeling.

'Poor Gabriel?' Charlotte turned from the French windows to face her father. 'What about Agnes? And Ellen herself? Can't you see the woman's point of view ever?'

Edward looked into his daughter's eyes.

'Gabriel entrusted her to me, first of all as a lady's maid to you, and then he agreed that she should accompany you to the Cape. That was a very difficult decision for him.'

'Yes, I know, Papa. I'm not denying that.'

'He will feel that we have not looked after her. And he has given us most of his life, working in the stables at Everhurst until he took over as head groom. He's had full responsibility for the stables for years and I've relied on him totally to buy and sell our horses and take care of them. And this is the reward for his loyal service: a daughter not only unmarried and pregnant, but also soiled with black blood.'

'How can you be so unfeeling, Papa?'

'On the contrary, I'm feeling a great deal for Ellen's hapless family.'

'Well, perhaps they don't have to know. Ellen can stay here with us. We'll look after her and the baby when it arrives.'

'That's out of the question, Charlotte. You should know

better than that. Our position here is delicate. Relations between the British and the Dutch are tense. They've been fighting over possession of the Cape Colony for years. The Dutch are puritanical in their outlook.'

'But why should they be concerned about Ellen's affairs? She means nothing to them.'

'My implicit support of an affair across the colour line would be perceived as a deliberate flouting of the Calvinistic moral code of the Dutch.'

'We can keep her hidden!' said Charlotte desperately.

Edward laughed. 'Charlotte, sometimes you are naïve. Do you really think that you can keep anything secret in a town like this? Walls have ears. Probably half of Simon's Town already knows that Ellen is having an affair with Sam. No, I'm afraid she can't stay here. She'll have to go back to England. Even though Gabriel and Agnes will be deeply shocked, they will stand by their only daughter in her hour of need. And I'll make sure that there is sufficient money to support her and the infant.'

'You think that money solves everything, don't you, Papa? That's why you wanted me to marry Lord Lascelles.'

'Charlotte, that's totally irrelevant to this situation. That would have been a very suitable social connection for you.'

'And this is not a suitable social connection for you, is it, Papa? And what about the scandal back at Everhurst? Gossip is every bit as vicious in England as you say it is here.'

'We'll manufacture a story that Ellen married a sailor who was killed in an accident at sea.'

'What a clever idea, Papa!' Edward was startled by the sharp irony in Charlotte's tone. 'What will happen, though, when a little brown baby pops out?'

'The child may well be more white than black,' said Edward with a slight air of irritation. 'The father is a mulatto after all. Let's worry about that when the infant comes. In the meanwhile we'll send her back to England with the fleet. My old friend, Captain Johnson, is returning to Portsmouth with his family. I'll ask him to take care of her. She'll be in good hands. In the meanwhile, if you'll excuse me,' said Edward with dismissive gesture, 'I must get back to my correspondence.' And he walked back to his desk.

Charlotte knew that there was no point in further argument. Suddenly the room seemed unbearably stifling, and she opened the French windows and ran across the garden and down to the beach.

* * *

Outside the door Ellen was kneeling with her ear to the keyhole. Back to England? Away from Sam and Charlotte? That awful voyage, three and a half to four months under sail? The fleet would not be leaving for another six weeks or so while they prepared for the return journey. Even now at least three of the ships were being careened in order to carry out underwater repairs. With general refurbishment and organisation and stocking up with fresh supplies, it would be the end of May or June before they left. By that time her pregnancy would be well advanced, and the weather off the Cape could also be uncertain. Many people fell ill and died on these long voyages. There was hardly a ship which could report a passage from England to Africa without at least one or two deaths. In any case, what would happen to her if she went back to England? No young man in the hamlet of Everhurst would want her with a child of mixed blood. And neither would she want anyone else anyway, she thought defiantly. Her parents, dear old Agnes and Gabriel, would be shocked, and humiliated in the traditional conservative English village society. No, she would rather take her chances here in Simon's Town with the one person who, she felt, both loved and understood her. She must find Sam.

CHAPTER NINE

Escape

Ellen ran silently from the study door, through the inner hall and down through the passages to the kitchen area at the back of the house. She had to find Sam as quickly as possible. In the warm spacious kitchen she found Elsie, the cook, singing quietly to herself as she kneaded dough for the bread which she was going to bake in the large brick oven. Elsie was a plump Cape Malay woman whose father, a freed slave, had been mission educated and had taught his daughter to speak English. It was this competence which had led to her employment at Admiralty House. She was a talented cook who ruled over the kitchens with a rod of iron. The coloured women, mainly freed slaves, who worked in her domain, were in awe of her. However, she had a compassionate nature and a very soft spot for Sam. She was distantly related to him through the network of legal and illegal family relationships in the Cape Malay community and was fiercely protective of him. She always made sure that Sam had the choicest morsels when he dropped by the kitchens for a visit. She was also fond of Ellen, the young, fresh-faced girl from the English countryside. She was aware of the growing affection between Ellen and Sam and though she feared for them, in her heart she was in sympathy with them and kept their relationship a closely guarded secret. Sam and Ellen had taken her into their confidence and she frequently acted as a go-between for them.

'Elsie! Elsie!'

'Ja, meisie. What's the matter?' Elsie turned around from her work with floured hands. She could sense the urgency in the young voice.

'Elsie, where's Sam?'

'Out in the stables as usual. The master's going into Cape Town early tomorrow and he is grooming the horses to have them ready for the journey. Why? What has happened, child?' She looked with concern at Ellen's tear-stained face.

'I've got to speak to him, Elsie!' cried Ellen, running to the door that led to the stables.

'Stop, Ellen! You can't just run across there! You know that the master doesn't like us to go to the stables. Our work is in the house. Also the other kêrels in the stables would talk if they saw you with Sam. Your secret would be all over Simon's Town by nightfall.'

The truth of Elsie's words stopped Ellen, who turned back towards the older woman.

'What can I do, Elsie? I have to see him soon!'

Elsie's heart went out to the distraught girl. Whatever the reason, she was clearly in deep distress.

'Come and sit down, meisie. Here, have a hot drink.' She led Ellen to an oak settle next to the fireplace and handed her a steaming mug. 'Now what is the matter?'

'I can't tell you, Elsie. Perhaps later when I've spoken to Sam,' said Ellen, the tears streaming down her face. Elsie's warm motherliness calmed her. 'But I need to talk to him as soon as I can.'

'He'll be over for dinner in a couple of hours' time. I'll tell him that you want to talk to him. Where will you meet him? In the usual place?'

'Yes, at Water's Edge, this evening at about eight when it's dark…then we're sure not to be seen.'

'Be careful, meisie. There's a ship just docked, and you know what the sailors are like when they first arrive. They're starved of fresh food, liquor and women. A young girl on her own is not safe on the streets at night.'

'Don't worry, Elsie, I'll be careful.'

***

At about seven-thirty that evening, as the sun was beginning to slide down behind the craggy heads of the Simonsberg, Ellen, holding a grey cloak around her like a tight cocoon against the wind, slipped out of the back gate of Admiralty House. She walked swiftly, willing herself not to run in order not to attract attention. As she passed the Studland wine-house on the other side of the road, without warning the door yawned open and three sailors lurched drunkenly into the street. Their raucous singing and laughter pierced the silence as they wove their way across the road aiming for the Dockyard gates. Ellen was just approaching the gates when they caught up with her.

'Well, what have we here?' said one.

'Let's have a look,' said one of his companions as he grabbed hold of Ellen's arms and pulled back her hood. Ellen screamed and wrenched herself away.

'Oh, she's a pretty wench, isn't she?' said the third. 'And she's got spirit as well!' He seized her round the waist, threw her back against the Dockyard wall and launched himself upon her, covering her small mouth with his own, reeking of alcohol. Ellen's stomach contracted with fear and nausea as she struggled to escape.

'Don't pretend that you want to get away! We all know you ladies of the night who wander the streets on your own, don't we, lads?'

'Aye, come on, George, don't keep her all to yerself. Let's go down to the beach and have some fun.'

With a drunken roar George lifted Ellen up across his broad chest and ran down past the Navy storehouses to the gravel beach. Hard on his heels were his two companions, breathless from their exertions and inflamed desire. As Ellen screamed in terror, George muffled her mouth with one huge hand while with the other he threw up her skirts, and in an instant was inside her, tearing into her fragile flesh. As he collapsed on her, his partners had already unbuckled their belts in anticipation.

Suddenly a light appeared around the corner of the Navy storehouses.

'It's the sentry on guard duty,' hissed George to his mates as they lay flat on the ground, still making sure that their victim was gagged. The sentry approached, waving a lantern around. Seeing and hearing nothing, he turned on his heel and walked away. The interruption had a sobering effect on the three sailors who stood up, looking at each other and at the girl who lay motionless on the beach. They were not hardened criminals. And as the alcoholic fumes cleared from their brains they were appalled at the deed which they had done. However, they were not heroes either, and had had hard experience of naval discipline. Their first instinct was to save their own skins.

'Think we'd better get out of here.'

'What about her?'

'Can't worry about that now. She's not dead.'

And the three miscreants disappeared into the night.

* * *

At Water's Edge, Sam sat patiently on a boulder and watched as the moon rose and made a silvery path across the water. If only the path led to some haven where he and Ellen could go. He wished he were a man of means, of any independent livelihood so that he could marry Ellen and offer her some kind of life, despite the scandal which would be sure to erupt over the liaison between a white English girl and a coloured man. He felt so powerless. As far as he could see his life would be one of serving others more richly endowed than he. No matter how benevolent his master, he still chafed at the sense of frustration and futility.

The moon was rising higher and higher and a chilly wind blew off the sea, bringing storm clouds with it. Where was she? She had especially asked to see him. Elsie's message had conveyed something urgent although when he had questioned her she could tell him nothing. Ellen might have been delayed by some domestic duties for a time but Charlotte was not a hard taskmaster and would have let her go by now. He began to feel a gnawing anxiety. All was not well. He decided to take the route which she usually followed from Admiralty House to Water's Edge. He walked up the hill from Seaforth Beach, turned right past the Burying Ground and walked down the hill into the town. There was unusual activity tonight: H.M.S. *Cornwallis* had docked the previous day and had spawned her crew into the streets of Simon's Town. There were sailors everywhere, and lights burned in every bar and hostelry in the town. Sam knew that they would be looking for fun and games and that a lone coloured youth might be viewed as a suitable target. He decided to turn off the main street and make his way back to Admiralty House along the beach. The moon lit his way and soon he was in sight of the Navy storehouses. He was just pondering whether to walk between the storehouses and the water or to move up above them to the road level again when he heard a low moan. He stopped in his tracks and saw a crumpled body on the beach. As he got nearer he registered with shock that it was a woman. Her skirts were torn and her lower body was bare. Then came the awful realisation: it was Ellen. He gathered her up into his arms and held her like a baby. Conflicting feelings of fierce love, deep compassion and savage anger swept through his being. Ellen's eyes flickered open. 'Sam?'

'Who has done this terrible thing to you?'

'The sailors,' she whispered.

'I'll kill them,' he vowed. 'Barbarians! The white man brings his civilisation to primitive Africa!' He was filled with unspeakable outrage that his precious Ellen had been violated. 'I'll find them and kill them. How many of them were there? What did they look like?'

'There were three of them, but I couldn't see their faces properly in the dark, Sam.'

'Any names?'

'One was called George. They were English.'

'From the *Cornwallis*. It docked this morning. I'll find them.'

'No, Sam. There are hundreds of sailors in town, not only from the *Cornwallis* but other ships as well. How do you think you'll find them?'

'I don't know, but I will. I've got friends in Simon's Town who'll help me…'

With a start, Sam noticed the growing stain of blood on Ellen's skirts.

'Ellen, you're bleeding. We must get help.'

'That's what I'm worried about, Sam – the baby.'

'Baby? What baby?'

For a moment Sam's mind was confused. Then comprehension dawned.

'Oh no, Ellen!'

'I'm sorry, Sam.'

'No, no, I'm not sorry about the baby. It's the damage that those skelms might have caused.'

As he stood up with Ellen in his arms he said, 'I understand now why you wanted to see me so urgently.'

Ellen nodded. 'Yes. And the Admiral knows and he wants to send me back to England. Oh, Sam, what am I to do? I don't want to go!' She was crying now from fear and exhaustion.

'No, you belong here with me. Don't worry. We'll make a plan.' Sam spoke reassuringly but his mind was racing. Where could he take Ellen? Not back to Admiralty House. There would be an outcry and too many questions. What was needed was immediate medical aid for Ellen and the baby.

'I'll take you to my cousin Christina. She is married to a fisherman and they live in a cottage on the outskirts of town.'

Sam was surprised at how light Ellen was as he made his way cautiously out of the Dockyard. He didn't want to meet any more sailors in his vulnerable position, so he walked as quickly as he could along the main road in the darkness. A wind had arisen and the clear moon of earlier was hidden by clouds. As he found the rough track leading to Christina's cottage the rain started biting at his arms and ankles. He would not have planned it this way, but now his path ahead was clear: he would not leave Ellen's side. He would protect her and keep her for the rest of his life.

CHAPTER TEN

Respite

Christina Jacob's cottage lay high up on a hill above Simon's Town. It was a simple rectangular white-washed structure with a thatched roof and a reed ceiling. From her home there was an unobstructed view of the harbour below and the fine stretch of water across to the other side of False Bay. The path up to the cottage was rough and ended in narrow steps which led to the front door. Christina's husband, Johannes, was a fisherman who made his living from the marine riches of False Bay. While there was never much money to spare, neither did his family starve. His young son Jacobus worked with him to supply the local boarding houses and hostelries with fresh fish, and they were negotiating a contract with the Royal Navy to provide salted fish for the fleet for their long voyages. The future looked good but in the meanwhile Johannes was content.

Christina had black hair, olive skin and dark brown eyes. Her individual features were not beautiful, but together they made up a picture that had its own unique loveliness. It was a quality in fact that came from within: warmth, compassion and caring that went beyond the bounds of her own family to encompass all with whom she came into contact.

On this particular evening she sat knitting quietly by the fireside. The children were already asleep. Johannes was also in bed because he was due to rise early for another fishing expedition. She hummed an ancient Malay folk tune quietly to herself as her nimble fingers progressed with the work. The fire crackled and occasionally a log would collapse with a soft sigh. It was comforting to be inside, embraced by the warmth of the fire, while outside the wind rose and rain began to spatter against the window panes.

Suddenly Christina's peace was disturbed by a thud on the front door. She got up quickly to look out of the window. In the darkness she could make out the shadow of a big man with a large bundle.

'Who is it?'

'It's me, Sam.'

Christina immediately opened the door.

'Sam! What are you doing here at this time of night? Come in! Come in!'

Sam struggled into the room with his burden. He was a strong man, used to hard manual labour, but the climb up the hill against wind and rain had demanded all his energy.

'What on earth have you got there?'

'It's a woman, Tina. I'll tell you the story later. Where can I put her down?'

Christina pointed to a wooden settle against the wall where Sam gently laid her. Ellen had fallen into an exhausted sleep. Christina looked at the drenched figure with tendrils of hair trailing across her white, drained face.

'It's one of the English women from Admiralty House. I've seen her in the town. What's happened to her?'

With someone to share the burden, Sam suddenly felt an overwhelming sense of relief. He sank down heavily on one of the oak benches and said, 'She's been raped. By sailors on a drunken rampage.'

'Bastards!' muttered Christina. 'But, as you say, we'll talk later. Right now this girl needs our help.'

Together they removed the sodden remains of Ellen's dress from her pale, bruised body.

'I hope she doesn't lose the baby. What do you think?' Sam asked.

'Baby? What baby? Is she with child?'

Christina looked up at Sam as understanding dawned on her face.

'Yours?'

Sam nodded.

'Oh no, Sam! This is dreadful.'

'No, it isn't, Tina, because I love her and will look after her. But will she keep the baby, my baby?'

Christina felt gently over Ellen's belly. 'That blood that you could see on her clothes comes from external wounds. I don't think it comes from the womb.'

An expression of anguish and rage washed over Sam's face. 'Do you think that my baby will live?' he whispered.

'It's too early to tell, but she can't be very far gone. We'll have to see what happens over the next few days. In the meanwhile she needs lots of rest and we must keep her warm and comfortable.'

She dried Ellen, put a cushion under her head, and covered her with a knitted blanket. Taking Sam by the hand she led him over to her own chair in front of the fire, poured him a hot drink from a pot on the hearth, drew up a stool and sat down next to him.

'Tell me what happened.'

Sam related the events of the evening and a short history of his relationship with Ellen. As he got to the end of his tale, Christina's heart went out to him.

'But why did you let yourself get involved with a white woman, Sam? You know from the experience with your own father that the relationship can go nowhere in this place.'

'I know, Tina, but I'm not my father and I'm not going to desert Ellen. She is my soulmate. She's like the other side of me,' he said, remembering the words Ellen had spoken to him at Water's Edge.

'Nee, Sam, you're being romantic. These are games that the rich, white people play. You need to choose someone of your own kind.'

'She is my own kind. It's just that our skins are of a different colour! I thought that you'd understand,' Sam said wearily.

'There's no going back now. Fate has made the decision for us and I'll look after her, but she needs someone to take care of her right now until I can work out the best thing to do.'

Christina paused. She knew that there would be difficulties ahead but there was only one course of action.

'She can stay here.'

Relief flooded Sam's features like the incoming tide over uneven sand.

'I hoped that you would say that. But what about Johannes?'

'Leave Johannes to me. He's a good man with a kind heart. He would never turn away anyone in trouble from his door and especially not you.'

Christina saw the dark smudges under Sam's eyes and how his shoulders drooped with fatigue. She had always been fond of her cousin, whom she knew well, and admired his gentle strength. As a young girl she had often been required to mind him when Sam's own mother, Lydia, came to live with them after his birth, and now that mothering instinct came to the fore.

'Enough talk now. You need to get some sleep.'

'You're right, Tina. I must get back to my quarters at the house,' said Sam, rising to his feet.

'Not tonight you won't. You'll sleep right here in Maria's bed and I'll take her into bed with me.'

Sam was too tired to protest and as soon as he got into the wooden cot he fell into a deep and sudden sleep.

* * *

Christina stood in the middle of the room and surveyed the dying fire. Things were not going to be easy. The girl would have to be kept hidden and secrets were not easily kept in Simon's Town ... the place was too small for that. She looked at the white pinched face of the young woman on the settle. Perhaps she would lose the baby. And that, under the circumstances, might be a blessing.

* * *

Ellen opened her eyes as the early morning rays streamed through the window. She was alarmed when the saw the unfamiliar surroundings of the simple cottage. She remembered the horror of the previous night and a cold shudder ran through her. Perhaps it was all just an awful nightmare and she would wake up back in her room at Admiralty House. Where was she? Where was Sam? She called out.

'Sam? Sam! Where are you?'

She was aware of a quiet presence which took her hand. Christina smiled down into her eyes.

'Hush, meisie. Sam has gone back to work in the stables at Admiralty House. I'm his cousin, Christina. He brought you here last night. Don't worry.'

Ellen's hands went to her belly.

'And the baby?'

'Well, we'll have to see. The next few days will tell whether you keep the baba or not. But now I want you to have something to eat.'

Ellen realised that despite everything she was hungry, and was pleased to take the hot drink and the bread which the older woman offered her.

'What about Miss Charlotte? She'll be worried.'

'Sam is going to speak to her today and tell her what has happened.'

'I should go back to the house,' said Ellen, starting to get up from the settle.

Christina restrained her with a firm but gentle hand. 'I think not. You need to rest for a while to try to make sure that you keep the baba. You want that, don't you?'

Ellen nodded and the words of the Admiral rang in her ears: '…we'll send her back to England with the fleet.'

'No, I can't go back to the house. Where can I go?' said Ellen as the desperation of her situation enveloped her like a dark cloud.

'Don't worry. You're going to stay here with me and Johannes and the children for a while. All you have to do is concentrate on getting strong again.'

Maria, Christina's youngest child, a girl of six with large soulful eyes and dark curly hair, came up and stood next to her mother. She had only seen white women at a distance before and felt a little frightened of them. However, her mother seemed to be happy so she was happy too.

'What a pretty child!' exclaimed Ellen. Suddenly she thought of the baby growing within her with a new sense of anticipation. Soon, if all went well, she too would have a beautiful child to love and care for. And she had Sam whom she loved and trusted with all her being. There was, really, much to be grateful for, she thought as she sank back into the cushions on the settle.

CHAPTER ELEVEN

Discovery

In the evening of the day after the engagement ball Charlotte missed Ellen. She was always punctual in her attendance on her young mistress, helping her to dress for dinner, but she was nowhere to be seen. Charlotte tried to reassure herself that Ellen was probably with Sam. She smiled in sympathy, but then remembered her father's words. It would not be a kindness to allow Ellen too many privileges. A cloud passed over her lovely features as she remembered the interview with her father that morning. How was she going to break the news to Ellen that she would have to go back to England with the fleet? The sooner Ellen knew the better. She must find her.

Before dinner she sought Elsie in the kitchen.

'Elsie, I'm looking for Ellen. Is she in the kitchen?'

'No, ma'am, she's not here.'

'Do you know where she is?'

Elsie averted her eyes.

'No, ma'am.'

Charlotte paused and looked at the comfortably proportioned woman. Everything about Elsie was round: her cheeks, her face, her ample bosom and her generous hips.

'I think that you know more than you're telling me, Elsie. I know that you want to protect Ellen, but perhaps you should know that I know about her and Sam.'

Elsie turned rapidly, her eyes rounder than ever. She hesitated, torn by divided loyalties to her mistress on the one hand and the young lovers on the other. At last her own genuine concern for Ellen combined with practical, down-to-earth common sense, swayed her decision.

'She's gone to meet him, ma'am.'

'What? Now! At night?'

'Yes, ma'am.'

'But it's dangerous. The sailors from the *Cornwallis* are in town. It's not safe for a young woman to be on her own in the street.'

'Yes, ma'am. I know. I tried to warn her, but she wouldn't listen. She'll be safe with Sam, ma'am, he's a sensible boy.'

'If she manages to evade the fleet,' Charlotte said wryly.

* * *

After another restless night Charlotte arose early the next morning. Rapid enquiries of Elsie revealed that Ellen had still not returned and her alarm grew. Sam was not in the stables either and Charlotte wondered wildly if they might have run off together. But where would they go? She decided to try to find out what had happened herself before raising a general alarm. She instructed James to saddle Amber and, refusing his offer to accompany her, went out to ride alone in the hope that she might find some clue as to Ellen's whereabouts.

As she rode through Simon's Town she recalled the carefree ride she had taken with John such a short time before. She rode up past Osmond's boatyard and the Martello Tower and followed the road around to Seaforth. This was where she had last seen Ellen and Sam together and she turned Amber down the rough track leading to Seaforth Beach. The bay with its fine stretch of sand showed no sign of human activity.

She urged her horse on past a rocky outcrop until she came to another smaller cove. This, she calculated, must be the exact spot where she had seen Ellen and Sam. This was Water's Edge where she and Ellen had collected perlemoen shells. She tethered Amber to a shrub and picked her way down through the rocks to the beach. The tide was high. She scrambled over a line of boulders, found herself a seat on a rock worn smooth by the constant pounding of the surf and sat down to think. The waves were chasing each other across the water, spume blowing high into the air. Noah's Ark projected the illusion of moving steadily southwards against the thrust of the current. Every now and then a great fan of foam rose out of the sea in front of it. Many of the rocks were submerged and the water clawed high up the sides of Roman Rock. Occasionally gulls flew past but there was no sign of the terns or the cormorants. The water soughed and sighed in its restless movement, straining ever higher up the beach until it reached the grassy bank of Water's Edge where it formed little whirlpools between the rocks on the edge of the shore. The sea threw up angry plumes of white water and the spray was blown back by the wind onto Charlotte's face.

She sat there, unaware of the passage of time, wrestling with the problem which had kept her awake all night and wondering if she should break the news of Ellen's departure to her father and how she could best help her once she found her. Her troubled spirits were reflected in the turbulent waters around her and in her heart she felt uneasy. At length she rose and returned to Amber and rode back to Admiralty House. By now the wind had risen and squalls of rain beat against her. She spurred her horse and quickly regained the stable where James was waiting for her with anxiety written all over his face.

Charlotte handed Amber over to him and ran back into the house by a side door and up to her room by the back stairs so that her father would not see her. Perhaps Ellen would be waiting for her with a reasonable excuse for her absence. She had her hand on her bedroom door-handle when she heard a whisper coming up the stairs.

'Miss Charlotte!'

She turned to see Elsie's ample frame labouring up the last few steps of the staircase.

'What is it, Elsie?'

Elsie struggled to catch her breath after the exertion of climbing the stairs. 'Please come down to the kitchen, ma'am. There's somebody who wants to talk to you.'

'Ellen?' Charlotte's heart rose.

Elsie shook her head and Charlotte followed her back down the stairs to the kitchen. There outside the kitchen door was Sam.

'Sam! Come inside out of the rain. Where's Ellen? What's happened to her? I've been so worried.'

Haltingly, in his heavily accented English, Sam related the events of the previous twenty-four hours. Charlotte was horrified at the tale which took shape. She had been anxious about Ellen going out alone into the night but her worst fears were realised when she heard about the sailors' violation of her friend. When Sam told her that Ellen knew that the Admiral intended to send her back to England with the fleet, Charlotte burst out, 'But how did Ellen know this? I haven't told her. I haven't seen her since the night of the ball!'

'That I don't know, ma'am, but she knows.'

'She must have heard my conversation with my father the morning after the ball. Perhaps she was outside the door.' As the realisation dawned she exclaimed, 'Then this is Papa's fault! If he hadn't been so unreasonable Ellen would never have run off like that! Poor Ellen!' Tears glistened in Charlotte's eyes. 'What a horrible experience. How is she?'

'As well as can be expected, ma'am. She's resting with Christina.'

Suddenly a thought struck Charlotte.

'Did you know that Ellen is with child?'

'Yes, ma'am, I do now,' said Sam steadily.

'Is the baby unharmed?'

'It's too early to tell yet, ma'am. But she's in good hands with Christina. She has delivered many babies.'

'I must go to her at once!' said Charlotte.

'If you'll excuse me, ma'am, I don't think that's a very good idea,' intervened Elsie, who had anticipated what Charlotte's reaction might be. 'It's best that as few people as possible know what's happened. If you was to go riding up to Christina's cottage you would draw attention to yourself and the secret would soon be out, which would do Ellen and Sam no good.'

Charlotte considered for a moment and realised the sense of Elsie's words.

'You're right, Elsie. Our first duty must be to help Ellen and that means keeping the whole business as quiet as we can, but we can at least send food, clothing and money,' said Charlotte. 'Come, Elsie, you can pack up some food.'

It helped to be doing something, and Charlotte wasted no time gathering together some warm garments and blankets which, together with the hamper of cheese, bread, meat and fruit that Elsie had put together, she handed over to Sam.

'Give this to Ellen with my love,' she said. 'Tell her not to worry. We'll find a way out of this somehow.'

Sam raised his hand to his head in a gesture of respect and disappeared into the gathering storm.

Charlotte walked slowly back up to her room. Should she tell her father of these latest developments? Would the knowledge of Ellen's rape at the hands of the sailors put him in a difficult position? How was it that life could have become so complicated in such a few short hours? The more she thought about it the more she realised that she would have to confide in him. Ellen's obvious disappearance would soon be remarked on and would have to be explained. She decided to speak to her father after dinner.

CHAPTER TWELVE

Revelations

The dinner that evening was the first time that Charlotte had talked to her father since she had told him about Ellen's pregnancy. John, who was unaware of the tension between them, kept up the small talk.

'This is an excellent meal, Charlotte. Elsie is a superb cook. Do you think that she might have an apprentice or a niece or someone who would like to come and work for us when we're married? She'd have to be prepared to come and live out on the eastern frontier though.'

'Are you still determined on that plan?' Edward enquired. 'I don't think that you realise how wild that part of the country is. It's unsettled except for the marauding Xhosa. You won't enjoy the elegant lifestyle that you are accustomed to, either here or in England. Even at sea you've had people to wait on you.'

'Perhaps I can train some Xhosas to be servants,' laughed John. 'Stop being so serious Uncle! This is a time for celebration.'

Edward smiled reluctantly. It was true that he was experiencing a deep content knowing that his daughter was to be married to a young man in whom he had confidence and who had a genuine regard for her.

Charlotte took little part in the conversation. She was preoccupied with Ellen's problems and how she should broach the subject with her father. After dinner she asked him to take a walk with her. The storm had blown away. It was a fine night and the moon rode high in the heavens.

'Let's go down to the beach, Papa,' Charlotte suggested. Edward nodded. He was keen to re-establish a happy rapport after their recent argument. Father and daughter strolled out onto the veranda and stepped into the garden where the fountain shimmered in the moonlight. They turned right past the rose garden and down to a path which led to the Admiral's private beach and jetty. The jetty had been recently constructed and enabled the Admiral to receive visitors from the fleet and to travel out to the ships with ease, without drawing attention to himself as he would do if he went down to the Dockyard.

'You must realise how happy I am about your engagement to John,' Edward began as they walked along the beach. 'What does concern me however, is his plan to settle on the eastern frontier. It's not the kind of place which I should wish for you. You have been gently reared and I fear that you would not be able to cope with the harsh conditions in the eastern Cape, let alone the danger.'

'You're underestimating me again, Papa,' Charlotte said with forced gaiety, 'but it's premature to worry about that. John may not be successful in his application. A great deal can happen in the next few months.'

'I suppose you're right,' her father agreed. 'By the way, I've been meaning to ask you, where is Ellen? For two days now I've noticed that she hasn't been there to help you dress for dinner. Is she not well?'

'That's what I wanted to speak to you about, Papa,' Charlotte said. 'There's been a mishap.'

'A mishap?' Edward stopped in his tracks and turned to look into his daughter's eyes. 'What on earth has happened? I hope that she hasn't been injured?'

'Yes, I'm afraid that she has, Papa,' Charlotte replied, and she told him the story. When she described Ellen's rape by the sailors, Edward's mouth stiffened into a hard line.

'I'll have them court-martialled,' he muttered.

'I've been thinking about that, Papa, and I don't know if that is a wise plan. It would cause such a stir. You would have to interrogate nearly every one of the sailors. It's unlikely that anyone would give himself up. You would have to drag Ellen into it. And also, with the background of mutiny, the sailors are restless and ready to rise up in defence of each other.'

Edward had to agree with the wisdom of this. The memory of the attempted mutiny on the *Argonaut* was fresh in his brain. It was not an isolated incident. The mutinies on the Spithead and the Noire had been alarming. Mutiny was ugly and destructive. It weakened the morale and spirit of the Navy, which at this time, with the threat of Napoleon ever present, even though he was imprisoned on Elba, must at all costs be preserved.

'Well, Charlotte, I must say that for a young woman you have an extraordinary understanding of naval matters.'

'Well, I am your daughter, sir. I have learnt most of it from you.'

Edward smiled, despite himself.

'Where is Ellen now?'

Charlotte recounted the history of Sam's rescue of Ellen and the haven which he had found for her with Christina.

Edward listened intently as Charlotte spoke. His eyes were fixed on the silhouettes of the ships swaying on the water. As she finished speaking he turned slowly to face his daughter.

'There's something I have to tell you, Charlotte. I think that, given the circumstances, you have a right to know. Ellen is your sister.'

CHAPTER THIRTEEN

The Confession

Charlotte was momentarily transfixed: Ellen, her sister?

'It was a long time ago, Charlotte, well over twenty-one years ago when I had a secret liaison. I came home on shore leave – I had been at sea for months. I'm ashamed to say that I was engaged to your mother at the time. But of course our courtship was conducted with the utmost decorum. I want to assure you that I loved your mother very much and I was heart-broken when she died.'

'But you were still able to have an affair with another woman?' questioned Charlotte bitterly.

Edward shrugged his shoulders.

'I don't understand. I've known Ellen all her life. She was born to Agnes and Gabriel not long before I was. Do you mean that Agnes...' The realisation dawned on her.

'Agnes was very beautiful, you know,' Edward said. 'Not that that excuses anything. Ellen looks very like her – the same dark hair and brilliant brown eyes. The same figure...' Edward's voice trailed off.

'But Agnes and Gabriel have been married for years! They are a devoted couple and loyal retainers at Everhurst.'

'I know it's difficult for you to understand. I had, as I say, just returned from sea. It was a warm day in September. I had been out riding and stopped to rest under an oak tree at Everhurst. I leaned back against the trunk of the tree watching the labourers working in the fields. One figure stood out, a tall slender woman who moved gracefully among the haystacks. I recognised her, of course, because she was the wife of Gabriel who worked in the stables.'

'Of course,' Charlotte smiled sardonically.

'You're not making this any easier, Charlotte. It was a passing passion you understand. We met a few times. Agnes was a little older than me and that made her even more attractive.'

'I don't think I want to hear any more of this.'

'No, I'm sure you don't. I've not spoken of this to anyone apart from my father since it happened. When Agnes found out that she was with child she came to see me. As I've said already by that time I was engaged to your mother. I had to tell my father who was furious. There was no question of marriage of course. There never would have been anyway with a girl of that class.'

'And in any case she was married,' interpolated Charlotte who found herself revolted by this upper-class arrogance. She was beginning to realise just how destructive class distinction could be. Ellen had been her close friend for years, but the spectre of class haunted her as it had her mother before her.

'Gabriel never knew. We had to make sure that Ellen was well provided for, of course. So my father gave him the management of the stables. It was fortunate that that position came up at the time and Gabriel had worked hard and had a talent with horses. We were able to promote him with a good house to live in and make sure that he and his family were comfortable.'

'You mean Gabriel never knew that Ellen was not his daughter?'

'No.'

'So Ellen has been living a lie all of these years.'

'Well, it depends on how you look at it. We thought that it would be the best solution for everyone. It wasn't easy for me. Ellen was born at much the same time that I was married to your mother. And I was sworn to silence.'

'How difficult for you,' Charlotte said with bitter irony. Edward flinched at the sharpness of her tone.

'After you were born and the shocking death of your mother, I was numb for a long time. I was very concerned about you too because you were the only child. It was wonderful for me when you started playing with Ellen. It brought great joy to my heart to see my daughters in close companionship, especially as the Navy required me to be away from home a good deal of the time. When the time came for you to have a lady's maid, Ellen was the obvious choice. You know the rest of the story.'

Charlotte found that it was difficult to speak. Her chest felt as though it was about to burst with suppressed passion. She fixed her eyes on the tall ships and eventually she whispered, 'It seems that Ellen's life has run a similar course to her mother's. Except that in Ellen's case there is no one to help her out.' She looked challengingly at her father.

'We can give her money, of course.'

'But we can't have her marrying Sam, can we? We can't have the daughter of the Admiral marrying a half-caste! We can't risk the remotest possibility of scandal, can we?'

'Charlotte, you're being unfair and unkind!'

'Am I? Am I? If you hadn't been so unsupportive and unsympathetic, decreeing that Ellen must go back to England, she would not have run off in such a panic into the arms of those drunken sailors.'

'What do you mean? She didn't hear me say that. She wasn't there. Unless perhaps you told her?' Edward said defensively.

'Oh yes, I'm afraid she was there – on the other side of the door. She heard everything you said and she didn't know how she was to carry on. So in desperation she ran away. It was your fault!'

'Oh Charlotte, don't!'

'Don't what? Don't make you face the truth about your past and your prejudices, let alone what you owe to your own legitimate daughter whose dearest friend, who also happens to be your daughter, is in desperate need?'

'Charlotte! Charlotte! What would you have me do?'

'Be human. Be the father that Ellen needs.'

'You don't know what you're asking. As I've said before the scandal would have serious repercussions. It's not only the family, but the Navy and the whole political situation.'

'How can you stand there and speak about your regard for your family? It's pretence. What you're worried about is appearances – the perfect Admiral, with the perfect family in a perfect house. Well, I think that it's a perfect disgrace!'

And with that Charlotte turned away from her father and ran up the beach to the path back to the house where the candlelight still spilled out from the great windows onto the garden.

CHAPTER FOURTEEN

Recovery

Autumn crept over Simon's Town with balmy days, clear blue skies and cold, crisp nights. Ellen made a good recovery physically, but the horror of that nightmare incident with the sailors was etched in her brain. She tried not to think of it, but if she did, the pieces were disconnected. She could not remember the order and sequence of events.

She helped Christina with domestic chores around the cottage, baking bread, learning to cook the traditional Malay dishes, washing, ironing and helping with the children. She had always been fond of children, and once they had become accustomed to having a strange white woman living with them, Christina's children became very attached to her. She learned to sing some of the haunting melodies of these fisher-people, and taught the children folk-songs which she had learned as a child in England. Meanwhile the baby grew within her and her belly began to swell. She gained a new glow and her beauty was more radiant than ever.

Sam came to visit her as often as he could, usually in the evening after his day's work in the stables was over. He brought with him food, clothing and messages from Charlotte. Charlotte herself longed to visit Ellen but the good sense of Elsie's words cautioned her. The whole affair needed to be kept as secret as possible.

Sam and Ellen were obliged to stay inside the cottage for fear of being seen, although occasionally in the evening they would walk out a little way into the hills behind Christina and Johannes' home to a concealed spot where they could talk. Sam was becoming increasingly frustrated by their situation and his inability to do anything about it. He felt keenly his responsibility towards Ellen and, while he was grateful for everything which Christina and Johannes were doing for her, he longed to take care of her himself. The prospect of doing that, however, seemed to be very remote. While up to now he had been content with his lot in the stables at Admiralty House, he could see life dragging on interminably. There was little prospect of any change in his future. What he earned as a stable-hand would be insufficient to keep a wife and young child. He might eventually be promoted to head groom, but James was a relatively young man and he would have to wait a long time for that. It was not that he was unhappy in his present situation. Admiral Lacey ruled with a benevolent discipline; working conditions were fair; he had clean and comfortable accommodation in the servants' quarters at Admiralty House. As he was not a slave, he was free to come and go as he wished. There was plenty of food and his relationship with Elsie ensured that he was well supplied with titbits. But that had been before. It seemed like another lifetime. Ellen's pregnancy had changed his whole world view. He did not shirk his new responsibilities and it was a sign of his moral fibre that he never once considered that he should leave Ellen's side. In fact, memories of his father's desertion of his mother when she was pregnant and the consequent struggle which she had had, before and after Sam's birth and throughout his growing years, made him more determined than ever to support Ellen.

Ellen and Sam talked endlessly of what they might do – move to another part of the country perhaps. Sam thought that he might have more chance of finding remunerative employment in Cape Town, but he worried about who would look after Ellen. Every time the conversation returned to the problem of the lack of money. Sam cast around in his mind. All he really knew was how to look after horses. He couldn't read or write but he was strong, energetic and prepared to work hard: there must be some opportunity for him he thought. One thing he was sure of was his love for Ellen. He had known that he loved her with a passion but now there was a new element, a desire to cherish her and protect her from all harm as he would a new born foal. Well he would just have to be alert to any opportunity which presented itself. As they sat in the growing dusk one evening, with a chill breeze blowing off the water, they saw Johannes toiling up the hill after a day's work down in the harbour.

'There's a contented man,' Sam said, 'going home to his wife and family. Perhaps he'll have some ideas. I'll talk to him later.'

As Johannes drew closer Sam realised that his appearance was deceptive. The expression in Johannes's eyes was anxious. Sam walked down to meet him as he climbed up the stairs to the cottage. He stepped laboriously as if he had suddenly aged since the morning.

'Johannes – what's the matter? What's happened?'

Johannes shook his head dumbly and stumbled into the cottage. He slumped onto the wooden settle. His face was white under the tanned skin. Christina turned from her cooking, her eyes widening in alarm.

'What's the matter?' She echoed Sam's words.

Johannes put his hand out to her.

'It's the boat.'

'The boat? Why? What's happened? You went out fishing early this morning.' Christina took his hand as she spoke.

'Ja, I had a good catch this morning and took some fish into the town to sell, and when I got back the boat was gone. I couldn't believe my eyes.'

'Do you know who took it?' Sam asked.

'Some sailors found it at its usual moorings. They took it out into the bay and crashed it into Noah's Ark. It is completely wrecked.'

'How do you know?' asked Christina.

'James, the head groom at Admiralty House, saw it when

he was exercising the Admiral's horse Champion on Seaforth Beach.'

'What happened to the sailors?'

'They drowned, I hope.' Sam's words were as bitter as bile.

'I'm not sure how many there were. James couldn't tell from the distance. He saw two of them who managed to swim back to shore.'

'We'll have to report this to the Admiral – the Royal Navy. They'll have to compensate us,' Christina said.

Johannes shook his head.

'Who would believe us? The sailors will lie. They'll be too frightened to tell the truth. I'm afraid we're finished.'

Sam could feel his anger rising to a passion. The sailors! The British! Who were they to come to Simon's Town and wreck other people's lives? He looked at his precious Ellen who had been violated by them. He looked at Johannes, a good, honest, noble man whose livelihood was now destroyed by the carelessness of the intruders. Feelings that he had not known before surged through his being. He wanted revenge. He would take revenge. It was not worth it to obey the law of the English invaders.

Christina for once was at a loss. They were totally dependent on the boat. There was very little money saved and they had children to provide for. Johannes knew no trade other than fishing. But without a boat he was powerless.

'We'll have to go to Cape Town,' she said at last, as she gave Johannes a hot drink. 'There's work there in the town. Perhaps Johannes can get a job with one of the fishing fleets.'

'No!' shouted Sam from the depth of his being. 'What will become of Ellen? You can't take her away from me!'

'What else is there to do?' Johannes said helplessly, lifting one hand like a broken wing.

Sam walked around the cottage, his mind turning and tumbling. Suddenly he hit on a plan, so daring that it took his breath away.

'Smuggling,' he said. 'I've heard that there's a fortune to be made in exporting brandy to England now that France is in such disorder with the war.'

Christina and Johannes were silent.

'It's illegal,' Christina said.

'If I could think of a legal way to make money, I would,' Sam said. 'There aren't many choices for the likes of us.'

'If we get caught the punishment will be dreadful,' Johannes said. 'The British authorities wouldn't listen to us for a minute, especially as we're coloured. They'd throw us into the Castle dungeons in Cape Town.' He shuddered. 'Death would be preferable to that.'

'Well I'm prepared to take the risk,' Sam said. 'I have a contact at a Constantia wine estate who would supply the brandy for a reward. I've been told about some English smugglers who are anchored just outside False Bay even now.'

'But we have no boat,' pointed out Johannes. 'How do you think that you'd get out to the ship with the brandy?'

'I'll get one,' Sam said. 'I'll beg, borrow or steal. Somehow I'll get one. Whatever it is that I have to do. I can't go on like this in a state of indecision.'

Johannes shook his head.

'I don't like it,' he said.

'But we've got nothing to lose!' Sam insisted. 'We don't owe any loyalty to these Englishmen!' For an instant there flashed into Sam's mind the image of Admiral Lacey, firm, yet fair. He had always been a kindly employer. And Miss Charlotte, always ready with a smile, who had been so good to Ellen. Resolutely he pushed these images away. It was easier to hate the brutes that had harmed his people.

'Look, Johannes, I don't think that you personally should be involved. There needs to be a man left to look after the women and children if anything goes wrong.'

Johannes started to protest but he was torn between loyalty to his family and the desire to provide for them.

'I'll need someone to help me with the boat though,' Sam continued. 'Petrus, my friend from Constantia, won't step off dry land. What about Jacobus?'

'No!' Christina cried out. 'He's only sixteen.'

'He's a strong lad,' Sam said. 'And he knows all about handling boats.'

Johannes nodded dumbly. He felt impotent in the face of the passion of the young man before him. Christina turned away, her eyes blinded with tears. Suddenly her peaceful, ordered life in the hills above Simon's Town was shaken to the core.

CHAPTER FIFTEEN

A Truce

After their confrontation on the Admiral's jetty, relations were strained between Charlotte and her father. She refused to speak to him unless absolutely necessary, but life had to go on. She was responsible for the domestic management of Admiralty House and was required to act as hostess for her father on social occasions. In addition there was the wedding to prepare for.

John had to be told about Ellen's disappearance and Edward took the opportunity to tell him one morning after breakfast on the veranda while Charlotte was busy with Elsie in the kitchen.

'Sex-starved bastards!' he said. 'Mind you, if she hadn't been so stupid as to consort with a nigger, none of this would have happened. She has only herself to blame.' Charlotte joined them on the veranda in time to hear this last utterance.

'John, how can you be so unfeeling?'

'Charlotte, in this world you have to stick to your own kind. Discipline at sea depends on absolute obedience of the crew to the officers who are drawn from the upper class. That's what has held the British aristocracy together for centuries.'

'None of that high-handed talk with me, if you please! English lords have been having affairs with working class girls for years.' Charlotte realised the implications of what she was saying and dared not look at her father. 'You've known Ellen, like me, for most of her life. How can you discard her as a useless toy?'

'There's nothing to be done, Charlotte. She's made her bed – if you'll excuse the pun,' he said with a coarse laugh, 'and now she must lie in it. We can't support her liaison with a Negro…'

'He's not a Negro!'

'We can't support it anyway. And if she won't go back to England then she must take the consequences here.'

'You're each as bad as each other,' said Charlotte, looking from John to her father, 'hidebound by your birth and colour!'

'What would you have us do, Charlotte?' Edward said in a conciliatory tone. 'Come and sit down and have some coffee with us.'

Charlotte sank into one of the upholstered wicker chairs and sighed. 'To tell you the truth, Papa, I really don't know the best course. Ellen has steadfastly refused to go back to England, and now her pregnancy is more advanced she would probably give birth on board ship, which is not to be recommended. As much as I would like to have her here at Admiralty House to look after her, I do understand that it would be very difficult. She would be subject to insults and ridicule from the other staff. She and Sam don't fit it in here any more.'

'In a way it would be easier if they were on a farm,' Edward said. 'I've been told that the Dutch farmers, despite their puritanical ways, are not averse to intimate relationships with their female slaves.'

'That's right, Uncle,' sniggered John. 'They read the Bible to the assembled household at the end of the day, and when their wives and family are safely in bed they go and have some fun in the slave huts.'

'That wouldn't do for Ellen at all,' said Charlotte, shocked at John's callousness. 'The one thing that Ellen knows is that she loves Sam and that he loves her, and they both want to have this child.'

'They would probably be better off in Cape Town,' Edward said. 'It's a much more cosmopolitan society than Simon's Town, which has a largely itinerant population. Perhaps after the baby is born we should encourage Sam to get a job in Cape Town. I would miss him because he's a good groom, but I can use my contacts to try to get him a suitable position in the stables of a decent family.'

'It still won't be easy,' Charlotte said, 'but perhaps that is a solution and I would be able to keep in touch with Ellen – even visit her, which I can't do here.'

'I'll talk to Sam when the moment is right,' Edward said. 'In the meanwhile we need to discuss the arrangements for your wedding. I've spoken to my old friend, Reverend Jarvis, the naval chaplain, who has agreed to conduct the ceremony.'

'But where are we going to have it?' Charlotte asked. 'St George's Church was damaged so badly in that storm last week that it is hardly likely to be in a fit state for a wedding in December.'

'Can't have been very well built then,' John commented.

'Perhaps not, but do you know that that was the first, and is at the moment the only consecrated Anglican Church in the Cape?' Edward said.

'That's surprising,' John said. 'I would have thought that there would be one in Cape Town.'

'There are plans for one but at the moment there is only the Dutch Groote Kerk.'

'This is all very interesting,' Charlotte said with an impatient shrug of her shoulders, 'but it doesn't solve the problem of the venue for our wedding.'

'I've had an idea,' Edward said. 'You know that I ordered the construction of the Mast House and Sail Loft as well as the Dockyard Wall earlier this year?'

'Yes, it's a sturdy building, unlikely to fall over in a storm,' John said.

'I went with John to see it,' Charlotte added. 'The Sail Loft is a lovely light room with a row of windows overlooking the Dockyard and bay.'

'Well what do you think of using that as a church?'

'A church?' John queried. 'But it will be full of dockworkers and their tools. Quite unsuitable.'

'No, listen a minute,' Edward said. 'The Loft is used for

storing sails – that's why it is so long – but the sail-makers are there only during the week. We needed plenty of light for them to be able to see to do their work.'

'But they're not there on Sundays!' said Charlotte. 'What a clever idea, Papa. Can you arrange it?'

'Very easily. The naval officers and their wives as well as the few local people are anxious to have a place to worship as soon as possible.'

'I couldn't think of a better setting for a naval wedding,' Charlotte said, 'but what about the reception?'

'I thought we'd have the reception here at the house,' Edward said.

'It'll be like that splendid ball in April,' John said. 'It's a capital plan, don't you think, Charlotte?' he said, taking her hand.

'Yes it is,' Charlotte replied, thinking as she spoke that it was that night when Ellen was helping her dress for the ball that she had told Charlotte about her pregnancy and her relationship with Sam. That was just a few short weeks ago, but it felt like another lifetime. She thought of Ellen up in Christina's cottage above Simon's Town. She never saw her nowadays but had regular news of her through Sam. She was aware that Ellen's disappearance and whereabouts had been the subject of much gossip both among the staff in both Admiralty House and among the people of Simon's Town, although she refused to engage in any talk herself. She missed Ellen. There was a gaping hole in her life which could never be filled, like a hollow in the sand that cannot hold the water of the sea. Although her father had not forbidden her to reveal the truth to Ellen about her real identity, Charlotte had decided not to tell her that they were sisters. It would not help the situation and might encourage her to feel dissatisfied. It was better that she continue to think of Agnes and Gabriel as her legitimate parents It was a tangled web, though, and she suddenly felt very tired.

'I think,' she said, 'that I would like to have a change of air before the wedding. I'm finding Simon's Town a trifle suffocating.'

'Would you like to come with me to the Franschhoek Valley next month, Charlotte?' Edward asked. 'I'm going to visit Etienne le Roux. He's a Huguenot farmer who owns a wine estate called L'Ourmarin, and he's invited me to stay for a week. He's hoping to get a contract to supply wine to the Navy, but he's a fine fellow and very hospitable. I'd be glad of your company and I think you would enjoy it.'

'I don't know if it's such a good idea for you to go gallivanting around the countryside,' John said, pouring himself another cup of coffee. 'You've got to be more circumspect now that you're an engaged woman.'

'Don't be so stuffy, John. Lady Anne Barnard travelled all over the Cape at the end of the last century and she acted as hostess to the governor.'

'Why don't you come with us as well, John?' Edward offered.

'Thank you, no, Uncle. I've planned to go to Cape Town to buy myself a horse.'

'Well, I like the idea,' said Charlotte. 'I think it's just what I need.'

CHAPTER SIXTEEN

The Plot

The four men hunched together over the candle on the bare wooden table sent distorted shadows up against the rough plaster wall of the cottage. Johannes and his son Jacobus, Sam, and Petrus, a middle-aged coloured man, were deep in conversation. Petrus, Sam's contact from the wine farm, Wittebomen, in Constantia, was also a groom and worked in the stables of the estate. He and Sam had met in Cape Town at a horse sale. Petrus was small and wiry and although he was only forty-five years old, he had a wizened face and a wide gap where his front teeth had been in his youth.

'Have you managed to get a boat?' Sam asked.

'Ja,' Johannes replied. 'Willem Smit says that I can borrow his boat for a few days while he's visiting his family on the other side of False Bay.'

'Does he know what you want the boat for?'

Johannes shook his head. He found this deception difficult. 'Willem thinks that I want to use it for fishing. He says I've got to pay him when I sell the fish.'

'You'll have enough to do that and more,' Sam said, with a show of confidence that was born of desperation.

'It's a risky business, Sam. If you get caught we'll never see you again.' Johannes's face was drawn with anxiety.

'Ja, you know what the Navy's like. They show no mercy with their own, leastways the likes of us,' Petrus said.

'Remember those men who were keelhauled last year,' Johannes continued. 'Their bodies were so scratched and broken that if they had survived, their lives wouldn't have been worth living.'

'Navy discipline is harsh, man. I can remember how they treated the mutineers in Table Bay in 1797. I was a young man then, but I still remember seeing the bodies of the leaders of the mutiny hanging from the yardarm of the *Sceptre*,' said Petrus, as an involuntary shudder rippled through his body.

'Ja!' Johannes agreed. 'It was the same here in Table Bay this last January. You saw the hanging on the *Argonaut* didn't you, Sam?'

'Yes, I did,' Sam nodded, 'but I'm prepared to take that chance.' The plot that Sam had devised was dangerous. Petrus would acquire a supply of brandy from the wine estate where he worked and would bring it over by ox-wagon to Muizenberg under the cover of darkness. It was too risky to attempt to bring it along the coast road to Simon's Town at night. At Muizenberg, Jacobus and Sam would receive the kegs of brandy and stow them away in the boat which they would then bring around to Simon's Bay by sea. Jacobus frequently went out at night to fish with his father and knew the location of the dangerous rocks.

'It's best to avoid the seafront of Simon's Town. We'll bring the boat around to Water's Edge where we can stow it under the sand behind some rocks,' said Sam, thinking of how the trysting place where he and Ellen used to meet was taking on a grim purpose.

'I'm worried about Jacobus going,' Johannes said.

'Ja, I know,' Sam agreed, 'but we need two of us to manage the boat.'

'I should be going!'

'I know that's how you feel, but someone has to stay with the women and children,' Sam said.

'And I want to go, Pa!' Jacobus said. 'I know these waters as well as you.'

Johannes looked at his son with a mixture of pride and trepidation. 'I wish there was another way...' he began.

'Well, there isn't!' Sam said flatly. 'The English smugglers will pay well for the brandy which they'll sell in England for a lot of money. And if it works this time, then we'll do it again!'

'Let's not be greedy now, Sam. We need some money to get us out of a hole – for me to buy a new boat and for you to have some capital to make a new start somewhere. I've no taste for a life trying to escape the law.'

'And I'm going to buy a couple of good horses to try some transport riding,' Petrus said.

'Good idea,' Johannes said. 'This is the first and last time, Sam.'

'You're both right, of course,' Sam said.

'So we're agreed then on Saturday in two weeks' time,' Petrus said. 'It's a good opportunity because the master's going to Cape Town for a party which Lord Charles Somerset is giving at Government House. I'll bribe the head groom to let me have a wagon for the night. I'll meet you at Peck's farmhouse near Fort Muizenberg at ten o'clock to hand over the brandy. After that it's up to you.'

'Right. Let's drink to the success of our venture,' Johannes said as he uncorked a bottle of red muscatel which stood on the table between them and poured a good measure into each of four tumblers. As they raised their glasses each met the eyes of the others in silent salute.

CHAPTER SEVENTEEN

L'Ourmarin

The carriage moved at a steady pace through the long avenue of oak trees which cast a deep shade over the dusty road. Ahead of them Charlotte could see carved wooden gates flanked by tall pillars which framed a white-washed farmhouse crowned with high Dutch gables. Inside the gates the driveway became a circle embracing an ornamental lake with a fountain at its centre. A veranda which extended the width of the house was roofed by a pergola covered with a prolific grape vine, which threw patterns of shade over the blinding white walls. Behind the house rose massive mountain peaks: on the right the towering crags of the Simonsberg; on the left the majestic range of the Groot Drakenstein. Purple-grey in the brilliant afternoon sunlight, the mountains cut a clearly defined outline against the sky.

As Charlotte stepped down from the carriage on the arm of her father, she found the heat almost overpowering and was glad to move into the shade of a giant oak tree which stood at the side of the house. Two tall, well-built men moved forward to greet them.

'Welcome to L'Ourmarin,' said the older of the two, holding out his hand.

'Ah, hello, Etienne, how very happy I am to see you again!' Edward Lacey said as he grasped the proffered hand. Although they came from very different backgrounds, one from the sea and the other from the land, Edward and Etienne had taken an instant liking to each other when they had met in Cape Town. There was an affinity between them which arose naturally. It was difficult to explain and neither cared to try to do so. They found an ease in their relationship and enjoyed each other's company.

'I'm delighted and honoured to be able to offer hospitality to you and …your daughter, I presume?'

'Ah, yes, of course, I was forgetting for a moment, you haven't met Charlotte, have you? Allow me to present my daughter, Charlotte Lacey. Charlotte, this is Mijnheer Etienne le Roux.'

Etienne, silver-haired and tanned, bowed over the delicate gloved hand which was offered to him and said, 'How do you do, Juffrouw Lacey.' As he stood up he turned and introduced his companion.

'This is my son Paul.'

'How do you do, Mijnheer le Roux,' said Charlotte, smiling sweetly and holding out her hand.

Paul le Roux was an athletic-looking young man of about twenty-six. His blonde hair fell forward over his eyes which seemed to reflect the brilliant blue of the sky. In repose his expression was serious but he had a wide smile which crinkled and lit up his face. He had a relaxed bearing and the confidence of a man who, despite his youth, had found his place in life. As he took her hand and bent over it for a moment her composure was disturbed.

'I'm delighted to meet you, Juffrouw Lacey.'

'Come in, come in. You must be tired and thirsty after that long drive,' Etienne said leading the way through the doorway into the cool of the house. On the other side of the square, highly polished flagstones Etienne's wife awaited them.

Marie le Roux was an angular woman with sharp features: a long nose, a straight humourless mouth and a set jaw. The black of her garments was relieved only by a white lace collar and bonnet tied under her chin. Even her hair, parted in the middle, was as dark as a crow's feathers. The hand that she extended to Charlotte was cold and her smile was tight.

'Welcome to L'Ourmarin, Juffrouw Lacey. You must feel in need of refreshment.'

'I certainly am,' Charlotte replied. 'It's been a long, dusty journey. Is it always so hot at this time of the year?'

'No, juffrouw. This is very unusual. We're experiencing what you English call an Indian summer,' Paul said, looking straight into her eyes with undisguised admiration.

'The heat may be uncomfortable for us, but it's very good for the grapes. It brings them to a fine maturity,' Etienne intervened.

'Will you men stop talking about your grapes and bring some chilled wine for our guests here!' Marie's sharp tones interrupted them.

She turned to Charlotte. 'Allow me to show you to your room while my husband is getting the wine,' she said. She led the way to a large bedroom on one side of the voorkamer. Two deep-set sash windows were shuttered against the afternoon sun. Marie opened them wide to reveal the view across the lake to the far hills.

'What a beautiful view!' Charlotte exclaimed.

'Ja,' agreed Marie, a shadow of a smile twitching her lip. 'We're very proud of our valley – Franschhoek. All of the inhabitants are descended from the Huguenots who escaped religious persecution in France in the seventeenth century. We made a fresh start here, and Franschhoek has been our home ever since.'

A young black woman appeared at the door with Charlotte's trunk on her head.

'Put it over there, Candaza.' Marie pointed to a low table where the slave deftly placed the trunk and then stood silently with her eyes downcast. It struck Charlotte how different this was from her relationship with Ellen, whom she remembered with a pang.

'I'm sure you will want to change.' Marie looked Charlotte up and down and Charlotte was suddenly aware of the low cut of her dress under her travelling cloak which contrasted sharply with Marie le Roux's high neckline and long sleeves.

'Yes, I would like to get out of these clothes which seem to have picked up a prodigious amount of the Cape dust.'

'There is fresh water in the pitcher,' Marie said unsmilingly. 'Candaza will help you to unpack and to dress. She is your slave for as long as you are here and will sleep next to you on the floor.'

'Thank you, but that won't be necessary,' Charlotte said. 'I packed my own clothes before I left Simon's Town and I'm sure that Candaza would be happier in her own bed.'

'She doesn't have one,' Marie said. 'But if you don't want her in the room she will sleep outside the door.' Her voice dripped with disapproval. 'You English have very free ways. But as you wish. Please join us in the voorkamer when you're ready.' And with that she silently withdrew.

Charlotte removed her poke-bonnet and poured some water from the pitcher into the basin in the oak washstand. Her skin tingled as she washed her face in the cold mountain water. She removed her travel-stained clothes and slipped into a cool, white muslin dress which hugged her figure. 'Mevrouw le Roux is not going to approve of this one either,' she said to herself. 'But I have a feeling that nothing that I do will please her – not that that matters at all!' She tossed her head and returned to the voorkamer which led directly into another room where the company was seated. It was not a large room but it was comfortably if austerely furnished and had wide French windows leading to a side veranda which gave access to the garden.

Etienne and Edward were engrossed in conversation, but they stood as she entered and Etienne invited her to sit in a chair next to him.

'Come and sit, Juffrouw Lacey, and tell me about yourself.'

'Just a moment, Pa. You cannot keep our beautiful guest to yourself.'

Etienne smiled indulgently at his son as Paul handed Charlotte a glass of chilled wine.

'Here, juffrouw, will you do us the honour of sampling our Chenin Blanc, the pride of L'Ourmarin?'

Charlotte was aware of a stiffening of Marie's expression, but she put out her hand to accept the glass.

'May this be the beginning of a long association,' Paul smiled as he raised his own glass, and together, as their eyes met, they savoured the wine.

CHAPTER EIGHTEEN

Paul

Charlotte woke up early the next morning, dressed, without the help of Candaza, and walked onto the veranda of L'Ourmarin. 'This is beautiful,' she said to herself as she took in the dramatic mountain scenery, so different from Simon's Town.

'Good morning, juffrouw.' The deep voice interrupted Charlotte's thoughts. She turned to see Paul standing at the corner of the veranda.

'Good morning, sir,' she replied, responding to his wide smile. His blonde hair caught the morning light as he walked towards her.

'It is a beautiful morning is it not?'

'It certainly is, sir.'

'Would you care to join me for a walk along the lakeside?' he said, holding out his hand to her.

'Why, sir, I'd be charmed,' said Charlotte taking his hand to walk down the veranda steps.

'How do you like our French Corner?' asked Paul, gesturing to the mountains and then neatly slipping Charlotte's hand under his arm.

'It's splendid. You are very fortunate to live here.'

'Ja, juffrouw. I am indeed blessed to live in this place.' agreed Paul, looking up towards the mountains behind the house. There was a note of seriousness in his voice. 'I have no wish to live elsewhere. I have no urge to travel. The trips to Cape Town to buy provisions or sell our wine are quite enough for me.'

'How long have your family lived here?' Charlotte asked.

'Over a hundred years,' Paul replied. 'Our ancestors were Huguenots who fled from France in the eighteenth century to escape religious persecution.'

Charlotte nodded. 'So your mother told me.'

'The Dutch East India Company assisted them in their passage,' continued Paul. 'Not that the Company had any religious sympathies, of course. Their interest was strictly commercial. They gave us land, implements and seed, all of which had to be paid for as soon as we made any money,' Paul laughed wryly.

'That sounds very familiar. Things don't change do they?' Charlotte replied. 'The colonial governor, Lord Charles Somerset, is planning with the British Government to bring out immigrants to settle the eastern Cape. Although it may seem to be philanthropic, it is in fact an expedient move. The colony needs to defend its eastern border and independent farmers will be far cheaper than soldiers.'

'Ja, I've heard rumours of the scheme,' Paul said. 'It will be no easier for today's British immigrants than it was for those Huguenots who came out here in the seventeenth century. It needs great courage to leave one's home and country.'

'I know what you mean,' Charlotte said. 'The voyage alone takes its toll. We were three and a half months at sea from the time we left England until we arrived at the Cape. I was thoroughly sick of being enclosed in a ship by the time we disembarked at Simon's Bay. At times I wondered if we would survive those terrible seas.'

'Well, I'm very pleased that you did,' Paul said. 'Otherwise I should never have had the opportunity of meeting you.' As he spoke he pulled her arm closer to his side. 'Many of those early adventurers did not survive the journey, you know. In fact the first wife of my great-great grandfather, Pierre, who came out here in 1688, died on board ship. But by the time they were in sight of Table Mountain Pierre had married again. His new bride was

Isabeau – you would call her Elizabeth in English. She was a widow, for her husband, also named Pierre, had died at sea as well.'

'My mother's name was Elizabeth,' Charlotte said. 'I never knew her. She died giving birth to me. It has always been a great sadness to me.' She paused for a moment as a melancholy shadow passed over her face. 'But tell me sir, how is it that you speak such good English? In fact, I expected that you would speak French with all the French words around here for names and places.'

'You won't find many, if any, Huguenots around here now who can speak French,' Paul said. 'The Dutch East India Company wanted our skills but didn't want a separate French identity especially when the Netherlands were at war with France. They wanted us to amalgamate with the local population, so by the early years of the last century, Dutch was the only language for government, education and religion.'

'But how did English come into it?'

'That's a more personal thing. My father realised that with the second British occupation of the Cape in 1806 that the English were here to stay, and that if he wanted a market for our wine and produce he and his family had better be able to communicate with the new government officials. So he arranged for us to have private tutors who were English-speaking and could teach us to speak properly.'

'That was a wise decision,' said Charlotte. 'I can speak a little French but I have no Dutch at all, which is a disadvantage when I try to speak to the local people.'

'Ja, English is very useful to me and enables me to have conversations with pretty Englishwomen,' Paul said looking down at Charlotte whose hand was resting lightly on his arm.

Charlotte laughed. She was a little embarrassed by the direct and obvious admiration of this handsome young man whom she had known for a very few hours. By now they had crossed the lawn in front of the manor house and were walking along a path beside the lake. There was not a sound to disturb the deep quiet other than the rhythmical splash of the fountain, the call of a bird or the occasional plop of a fish as it surfaced and fell back into the water again. They paused at the far side of the lake to look back at the house.

'It's a fine building,' Charlotte said. 'Did your great-great grandfather build it?'

'Ja, he did. He came to this valley in 1694 and named it, as many of the Huguenot settlers did, after his home in France. He came from a village called L'Ourmarin which was staunchly loyal to the Protestant faith. Before he died he had planted a thousand vines. He had been a vine-grower and wine-maker in France so this was an easy transition for him. Fortunately, this part of the Cape provides ideal conditions for growing grapes: cold, wet winters and long, hot, dry summers which allow the grapes to grow to full maturity.'

'It may interest you to know that I also have French connections in my ancestry,' Charlotte said. 'Going way back on my father's side, a du Lassey is said to have come over from Normandy with William the Conqueror to fight the Battle of Hastings in 1066. There is still a town in Normandy called Lassey. There are Laceys in Sussex today, but our branch of the family has been living in Hampshire for generations. That's where our family estate is.'

'You are a long way from home, juffrouw. Do you miss it?'

'Yes, in many ways I do. Everhurst has been my home all my life. I've never been as far away from it as I am at this moment. But people are more important than places, aren't they? And the people whom I love most are here with me in the Cape. Also it's very exciting being here. It's all so extravagantly beautiful. Everything is on a much bigger scale than it is in England.'

'Well, as I said before, I'm very pleased that you decided to come, and more particularly that you came on this trip with your father,' said Paul, catching her eye.

After a moment Charlotte had to look away for fear that her eyes might betray the sudden intensity of her emotions. She reminded herself that she was in love with John and was engaged to be married to him. She felt confused and disquieted and wished momentarily that she had not agreed to come on this visit.

'All this exertion in the bracing country air has made me hungry,' she said. 'Do you think that we could go back to the house for breakfast?'

'Of course, juffrouw,' replied Paul as he led her back to the family homestead.

* * *

The days at L'Ourmarin slipped easily one into another. Paul took Charlotte on a tour by horseback of the estate where she saw the coloured slaves working in the vineyards. He took her to the wine cellar, deep and cool and aromatic, where she met Moses, a Hottentot, who was in charge.

'The slaves bring the grapes in here in large baskets – we call them "ballasmandjies" because of their shape – and then they are thrown into these vats.' He pointed to the vats which were built into the floor. 'Here they ferment and we have to scoop the top frequently to ensure that all the grapes ferment.' He pointed to a slave who was standing at the top of a vat with a large scoop.

'What happens next?' Charlotte asked.

'After three or four weeks the wine is released through this tap,' he pointed to a tap at the base of the vat, 'and carried through to the barrels in the room where we came in. That is where the wine matures.'

'What kind of grapes do you use for making wine?' Charlotte asked.

'Semillon, Hanepoot and Chenin Blanc, but we are keen to try other cultivars. You've tried our Chenin Blanc. Have a taste of the red muscatel.' He indicated to Moses who collected a glass of red wine from one of the barrels and gave it to Charlotte.

'Delicious,' Charlotte said, sniffing and savouring the wine. 'I'll have to make sure that Papa takes some of this back home to Simon's Town.'

* * *

Charlotte enjoyed walking around the estate in the early evenings and often Paul accompanied her. She was especially fond of the avenue of oaks.

'This reminds me of my home,' she remarked to Paul. 'We also have oak trees growing on our estate in England. Oak trees make me feel secure. They are somehow permanent. One has the sense that they will be here long after you and I are gone.'

'Well, that's perfectly true, juffrouw, but let us not be sad. We are young and must celebrate life not be miserable and mourn its passing.'

'I'm sorry. I didn't mean to sound gloomy. In truth I am very happy. This has been a wonderful holiday.'

And Charlotte was happy. Happier than she cared to admit to herself.

* * *

It was the last night before the Laceys' return to Simon's Town. The le Rouxs put on a splendid dinner of lamb and vegetables followed by stewed fruit, jellies and cream, washed down with a selection of their finest wines. They sat at the long oak table in the agterkamer which was lit by fat candles in pewter holders. There were seven of them altogether: Etienne, Marie, Paul, his younger brother Guy, and his older sister Marie-Louise, engaged to be married to a farmer of a neighbouring estate.

Edward rose to his feet. 'I would like us to drink two toasts,' he said, 'one to our business contract, and the other to you, Etienne and Marie, and your family.' Edward grinned broadly. He had not looked so relaxed for ages, Charlotte thought. He lifted his goblet of wine to the assembled company. 'Charlotte and I would like to thank you for your hospitality. We hope to return the favour when you visit us at Admiralty House in Simon's Town. When do you think that might be?'

'In six or eight weeks,' Etienne replied. 'I shall be delivering the first supply of wine that you ordered for the fleet towards the end of August or September. The wine should be well-matured by then.'

'We shall look forward to that, won't we, Charlotte?' Edward smiled at his daughter.

Charlotte smiled too and answered appropriately. But within she felt discomposed. She was alarmed by the attraction she felt for Paul. On one level she was pleased that they were returning to their life in Simon's Town, but on another level she was drawn to this man whom she had so recently met and who had invaded her emotional life in spite of her better judgement.

Later that night as they rose from the dinner table and moved to the drawing room, Paul approached Charlotte. 'Would you do me the honour of accompanying me onto the veranda? There's a full moon tonight and I'd like to show you the view of the estate in the moonlight.'

Charlotte had mixed feelings about such an invitation. It was safer in the house with her father and the le Rouxs. She glanced at her father and saw that he was smiling and nodding his assent. She could hardly refuse.

'Why thank you, sir,' said Charlotte, wondering if he would notice how her hand trembled as she picked up her shawl. She followed him through the French windows to the veranda.

Charlotte gave an involuntary gasp as she looked at the scene. The moon, large and yellow-white, was reflected in the glistening sheet of the lake, and the night was almost as bright as day, but different, less harsh.

'Step down onto the terrace a moment and look up at the house,' Paul invited. He held out his hand in that same gesture of support that he had made when they had first walked together. They walked a few paces and stood transfixed. The house with its imposing gables shone with an unearthly splendour against the gleaming mountains. Charlotte was overwhelmed. 'And now it is the witching time of night,' she murmured. 'One almost expects fairies or fey creatures to emerge from the shadows.' She didn't know whether he had pulled her or whether she had moved towards him. All she knew was that the next moment she was in his arms. She looked up at him: his blonde hair had a radiance like a halo. He bent his head to her and involuntarily she raised hers to him. He kissed her gently and she pulled away.

'No, sir.'

But the attraction was irresistible. They were drawn to each other and as he kissed her again Charlotte could feel the pressure of his body against hers which was responding and yielding to him. She wanted him as much as he did her. Suddenly the image of John and her other life in Simon's Town intruded into her consciousness. She heard John's words: 'You know that I've always loved you, Charlotte.'

'No, sir,' she said again and stepped out of his embrace.

'I'm sorry, juffrouw, I forgot myself.'

'I'm sorry too. But I think that you don't understand my situation.'

'What is that?' Paul looked puzzled.

'Don't you know that I'm engaged to be married?'

Paul's face fell like a curtain falling to the floor. His arms dropped down by his side. He was discomfited and also deeply disappointed. He turned away from her to look back at the house.

'Why didn't you tell me?'

'I...I don't know. I thought Papa had told your father...it didn't seem necessary...there wasn't an opportunity...' she ended lamely.

'Juffrouw Lacey,' he said, gathering himself together. 'I beg your pardon for embarrassing you. It was inexcusable to have taken such liberties with an affianced lady. Please forgive me.' He bowed low and offered her his arm to escort her back to the house.

Once inside, Paul excused himself from the company, saying that he had to rise early the next day to see to his duties on the estate.

Shortly afterwards Edward and Charlotte bade their hosts goodnight and retired to their respective rooms. Charlotte was left feeling disconsolate. She tossed and turned as conflicting thoughts and emotions overtook her being. The one strand of her life which had seemed so straightforward before this visit to L'Ourmarin was her relationship with John. Their future had been neatly and happily mapped out. Now she was in turmoil. She wished that she had never come. And yet that newly-awakened fire within her was something that she would not easily forget – if at all. The sun was sending its first tentative fingers over the horizon before she finally slept.

CHAPTER NINETEEN

The Waters of the Bay

Sam and Jacobus were down at Water's Edge waiting for the signal from the smugglers' ship. Against the light of the moon, which was scudding across the sky between a forest of clouds, they could see the ghostly outline of the pirate ship.

'When we see the light flash three times that's our cue,' Sam said. 'We must pull out the boat as quickly and quietly as we can.'

'Those kegs of brandy will make it heavy and difficult to move,' Jacobus objected.

'Don't worry. They're securely lashed down and it will be easier once we have launched the boat in the water,' Sam said. 'The difficult part will be to push it through the breakers.'

'I don't like it,' Jacobus said, rubbing his hands together. 'There're just too many rocks in this bay.'

'That's why you're here, Jacobus. Remember? You have learnt about these waters from your pa.'

Sam could see that, despite his brave words in front of his father, Jacobus was afraid. His voice softened and he put his hand on the boy's shoulder.

'This is the only way, Jacobus. We have to avoid the main jetty in town and Cole's Point. Seaforth is too exposed as well.'

'The weather's not good,' Jacobus said, looking up at the sky.

'There's no other time,' Sam said. He left Jacobus and the boat concealed behind some fynbos and positioned himself in a crevice from which he had a clear vantage point. Even as he watched he could see storm clouds blowing up from the north-west. A lowering black canopy seemed to cover the sky and snuff out the moon in a matter of seconds. The wind grew stronger and stronger and the waves grew in size chasing one another, each more impatient than the last to get to shore. Observing these ominous changes in the weather Sam was very grateful that he had Jacobus with him as it would be a hard row back to Water's Edge into the teeth of the wind. He fixed his eyes on the shadowy shape of the ship beyond Roman Rock: waiting for the signal.

Suddenly he saw three flashes of light beam across the slatey waters. Now was their chance. The wind seemed to have dropped a little. He ran over to Jacobus and together they dragged the boat out of the undergrowth and pulled it down the sandy beach. Even with their combined strength it was a struggle to push the craft through the waves which were crashing onto the shore. They pushed the boat out until they were waist deep in water. Sam jumped in first to grab the oars. Jacobus gave the boat a final shove and scrambled aboard from the stern. As they reached the relative calm of the water beyond the breakers they began to row out towards Noah's Ark. It was strenuous work and they seemed to be making little headway but gradually they approached the steep sides of the giant rock. They steered a passage through the channel between Noah's Ark and Roman Rock to the smugglers' ship which was anchored beyond. Sam looked up in alarm. The wind was growing in force and was whipping the waves into mountainous peaks. They smashed against the side of Noah's Ark, sending up great plumes of spray. Roman Rock was completely covered over but he knew that, above all, he must keep control of his emotions and focus on his goal.

'How are we doing, Jacobus?'

'Well. As you said, I know the waters here. I've often been out with Pa on fishing trips. We just need to steer straight ahead.'

Sam was plying the oars while Jacobus was sitting in the stern in charge of the rudder. Sam was aware of his muscles taut and straining across his back, shoulders and arms as he attempted to propel the boat through the raging water. He needed help.

'Jacobus! Come, take the other oar!' he shouted although his voice was barely audible above the cacophony of wind and water. Jacobus scrambled over the kegs of brandy, grabbed the oar from Sam and was about to sit down when the boat slewed and he stumbled and let go of the oar which slipped out of the rowlocks into the foaming sea. Jacobus instinctively stretched out to retrieve it and lost his balance. With wildly flailing arms and a spine-chilling howl, which penetrated the roar of the wind and sea, he fell into the churning water. Sam impulsively reached out to grab the boy but he was unable to hold him. He watched in cold and helpless horror as Jacobus and the oar were snatched away and the boy, dragged down by the weight of his clothes, disappeared under the water. The distance between the boat and the oar became greater with every second. The image of Christina and Johannes rose up before his eyes. How could he face them? The agony was unspeakable.

Sam was now made forcibly aware of his own precarious predicament. One oar was useless. The boat was careering out of control at the mercy of the angry waters. If he could use the oar over the transom as a rudder he might be able to steer the boat towards the ship. Otherwise he had visions of being swept out beyond Hangklip into the open seas, if he survived the night.

Then the rain began. It came at him like horizontal sheets cutting at his body. He could no longer make out the division between the sea and the sky. His hair was plastered down onto his head and icy needles stung his eyes. The cold blew through him like metal knives and the rain streamed down under his collar, soaking him to the skin. His could hear nothing but the continuous roar of the water and the wind screaming like a banshee. The waves rose higher and higher all around; insane peaks whose white tops were whipped away by the wind. Crouching with his oar over the stern Sam tried to make out the ship, which was carrying no lights. The air was full of foam and spray and the waves were growing taller and steeper. He was carried up to the crest of a wave when the sudden squall ceased and the wind dropped. He climbed dizzily to the top of the next wave and caught sight of the hulk of the ship to his left. Hope rose in his being as he plunged down into the next valley in the valiant little craft. Then an awesome calm. He looked up in terror as a massive wave rose up and towered over him where he sat, defenceless. As it reached its full height he could see the white water at the top of the wave. For a timeless moment it seemed to hover over him. Then the fall. It smashed down over him. And as it continued on its inexorable path to the shore, there was nothing more to be seen.

CHAPTER TWENTY

Sam

Charlotte sat on her favourite boulder at Water's Edge and looked north towards the harbour of Simon's Bay. The sea was angry today and its slate-grey waters heaved and rolled. She could see the tall-masted ships in the bay with their sails tightly furled against the blustery northerly wind that was blowing. The external turbulence echoed her own inner turmoil. It was a month since she and her father had returned from L'Ourmarin to Admiralty House where John was waiting for them. He was overjoyed to see them again.

Life had been insufferably dull in Simon's Town although he had alleviated the boredom by a trip to Cape Town. Charlotte was pleased to see him too but as she moved into the warmth of his welcoming arms she was aware of a deep unease within her being. During her stay at L'Ourmarin she had become increasingly aware of a space between her and John. From the moment that she had told Paul the truth about her engagement to John he had kept his distance. It had to be that way. But she was not at peace. She had hoped that with the passage of time matters would resolve themselves but the image of the sun-bronzed face with the laughing blue eyes would not leave her. There was no denying that she felt a deep affinity with Paul yet she loved John too. She wished that her life could be more ordered. This tumult of emotions was very uncomfortable.

'And really, what have I got to complain about?' Charlotte said to herself. 'I have a man who loves me and a promising future ahead. Whereas poor Ellen, sitting up there in that cottage on the hill – what is she going to do? What sort of future will she and Sam have? They won't be accepted here by either the colonists or the local coloured community. They'll have to move away. Papa hasn't been able to find anything suitable for Sam in Cape Town yet. Come to think of it, I haven't seen Sam for a few days. I wonder where he is. Maybe he has gone to look for a job in Cape Town himself? Perhaps he and Ellen can come and join us when John and I go to the eastern frontier.' But even as she articulated these thoughts she remembered John's outburst when he had seen Ellen and Sam down on the beach: 'She's holding hands with a nigger!' Would he be able to change his prejudices? Would he even want to? She had never told him the truth about Ellen and her father either. She knew that he would be offended by the idea of being related to a working-class girl. His life at sea as an officer had only served to strengthen his perception of the class divide that she found so suffocating.

The tide was running high now and there was no beach to be seen as the waves crashed up against the grassy bank. The sandstone rocks and hills above her seemed to be menacing as heavy clouds rolled across them. Showers of spray were thrown up by the waters and her skirt and shawl were becoming drenched. She looked at the kelp – strange, dark outgrowths from the sea that looked like the root ends of small unturned trees or even the misshapen arms of a man, grotesque and clawing. A clutch of horror grabbed her. The arm of a man. It couldn't be. But it was. Caught in a tangle of seaweed, it was being relentlessly drawn into the shore.

Charlotte gathered up her skirts and scrambled over the boulders towards the narrow path which led to the beach. At the end of the rocky pathway there was a boiling cauldron of white water where the golden sand usually lay. She knew that with the next withdrawal of the waves she could leap across the shallows. Without waiting to consider, she threw herself at the first opportunity across to the comparative safety of the upper beach. She edged her way against the grassy bank and watched the burden of death move towards her.

As soon as it was within what she judged to be reasonable reach, she waded out into the heaving waters. There caught in the web of kelp, was the figure of a man, familiar and well-loved – Sam.

* * *

Charlotte grabbed hold of Sam's hand and started to pull. He was unbelievably heavy as his clothes and limbs were caught in the kelp. She untangled him with difficulty as the waves crashed around her. Fortunately the tide was coming in and as soon as the body was free of the kelp she was able to take advantage of a breaking wave to help pull it onto the sand. She hauled the body onto the bank and collapsed onto the ground herself. She was exhausted and sodden but her mind was racing. She must get help. She wrung out her long skirts; her shawl had been lost to the waters. She ran to where she had tethered Amber.

Charlotte leaped into the saddle and spurred Amber into a gallop. As she raced down towards the main street of the town large drops of rain obscured her vision but Amber knew the way well and before long she was at the entrance of Admiralty House stables where she saw James.

'James! James!' she called. 'Quickly! I need help.'

'What's the matter, Miss Charlotte?' Concern was drawn on James' open, wide-eyed face.

As Charlotte quickly recounted her ordeal, James took charge and summoned two other stablehands.

'Don't worry, Miss Charlotte, we'll bring him back! You go into the house and get dry.'

Charlotte started to protest but she suddenly realised just how tired she was and as the three men galloped off through the town towards Water's Edge, she dragged herself through the back door of the house and into the kitchen.

'Elsie!'

'What is it, ma'am?' Elsie's cheeks were flushed from tending the meal which was cooking in the huge oven.

Charlotte collapsed onto a chair. As she told the older woman the story Elsie threw her apron over her head, sank down onto a wooden bench and wailed. It was like losing a son.

'What about Ellen?' she whispered at last.

'We'll have to tell her. She has to know.'

'Ja, but I fear for her and the baby. How much more does she have to go through? It will be a terrible shock.'

Charlotte got up from the bench with a sudden burst of energy.

'Elsie, I've got to go and tell her,' she said, 'before anyone else does!' And she started to run to the kitchen door.

'No, ma'am!' Elsie took hold of her. 'You can't go out again tonight. You're already soaked to the skin.'

'I must,' Charlotte said, but even as she pushed open the kitchen door, the wind took hold of it like an enormous hand and blew it back in against the wall with an ear-splitting crash. As if on cue, the rain intensified like an angry attacking army.

'You'd best wait until the morning, ma'am. And then perhaps James can go with you as well!' Elsie's voice was shrill against the roar of the elements as she and Charlotte dragged the door closed.

Drooping with the effort of struggling with the door, Charlotte agreed

'Yes, I suppose you're right,' she said as she climbed wearily up the stairs to bed.

'If Papa asks after me, tell him that I've gone to bed because I am unwell.'

Suddenly the world felt very dark indeed, like the dark clouds outside which had exploded into the storm.

* * *

The next day the sky had cleared and the birds were singing their dawn chorus in the milkwood trees outside Admiralty House as

Charlotte ran down the street towards the Dockyard. She had never been to Christina's cottage before as Sam had always taken the supplies that she had sent for Ellen, but Elsie had told her where it was.

'Go through the town, as far as Cole's Point and Mr Osmond's buildings. On the right there's a narrow lane that goes up past the new naval hospital. Follow it until you come to the cottage. It's like any of the fishermen's cottages that you see around here – white with a thatched roof – but there's a lemon tree in the garden that marks it out.'

At this early hour there were few people about in Simon's Town. The fishermen had long gone out and she could see their boats in the bay. She found the narrow footpath and began the climb. At the end of the path she followed rough-hewn steps to a wooden gate. 'There's the lemon tree,' she said to herself. 'This must be Christina's cottage.' As she paused to catch her breath she caught sight of the back of a young woman with long chestnut hair hanging out some washing. Emotion tensed Charlotte's throat. This was the first time that she had seen Ellen since that fateful night when she had gone to meet Sam and had ended up in the clutches of the sailors.

'Ellen!'

Ellen turned at the sound of her voice. 'Miss Charlotte!' Her face lit up and she dropped the washing as she ran to Charlotte and flung herself into her arms. The two women hugged each other, laughing and crying. Eventually Charlotte drew back and with her hands on Ellen's shoulders looked her up and down, noticing her protruding belly.

'You're looking well, Ellen, despite everything.'

'Thanks, Miss Charlotte, but we've had such a worrying few days. Sam and Jacobus went out fishing two nights ago and we haven't seen them since. We're very afraid that they may have been lost in that storm.'

'Is there somewhere we can sit down?' Charlotte said, dropping her eyes from Ellen's face.

'Yes, of course. Let's go into the cottage. There's no-one else here. Johannes has gone out with a fisherman friend to see if he can see any sign of the boat that Sam and Jacobus were in, and Christina has taken Maria into the village to see if anyone has any news.' Ellen led Charlotte into the cottage where they sat down on the wooden settle. 'Would you like a drink?' Ellen offered. 'You must be thirsty after your climb up the hill.'

'Yes – no. Ellen, I don't know how to say this. There isn't a right way to deliver awful news.'

The silence between them lay like a sheet of lead. Eventually Ellen spoke.

'It's Sam, isn't it?' Her face was drained of colour.

'Yes, I'm afraid so. Yesterday afternoon I went riding and went to our favourite place where we used to gather shells – Water's Edge – you will remember it.' Ellen nodded her head – how could she forget it? 'The tide was high and I found Sam's body washed up among the kelp.'

'No,' Ellen whispered. 'This is what I've feared most of all. Somewhere in my being I knew it. He's left me.'

She stood up and walked over to the window from where she could look out over the bay. 'He was so brave and he took this unnecessary risk for us – for the baby and our future together. I never liked the plan but he insisted that it was the only way out for us.'

'Plan? What plan?'

Ellen turned back to Charlotte. 'Of course, you don't know but it doesn't matter now. You may as well know. He and Jacobus didn't go fishing. Sam was involved with some English smugglers exchanging Constantia brandy for good money. He said it would make our fortune and that we could go away and make a new start somewhere. He and Jacobus borrowed a boat and were delivering the first haul of brandy that night.'

'But smuggling's illegal in the Colony. He would have had a harsh sentence if he had been discovered – prison in the Castle at the very least.'

'Well, it doesn't matter any more, does it? This is all that's left of him,' Ellen said, holding her bulging belly on both sides, 'and so it's even more precious. Promise me, Miss Charlotte,' she said as she turned to face her, 'that if anything happens to me you will see that our baby is taken care of.'

Charlotte felt a clutch of alarm but smiled as she said, 'Of course Ellen, but now is not the time to have morbid thoughts. Your baby is due to be born very soon and you must keep well for that.'

'You're right,' Ellen said as she walked over to Charlotte who opened her arms in a wide embrace. And as they clung to each other, great shuddering sobs racked Ellen's body.

'Don't worry, Ellen,' Charlotte whispered. 'All will be well, but if anything should happen I'll look after this child as if it were my own flesh and blood.' 'Which it is,' she said to herself.

* * *

As Charlotte made her way back to Admiralty House, she thought about how she would tell her father of these latest developments. Would this change his view? Would he feel that he could take Ellen in now that she was really alone? She decided that there was no time to lose and sought her father in his study.

At the sound of her light knock Edward got up from his desk and opened the door. The lines on his face were deep with anxiety.

'Charlotte, where have you been?'

'I've been to visit Ellen at Christina's house.'

'But we agreed that you wouldn't visit her to avoid suspicion. And you know that I don't want you to wander around the streets of Simon's Town by yourself. Look what happened to Ellen.'

'I don't think that anyone would dare to do anything to the Admiral's daughter, but in any event I had to go to tell her about Sam.'

'Yes, I heard about Sam,' Edward said with a sigh. 'James told me last night when he brought his body back in the wagon. It's a damn shame. The boy had a good future in the stables and I'll have to find someone to replace him.'

'Don't you care what happens to Ellen now?' Charlotte challenged him.

'Yes, of course I do.'

'Well, can we bring her to live here now that she's alone? Her baby's due soon!'

'Charlotte, Charlotte! We've been through this before. You know we can't have Ellen here with the baby. The scandal would be too much.'

'The baby is your grandchild, remember! Don't you care about that?'

'Charlotte, I'm not as unfeeling as you seem to think I am. I care very much abut Ellen. That's why I've always made sure that she was looked after. I care very much about my grandchild too but I have to be mindful of my position here: our relations with the Dutch, our standing with the local population.'

'That's what you really care about, isn't it!' sneered Charlotte. 'Class and position! There are other more important things in life!'

'Charlotte, I know that you are right. There is nothing more important than family, and I have been trying to work out the best solution for Ellen even before this tragedy. I don't think that it is in Ellen's best interests for her to be here at the house. However, she can't stay indefinitely in a Malay fisherman's cottage in Simon's Town. I know she doesn't want to go back to England, but perhaps she'd like to go to Cape Town. I think that I'd be able to find a position for her with a family in Cape Town, but she wouldn't be able to take the baby. We'll have to find a home…'

'Ellen would never agree to that and neither would I! She will not be separated from her baby who is the only link that she has with Sam. And I'm the child's aunt and I want to watch him or her grow up too. You seem to be quite willing to lose contact with your only grandchild. Sometimes, Papa,' Charlotte stood up, 'I find it extremely difficult to understand you and wonder if I really am your daughter.' With that barbed comment she marched out of the room.

CHAPTER TWENTY-ONE

The Funeral

The Seaforth Burying Ground was on the outskirts of Simon's Town on a hill overlooking False Bay. It was always a place for sober reflection with its memorial stones to so many who had died prematurely, particularly sailors who had perished in the shipwrecks along the coast.

On this August afternoon in 1815, the occasion of the funeral of Samuel van Aardt, for that was the name of his Dutch father, the canopy of clouds was unbroken and the wind blowing in from the north brought squalls of rain. In contrast to the big, angry sky the human gathering seemed small and vulnerable. Charlotte was there, wrapped in a dark cloak and hood for protection against the rain. Ellen, heavily pregnant, leaned against her. There was no colour in her face, which was swollen from weeping. As the only two white women they stood out in stark contrast against the huddle of dark Malay fisher folk. Elsie wept copiously. Johannes and Christina stood close together for comfort, rigid like stone images. Apart from these there was a smattering of people: James, his mouth set in a grim line, come to pay his respects to his colleague and Willem Smit, Johannes' fishing friend who had lent them the boat. Most of the workers from Admiralty House came but no other white people. The Admiral himself, to his secret relief, had been summoned by Lord Somerset to a meeting of all the officers of the fleet in Cape Town. John had flatly refused to go.

Although most of the coloured people were Muslim, it had been decided to give Sam a Christian burial as his father, even though he had deserted him a baby, had been a Christian as he had been a Dutch burger. Out of respect for Ellen as well, it had seemed appropriate to follow the Christian funeral rites. Admiral Lacey had commissioned the naval chaplain, Captain Jarvis, to conduct the funeral. There was some resistance to this from Johannes and Christina who wanted a Muslim ritual, but in truth they were so broken by the loss of Jacobus that they did not have the spirit to fight the decisions of Charlotte and her father. There had been a separate Muslim service for Jacobus.

The coffin was brought from Admiralty House on a wagon by James, who acted as a pall bearer with Johannes and two of the stable hands. The plain wooden box was lowered into the muddy grave while Reverend Jarvis intoned from the Anglican prayer book: 'Forasmuch as it hath pleased Almighty God of his great mercy to receive unto himself the soul of our dear brother here departed, we therefore commit his body to the ground; earth to earth, ashes to ashes, dust to dust; in sure and certain hope…' Charlotte thought how a few short months ago she and Ellen had heard these words echoing across the bay when John had arrived and the execution of the mutineer had taken place. Such a short time and yet so much had happened: love, new life, death…Suddenly she felt a weight against her as with a soft moan Ellen fainted. Despite Charlotte's effort to hold her, she crumpled onto to the ground next to the grave.

Johannes moved forward quickly and picked her up in his strong arms. 'She needs a doctor,' he muttered as he looked at Ellen's chalk-white face.

'We'll take her to the naval hospital. It's the closest and this is an emergency,' Charlotte said. 'We can take her in my carriage.'

She led the way to her carriage where James took charge of the horses, followed by Johannes carrying the young woman who looked hardly more than a child herself. Behind him walked Christina with her head bowed in grief. It was a sad little party which moved slowly away from the desolate scene on the hillside overlooking Simon's Bay.

CHAPTER TWENTY-TWO

Samuel Joseph

The candle in the lantern burned low. The fragile flame flickered and sputtered as the wind howled outside and the rain rattled against the window panes of the small ward in the naval hospital. Normally Simon's Bay was sheltered, which was why the British, and before them the Dutch, had decided to move the winter anchorage from Table Bay to Simon's Bay. But on occasions like this, when the storm swept in from the Atlantic, the little settlement was vulnerable.

In a narrow bed Ellen lay moaning and writhing in the pangs of childbirth. Ellen knew nothing of the storm outside: she was too consumed by the storm within her own body. She was barely conscious as a fever ravaged her as well. By her side sat old Rachel, the midwife: a toothless crone with a wizened face, yet she knew her job thoroughly. She had brought many infants into the world in Simon's Town, but this time she was worried. All was not well. The baby was not coming and the girl was not helping. She had seen cases like this before, although this was the first time that she had been asked to deliver a white baby in a hospital.

She had felt a deep unease as she had hurried to the hospital that evening hugging her cloak close to her against the wind. It was not a night to be outside, but Elsie had arrived in her cottage, breathless and heaving from exertion in climbing up the steep lane from the town, and had implored her to come. They had known each other for many years and when Rachel realised the depth of her friend's distress, she didn't hesitate.

'I have to go back to the house now because the Admiral is arriving from Cape Town tonight and is giving a dinner for all the naval officers in Simon's Town. Miss Charlotte is taking care of Ellen at the hospital until you come but she has to be back to entertain the ladies.'

'But they won't let me into the Naval Hospital,' Rachel protested.

'I told you Miss Charlotte is there and will make sure that you're allowed in. There's no time to lose, Rachel. The girl needs your help. Promise me that you'll go.'

'Ja, I'm coming,' Rachel said as she hoisted herself from the comfortable chair next to the fire where she had been dozing after her meal. 'I'll just gather my things.'

And so Rachel had come down to the hospital where Charlotte was waiting for her at the entrance.

'Thank you for coming, Rachel,' said Charlotte as she led the way into the ward where Ellen lay sleeping. 'Take good care of her, won't you? She's very precious to me.' She kissed Ellen gently on the forehead as she gathered up her cloak. 'I have to go now to entertain my father's guests but I'll be back as soon as I can.'

With Charlotte's departure Rachel had taken her place in the chair by the bed.

* * *

Suddenly Ellen groaned in agony and bent up her legs. Rachel felt her abdomen with practised hands.

'Kom, meisie,' she whispered into Ellen's ear. 'The baba wants to come now. Push now. Let the baba come.'

'I can't,' Ellen whimpered. 'It's tearing me apart. Oh God, help me, help me!'

Her slight body thrashed around on the bed. She clung onto

Rachel's hand and bit into the cloth which the old woman offered her. Finally Ellen gave a scream which seemed to echo throughout the whole hospital and with a superhuman shove and the help of Rachel's expert hands a little scrap of humanity was forced into the cold air of the dark room.

Rachel took hold of the infant, deftly cut the cord, washed the child in warm water and wrapped it in a soft woollen blanket.

'Look, meisie, you have a son,' she said.

Ellen looked up with glazed eyes. 'Let me hold him,' she said.

Rachel raised Ellen up so that she was sitting up against the pillows and placed the small bundle in the crook of her arm. As she cradled her baby and looked down on him, Ellen forgot all of the pain and suffering. She felt a warm glow suffuse her tormented body.

She smiled up at Rachel. 'He's beautiful,' she said. 'He's worth it all. He's just like his father with those green eyes, don't you think?'

'Ja, meisie. Those are his pa's eyes all right.' Rachel had often seen Sam out and about with the horses in and around Simon's Town.

'And he'll have his father's name – Sam,' Ellen said. 'And another one just for him – Joseph. Samuel Joseph he'll be, Rachel.'

A lump came into old Rachel's throat as she looked at the young white woman. She had seen much pain and tragedy in her lifetime, but the moment of birth never failed to move her. It was like a miracle re-enacted over and over again. But there was death in the room as well. 'Who will care for the child?' she thought to herself.

As if she had read her thoughts Ellen said, 'If I don't come out of here, Rachel, please take my son to Miss Charlotte at Admiralty House. She will take care of him.'

Rachel was sceptical. She knew about Ellen's connection with the Admiral and his family and that Charlotte had arranged matters at the hospital so that Ellen could give birth there with Rachel's help. She had also seen Charlotte's obvious affection for her former maid, but a long term arrangement was another thing. She had a deep-seated suspicion of the white colonists and she could hardly imagine that a privileged white woman would want to be permanently connected to a child of mixed blood.

'Are you sure, meisie? You know I have a cousin on a small farm just outside of Simon's Town who would probably take care of him. She lost her own baby last year and has been pining for another. I'm sure that she and her husband, who is a kind man, would be happy to take him in.'

'No!' Ellen burst out fiercely, raising herself from the pillows of the bed. 'You must do as I say! Promise me.'

Rachel was taken aback by this sudden energy from the feeble frame of the young woman. It was the second time that night that she had been urged to make a promise.

'Ja, meisie. Don't worry. I'll do as you ask. Sleep now.'

As Ellen closed her eyes, Rachel gently took the small bundle from her and placed it in a wicker basket next to the bed and sat back herself in the wooden chair. The light from the lantern projected her shadow, grotesque and disproportionate, against the opposite wall of the room. As she turned her head to look at the quiet form in the bed, she noticed a dark stain spreading over the white bed-clothes and felt a surge of fear. The girl was bleeding too much and needed more than a midwife's expertise. She ran out of the room to find the doctor.

'He's not here,' said an orderly on duty, a young English sailor who had been press-ganged into the Navy in Portsmouth. He looked the shabby old woman up and down. In the ordinary way he would not have allowed her into the hospital but the Admiral's daughter had authorised her admission. 'There's been an accident down at the Dockyard. A crewman fell off a mast in the wind and has been badly injured. The surgeon won't be back until the morning.'

'We've got to find someone to help,' urged Rachel. 'There's a young woman in the ward up there who will die unless she has a doctor's help.'

'I'm sorry,' the orderly said. 'There's nothing I can do. I'll tell the surgeon as soon as he comes back. He's bound to bring the lad in here for treatment, if he has survived the fall.'

'Can't we send someone to fetch him or at least ask for advice?'

'I'm the only one here,' the orderly replied. 'Why don't you go yourself?'

'I can't leave the mother,' Rachel said. 'She needs to have someone with her all the time.'

The orderly shook his head. 'I'm sorry,' he repeated. 'I'll tell the surgeon as soon as he comes back.'

'I just hope it won't be too late,' Rachel muttered ominously as she turned and walked slowly back up the stairs to the ward.

The linen on the bed was scarlet with blood and the girl lay very quietly, unnaturally quietly, after all the struggle of the past few hours. Rachel hurried over and felt her pulse. It was still there, but faint and irregular. She held the small white hand and willed Ellen to live.

'Kom, meisie,' she said. 'You have the child to live for.'

But even as she held the slender hand in her own gnarled one, she felt the life ebb out of it and, as the first streaks of light shone across the waters of the bay and found their way into the ward, Ellen slipped away into oblivion.

CHAPTER TWENTY-THREE

Drama at Home and Abroad

The long mahogany table in the main dining-room in Admiralty House shone in the soft candlelight. The silver candelabra and cutlery glinted while the crystal wine goblets winked like diamonds. A large arched mirror with bevelled edges and a gold-leaf frame intensified the interplay of light and shade. At the long, deep-set windows, blue velvet drapes with valances edged with gold brocade enclosed the whole with a quiet opulence. The blue and gold was echoed in the dress uniforms of the assembled naval officers in blue high-collared tailcoats with gold epaulettes and braiding. It was a scene of convivial warmth, boasting all the best that European civilisation could offer, yet the locale was the tip of Africa. At the head of the table sat Admiral Lacey in blue frockcoat; at the other end sat Charlotte in a white silk dress that shimmered in the incandescent glow of the candles.

The talk was all of the glorious victory at Waterloo in June.

'Wellington certainly put paid to Boney's career,' said Thomas Devenish, a young naval officer newly arrived in the Cape with his bride Lucy, a pretty, demure English rose, who had found the Atlantic crossing quite appalling and life in the young colony raw and intimidating.

'It's true he takes the glory,' Edward Lacey agreed, 'but had Boney's army not been decimated and demoralised at Borodino, the outcome might have been very different.'

'You're right, Uncle Edward,' volunteered John, 'although he had amazing resources. Do you know that Napoleon had an army of 610,000 men before the Russian campaign, but that he returned with only 20,000, and that only 1,000 of those were of any further military use? Yet within three months he had mustered an army of 25,000 and had won three victories before he was defeated at Leipzig. They say that in the end, when he was defending French soil, he even had youngsters who did not know how to handle a rifle fighting for him.'

'He must certainly go down in history as one of the greatest military geniuses that the world has ever known,' Edward said. 'He seemed to have an almost hypnotic ability to inspire men to follow him. It still amazes me that he could arrive from Elba with only a few hundred soldiers and yet, within weeks, have gathered forces behind him, recaptured Paris again and had taken the offensive against the allies in Belgium.'

'It was certainly touch and go at one stage,' commented Richard, Lord Clarendon. 'If it hadn't been for Blucher and the Prussians intervening when they did, I doubt the outcome would have been quite so decisive.'

'Well at least we can sleep easy in our beds now,' offered Kitty Clarendon, in Charlotte's eyes a silly affected woman who seemed to be able to think of nothing beyond the latest fashions in England and Europe and the frightful natives in the colony.

'We were never in any danger here,' Charlotte said. 'In fact, if it were not for the despatches coming in with the ships at frequent intervals, we should never even have been aware of a war at all.'

'Mind you, when you hear reports of the great ball given by the Duchess of Richmond in Brussels on the eve of Waterloo, you might be forgiven for thinking that some people regarded it all as some grand social occasion,' John remarked with heavy irony.

William Lamplough, a large, phlegmatic bachelor of about forty, raised his head at this. 'War is never just a display of strength you know. It's most often tied up with economic necessity and it has its effect on the social world as well. Just look at the elegant robes our young ladies are wearing this evening. They find their inspiration in the court of Napoleon!'

'Oh, surely you can't mean that,' wailed Kitty Clarendon. 'Had I known of the connection of these styles with that barbaric upstart, I'm sure I would have worn my grandmother's hooped petticoats!'

There was a slight embarrassed pause, broken by Edward, always the diplomat. 'On this occasion, you know, I think we at the Cape are going to feel the reverberations of international events. The latest rumour that I have heard is that they are going to exile Bonaparte to St Helena and it's likely to have considerable impact on the economy here.'

'By Jove, I think you're right,' Clarendon said. 'They're going to have to get their supplies and reinforcements from the Cape. And that means us.'

'It could mean something of a boom for the settlement here in Simon's Town as well as a boost for the rural economy,' Lamplough added. 'We could do with a bit more activity around here.'

'Oh, I do hope that there's no danger of that savage coming here!' shrieked Kitty.

'Hardly likely,' remarked Lamplough laconically, 'seeing that he will be heavily guarded and would have to be a remarkably good swimmer to swim the 1,700 miles from St Helena to Cape Town!'

Charlotte thought that this was an appropriate moment to suggest that the ladies withdraw to the drawing-room while the gentlemen enjoyed their port.

* * *

Alone with his naval colleagues, Edward Lacey was able to talk more freely. He had always found it difficult to speak of matters of politics and national interest with women, apart from his daughter, and anyway the subject required a degree of confidentiality. He relaxed visibly as he passed the crystal decanter of port around the highly polished table.

'I heard from Somerset in Cape Town that, according to the latest despatches, the governor of St Helena himself, Sir George Cockburn, is to escort Napoleon to the island in the *Northumberland*.'

'Not your usual prisoner of war!' chuckled Devenish. 'An emperor, even if he is self-appointed, will need to be treated with a measure of respect.'

'And live in the style to which he was not born,' Lamplough said ironically.

'There is talk of him living at Longwood, the country house in the green uplands of the island,' Edward continued. 'But of course, even a mansion can become a suffocating prison, which will in fact be the case.'

'You can bet your life that the garrison will be strengthened,' John said. 'They're not going to take any chances this time. Incidentally, Uncle, what sort of people live in St Helena?'

'Well, apart from the small diplomatic circle, there are of course the descendants of the ruined Londoners who settled there from England after the Great Fire of 1666. Then there are the Chinese and Indian labourers and African slaves brought out by the East India Company. There has been quite a lot of intermarriage, so the inhabitants are emerging as almost a unique racial type.'

'And now, as John has already indicated, there is likely to be an influx of His Majesty's forces to ensure that their prize does not escape,' added Lamplough.

* * *

Charlotte left the ladies chatting aimlessly in the drawing-room and moved quietly out onto the veranda. Before her the fountain in the centre of the rose garden played softly into the pond and beyond the gate the moon trod a silver pathway over the still waters of the bay. The night was remarkably tranquil, particularly after the storm of the previous night. Charlotte wondered afresh at the changeable nature of the weather at the Cape. It was all apparently so peaceful yet within Charlotte there was disquiet.

Her thoughts were with poor Ellen in the naval hospital. She had not been able to visit her since she had left her there in Rachel's charge the previous evening because of entertaining her father's guests. She had taken the ladies on a carriage ride to view the sights of Simon's Town which was shaking off the storm water in the winter sun. She had found the company of the ladies unbearably tedious: all she wanted to do was sit by Ellen's side in the hospital. The day had worn on, punctuated by a luncheon and a recital, until the dinner party that night. She had not even had a chance to talk to Elsie.

The other matter on her mind was the long-awaited visit of the Le Rouxs from L'Ourmarin the next month. Since the discovery of Sam's body and the subsequent events, Paul had been pushed from her mind. At the very thought of him a warm glow suffused her being. She felt very attracted to him. There was no denying that, and yet here she was engaged to John whom she had known and loved for so long. Her father was delighted with the match and they all had so much to look forward to. Nothing should be holding her back. But how could she marry him feeling as she did about Paul? Perhaps her feelings for Paul arose from the attraction of someone who came from a different background. She was probably just another girl whom he had kissed in the moonlight on a night much like tonight. It was better just to forget about him. But, unfortunately it was not quite as easy as that. Her recalcitrant heart would not listen to her mind. Why was life so complex? Things had been simple and straightforward before the visit to L'Ourmarin. How was she to react when they came? Would she be able to hide her feelings?

Charlotte stepped down from the veranda to take a turn about the garden when suddenly she was aware of a shadow moving in the shrubbery. Startled, she called out, 'Who is it? Is someone there?'

'Sh, ma'am. It's me – Elsie!' came a whisper.

'What are you doing here? I thought you went off duty hours ago.'

'Yes, ma'am. But please can you come to the quarters? I have an urgent message for you.'

'Can't you tell me now?'

'No, ma'am, I don't want us to be seen. Please be quick.'

At that moment someone opened the French windows leading from the drawing-room onto the veranda.

'Charlotte!'

'Yes, Papa.' She turned quickly, hoping that her face would not betray her inner agitation.

'I've been looking for you. Our guests would like some entertainment. We'd like you come and play the piano for us.'

'Oh, must I, Papa? I'm feeling very tired this evening.'

'Come, my dear. You know how our friends from England love to be reminded of life at home. They have so few opportunities for refined entertainment here.'

As she walked back into the brightly lit drawing room Charlotte realised that she would have no alternative but to oblige. She sat down at the piano while her heart was thudding within her. What could Elsie want? There must be something amiss with Ellen for her to come in search of Charlotte like this. She managed to get through a few pieces and then retired gracefully when Lucy Devenish was persuaded to take her place. Lucy played with a delicate air befitting her genteel upbringing.

Kitty Clarendon applauded slightly too loudly. Trying as she always must to draw attention to herself, she called out, 'Oh, that was marvellous! I do wish I could play like that. What a great talent you have, Lucy!'

Lucy smiled and withdrew from the piano stool to her seat next to her husband. It seemed to Charlotte that the evening would never end. How long were they to continue with these social niceties? She was longing to discover the reason for Elsie's visit, although an intuitive dread clawed at her stomach.

After what seemed like an eternity the guests made signs of leaving. The carriages were called for but Charlotte's duties were not yet over. She had to stand with her father and John at the front door and bid them all farewell. As soon as everyone had gone, she made her excuses and escaped up the stairs to her bedroom, with her father and John looking a little anxiously after her.

'Is all well with Charlotte, do you think?' enquired John.

'Oh yes,' Edward reassured him. 'She told me that she's tired. I know that she finds Lady Clarendon rather a trial.'

'Well I agree with her there,' said John. 'She's tiresome – quite the worst kind of Englishwoman as far as I'm concerned, and not one who is going to make any worthwhile contribution to the Colony.'

'I should think that there's little danger of her making any contribution at all,' Edward said. 'She won't last long here. She'll want to get back to the glamour and bright lights of London as soon as possible!'

* * *

Charlotte waited until she heard her father and John retire to their rooms. She had changed out of her elegant evening clothes into a plain brown dress and as soon as all was quiet she slipped down the backstairs and ran silently towards Elsie's room in the servants' quarters. She knocked softly on the door.

'Who is it?' Elsie whispered at the keyhole.

'It's me, Miss Charlotte.' Quickly and silently the door was opened to admit Charlotte to the plain but comfortable room. Immediately she saw Rachel sitting on a chair against the wall with a bundle in her arms. Fear clasped Charlotte's heart.

'What's happened Elsie?'

Elsie's eyes filled with tears. She could not speak.

'Is that Ellen's baby?'

Elsie nodded.

'And Ellen?'

Elsie averted her eyes and shook her head. The tears coursed down her cheeks.

'I'm sorry ma'am.'

'Oh no Elsie! Why? She seemed to be sleeping peacefully when I left her with Rachel last night. When?'

'Just before dawn this morning ma'am. After you left she went into labour.'

'I wasn't surprised when she collapsed at the funeral. The strain was too much to bear but she recovered consciousness when we took her to the hospital,' Charlotte said.

'Yes, ma'am, but the pains started and the baby came before its time and Ellen bled too much. Rachel did all she could but the doctor couldn't come and there was nothing that she could do to save her.'

'Oh why didn't she call for me? I should have been with her! Perhaps I could have helped,' Charlotte groaned.

'I don't know, ma'am. She could have called for me as well. I've helped bring many babies into the world. Perhaps she didn't want to make a fuss or maybe she was just too ill to think. Rachel tried to get help, but there was no-one to send and she wouldn't leave Ellen alone. All I know is that she lost the will to live when Sam had gone. She never recovered from his death. The light went out of her eyes.'

Charlotte nodded. It was true: bright vivacious, loving Ellen had gone with her lover into the waters of the Bay.

'And the baby?'

Rachel spoke for the first time. 'It's a boy Miss Lacey. She named him Samuel Joseph and made me promise that I'd bring him to you.'

Charlotte moved over to old Rachel who held up the tiny bundle to Charlotte. As Charlotte took her nephew into her arms she felt a surge of fierce protective love. She would care for this child and see that he was given every chance in life. For the sake of Ellen. And Sam.

CHAPTER TWENTY-FOUR

Reunion

From the north-facing window of her room Charlotte could see the main road coming in to Simon's Town from Visch Hoek. She became aware of a cloud of dust on the curve of the road in the far distance. As it came closer she saw that it was an ox wagon escorted by two riders. It must be Paul and Etienne. Charlotte watched the slow progress of the vehicle with mounting excitement. Eventually she could contain herself no longer and she ran down the stairs to the inner hall where her father was just emerging from his study.

'They're here, Papa!'

'Already? Well, they've made good time haven't they? I thought that they would arrive some time this afternoon. Let's go and meet them,' Edward said with a smile. 'I'm pleased to be relieved of this never-ending pile of paper work.'

Together father and daughter walked through the entrance hall and opened the elegant front door to Admiralty House. As they stepped into the spring sunshine Paul and Etienne trotted through the tollgate and stopped at the imposing entrance gates. They sat side by side atop their mounts, handsome men both, dignified and at peace with themselves. Behind them in the dusty street was the wagon full of wine barrels firmly lashed together as well as cases of bottled wine. The driver, who sat jauntily at the front of the wagon, raised his hat to the Admiral while the oxen stood stolidly and patiently in their yokes. Born to slavery, they had known nothing else, and Charlotte was reminded of the plight of those thousands in human bondage with whom she had come to sympathise during these last months. However, her thoughts were interrupted by the demands of courtesy and her very real pleasure at seeing Paul and his father again. She stepped back slightly into the porch to allow the men to exchange greetings first.

'How very happy I am to see you Etienne. And you too, Paul.' Edward extended his hand. 'Welcome to Simon's Town and Admiralty House.'

'Good morning Edward,' returned Etienne, dismounting and grasping his friend's hand. Paul followed closely behind him and shook his hand as well.

'I hope you enjoy the fruits of our labours.' Etienne pointed to the wine on the wagon. 'I have some barrels suitable for transport on your ships and also some of my choice bottles for your own cellar. These last are a gift from us.'

'Why, thank you, Etienne. That's extremely generous of you. Come inside. You must be tired and thirsty after your long ride.'

Admiral Lacey beckoned to one of the sentries on duty at the gates.

'Call James to take care of the horses, the oxen and the wagon driver, and instruct him to see that this precious cargo is brought over to the cellars of the house immediately.'

The three men walked into the shade of the porch where Charlotte was waiting quietly with a pounding heart.

'Good morning, Juffrouw Lacey.' Etienne bowed low over her hand and then Paul was raising her hand to his lips and looking directly into her eyes with his own brilliant blue ones. Charlotte experienced once again the inner stirring that this man aroused in her, and she wondered whether he would notice that her palms were sweating. She had a sudden irrational impulse to throw herself into his arms. But she recollected herself and assumed her role of the gracious hostess, mistress of Admiralty House.

'Good morning, gentlemen. I'm delighted to be able to

welcome you to our home. Please come in,' she said, leading the way into the deep cool of the entrance hall. 'Anna will show you to your rooms and then please join us for coffee on the veranda.'

* * *

A short while later Paul, Etienne, Charlotte and Edward were seated in the comfortable wicker chairs on the veranda. Below on the terrace the fountain played into the ornamental pool, surrounded by lush lawns and vivid flowers. Etienne breathed a sigh of contentment as he raised his coffee cup to his lips. 'This place is an oasis after our journey,' he said.

'Was it difficult?' Edward asked.

'In parts,' Etienne replied. 'We know the first part of the journey well. We outspanned at Meerlust, which is where Simon van der Stel used to outspan his teams when he travelled from Stellenbosch to Cape Town.'

'Simon van der Stel? I've been reading about him,' Charlotte said. 'Simon's Town gets its name from him.'

'And Stellenbosch as well,' Etienne said. 'He was the first governor of the Dutch colony – a remarkable man. He established the first wine estate at Groot Constantia, named after his wife Constance.'

'We owe a particular debt to him,' Paul intervened, 'as it was under his rule that the first Huguenots came to the Cape and were to settle in the Franschhoek valley which was established by van der Stel in 1687. You may remember me telling you about our family who came out from France to escape religious persecution?' he said to Charlotte.

'Of course I do,' Charlotte replied. 'It's a stirring history.'

'Van der Stel called the valley Drakenstein, after the great estate in Holland belonging to the Lords of Mydrecht, but with the settling of the Huguenots, it became known as Franschhoek – or French corner as the English would say.'

'Did you break your journey in Cape Town?' Edward asked, pouring another cup of coffee.

'Ja, we spent the night with some old friends in the city and then began our journey to Simon's Town early this morning.'

'The roads leave much to be desired,' Edward said, 'although to give Somerset his due, he has spent sixteen thousand pounds on their improvement. It's a reflection of a changed attitude now that the British Government has taken permanent possession of the Cape.'

'The road immediately outside Cape Town itself is not too bad around Wynberg Hill to Groot Constantia, Tokai and around the foot of the Steenberg Mountain. It's the route from Muizenberg that is most difficult,' Etienne said. 'The road is literally hacked out of the mountains, so we had to make our way over ridges and rocky outcrops and through streams, sometimes just above the waves so we were splashed by the spray.'

'We have an excellent driver,' Paul said. 'Moses can manage a team of oxen like you or I might handle a pack of hunting dogs. He certainly showed his skill in negotiating the Trappe, that series of ledges cut into the rock leading down to Visch Hoek Bay. He coaxed and wheedled those great beasts like kittens until he got them onto the sand.'

'That's known locally as Keppel's Folly,' Edward chuckled. 'A crazy Irishman, Lieutenant Henry Keppel, drove a tandem down the "Trappe" on his journey from Cape Town to Simon's Town. To top it all he had a passenger, a man with a broken arm.'

'Well, we didn't even think of trying that.' Etienne laughed too. 'We led our horses down the cutting but the oxen had faith in Moses.'

'Where did you find a driver like that?' Edward asked.

'He's a Hottentot, a Khoi, not a slave. His family have worked at L'Ourmarin for generations. The Hottentots have a way with animals,' Etienne said. 'I suppose they've lived close to nature for thousands of years and have learnt how to befriend the land, not see it as an enemy.'

'He's a valuable worker. He manages the wine cellar for us as well,' Paul said.

'Oh yes, I remember meeting him,' Charlotte said, 'when you

took me on the tour of the estate and showed me how the wines are made. I didn't realise that it was him.'

'I told James to look after him,' Edward said, 'and Elsie will make sure that he has plenty to eat.'

'I'm glad you warned us about the quicksand at the mouth of the Silvermyn River,' Paul said. 'Fortunately the tide was out when we got to Visch Hoek so we took the horses and oxen over the firm, wet sands. After that we had only the humps of Elsie's Peak to negotiate before we got here.'

'We're delighted that you have arrived safely,' Edward said. 'How long will you be able to stay with us?'

'We've given ourselves a week's rest. We've left L'Ourmarin in the competent hands of Guy and Marie, so we can rest easy.' Etienne leaned back in his chair as he spoke.

'It's a pity that you are only here for a week as you probably won't have the opportunity to meet John, Charlotte's fiancé. He has gone into Cape Town for a meeting with Lord Somerset. He's keen to settle on the eastern frontier and has gone to put in an application for land and the formalities are likely to take a few days.'

'That's disappointing,' Paul said. 'We'll have to meet him another time. We've been looking forward to this holiday with you very much.' As Paul spoke, his eyes caught Charlotte's and she had to look away lest her expression betray her feelings.

CHAPTER TWENTY-FIVE

The End of the Beginning

The company was to gather on the veranda of Admiralty House for breakfast. A long table covered by a damask cloth was laden with the choicest of Cape fruits: downy, golden peaches; fat, purple plums and clusters of green grapes. The air was redolent with the succulent aroma of freshly baked bread from the kitchen. Platters of cold meats and cheeses lay on a serving table.

Beyond the veranda, the garden shimmered in the morning dew. The roses were in prolific bloom and huge trees cast a deep shade on the perimeter of the lawn. As Charlotte walked out onto the veranda she felt a surge of pleasure at this extravagant beauty which contrasted with the barren hills above the town.

'Goeie more, juffrouw,' came a well-known voice as Paul appeared from round the corner of the veranda.

'Good morning, sir. Can I help you to some breakfast?' Charlotte said, curtseying in mock gentility.

Paul responded by bowing and saying, 'I thought perhaps we might take a turn around the garden before breakfast?'

'Why certainly, sir,' Charlotte replied, with memories of another garden walk with this handsome man fresh in her memory. She was pleased that the awkwardness of their last meeting at L'Ourmarin seemed to have passed, and taking Paul's outstretched hand, she stepped down from the veranda. The grass was wet underfoot and they left a trail as they walked towards the avenue which framed one side of the garden.

'It's very beautiful here, juffrouw. This is a fine house, and with the prospect of your marriage, you must be extremely happy.'

Charlotte paused. She found it impossible to be insincere with Paul.

'Aren't you happy?' he asked into the silence.

Charlotte looked directly into his eyes. 'A great deal has happened since we last met,' she said. Paul nodded, encouraging her to continue.

'Two young people I knew have died. I was particularly close to one of them.'

'I'm sorry,' he said simply. 'Do you want to talk about it?'

'Yes, I think I do,' Charlotte said.

In their walk around the garden they had arrived at the path leading down to the Admiral's jetty.

'Shall we go down to the beach?' he said.

'What about breakfast? I ought to get back to play the gracious hostess,' said Charlotte looking back at the house.

'I don't think that you need to worry about that,' Paul said. 'Our fathers are totally engrossed in each others' company and they will hardly miss us. Come, let's go down to a place where we can look at the water.' He took her arm in his and they walked through the deep shade of the grove of milkwood trees and across the beach to the jetty. They stood for a while watching the early morning sun dancing on the water. Eventually Charlotte started to talk and unfolded the whole tragic story of Sam and Ellen and baby Joseph.

'Where is the baby now?'

'At this moment he's being cared for by a Malay woman, the wife of a fisherman who lives up on a hill above Simon's Town. Christina is kind and a good mother. She is Sam's cousin and Ellen went to stay with her before she had the baby. After Ellen died Christina offered to look after the child. It was a hard decision as Ellen had entrusted Samuel Joseph to me, but, in the end, I decided that it was the best thing to do. I have been helping where I can with food, clothing and money but it was never going to be a permanent arrangement. That is why Sam got caught up in the smuggling venture. He was hoping that he would be able to buy a new life for Ellen and himself somewhere else.'

'It sounds like an act born of desperation,' Paul commented.

'I'm sure that it was, but now the arrangement can't continue. Even as we talk, Christina's husband Johannes is looking for work in Cape Town. They want to make a fresh start somewhere new. They are grappling with the loss of their son Jacobus who was drowned with Sam that dreadful night. On top of that, without a boat he has no means of making a living here, and he has also to replace the one that he borrowed.'

'So that means that Samuel Joseph will go with them to Cape Town?'

'No, I won't let that happen. It's too much of a burden on Christina and Johannes when they are trying to re-establish themselves. And in any case, a baby demands a great deal of time and Christina has children of her own to care for. Then, of course, there is the fact that the boy is half-caste for his father was half white and his mother was totally white. In fact, if you were to see him you would think that he is a white baby. And that is the basis of the problem. He will not be accepted by the Malay community and neither will he be accepted by the white community. He faces a future of being an outcast. Simon's Town is just too small for him.'

'Perhaps the Cape is too small for him,' Paul said thoughtfully.

'I truly loved Ellen, you know. She was so much more than a servant to me. I never thought of her in that way.' Charlotte paused. She wondered if she should tell Paul that Ellen was her half-sister but she decided that, although she had an intuitive trust in Paul, it was not yet time to share the secret that only she and her father knew in the Cape. 'She was my friend,' Charlotte continued. 'We were of much the same age. We were both in love with life. I can't believe that she's gone…' Charlotte's voice broke and Paul put his arm around her trembling shoulders. 'It all seems such an unnecessary waste. I wish that I could do something for the child. I would feel that I was somehow doing something to help Ellen. I would take care of him myself, but, of course, my father won't hear of that.'

'It's difficult for him,' Paul commented. 'Don't be too harsh in your judgement of him. He is in a delicate position here in Simon's Town and can't afford any scandal.'

'I do understand that. If the truth be told, it's probably more convenient that Ellen is dead,' she said bitterly. 'Now she can't be a social embarrassment, but the inconvenient truth is the existence of the baby.'

Paul took Charlotte's hand and led her to the end of the jetty. They stood there together for a while looking at the tall ships swaying rhythmically in the water, which was ruffled by a skittish breeze. The warmth of the morning sun washed over them, restoring some peace to Charlotte's agitated spirit.

Eventually Paul spoke. 'Who is legally responsible for the child?'

'That's a good question,' Charlotte said, thinking as she spoke that she and her father were probably the next of kin. 'Both his parents are dead and, as far as I know, both of Sam's parents are too. Ellen's parents are in England, and even if they are legally responsible, how would we get the baby there? Who would be prepared to take him?'

'Your country has abolished the slave trade but the practice of slavery is still alive and well in the Cape. I don't think that too many questions would be asked about the movement of a small infant. But perhaps, Charlotte, I can do something to help this child. He could come back with us to L'Ourmarin.'

Charlotte turned in astonishment and looked at Paul. Yes, those blue eyes were serious and considering. This was a side of him that she had not seen. Why should he do this? And how was he to do it? Paul sensed her questions.

'You have met my mother.' The image of the humourless, forbidding Marie le Roux rose in Charlotte's mind. 'She is a fine woman: good, upright and Christian. She would, I am sure, be prepared to oversee the upbringing of this child.'

'You're not suggesting that he would come and live with you in your home at L'Ourmarin, are you?' Charlotte exclaimed.

'No,' Paul laughed. 'My mother is not quite as Christian as that! She would, however, not object to the boy living on the estate. We have a woman of mixed blood whose husband manages the wine cellars at L'Ourmarin. In fact, you've met him. He's here right now in your servants' quarters.'

'Moses! The intrepid wagon driver?'

'The very one. His wife is a young woman of Malay stock but childless. I think that she would be pleased to have a baby to care for and my mother would feel that she was doing her Christian duty in allowing this to take place.'

Charlotte still did not speak. She was deeply moved by this generous offer. It was not something for which she would have asked. Neither would she have looked to Paul for help. Sharing the problem with him had not only lightened the load for her but had also presented new and creative possibilities for its solution. L'Ourmarin was far enough away from Simon's Town to provide a safe haven for Samuel Joseph and yet close enough that she could see him regularly. As an adopted child of a cellar manager he would have some respectability and security in society. It would be a healthy life.

'This is a very fine gesture, sir.'

'It's not a gesture. It's a serious offer. Obviously I'll have to discuss it with my parents and with Moses and Heloise. But I feel hopeful of the outcome.'

Charlotte bowed her head so that the many conflicting emotions that were racing through her being would not be obvious. 'Thank you,' she whispered.

'There is no need for thanks,' he said.

CHAPTER TWENTY-SIX

Conflict at Water's Edge

When Paul broached the subject of Samuel Joseph to Etienne he was surprised, but, being essentially a kind and God-fearing man, who had good relationships with his employees, whether slaves or free men, he saw this as an opportunity to do good. He and Paul spoke to Moses whose grin was as wide as the mouth of the Silvermyn River.

'Ja, Baas. Heloise will be very happy. But what about the Nooi?'

'I'll write to her and ask her to speak to Heloise.' And Etienne sent a rider through to L'Ourmarin with a letter to Marie, informing her of the plan. While not particularly wanting to encourage connections with the English family, Marie, nevertheless, generally submitted to her husband's wishes, and so she told Heloise who was delighted with the idea. She and Moses had been married for several years and yet no child had arrived. She was eager to receive the baby as soon as possible.

John returned from Cape Town in high spirits, as his meeting with Lord Somerset had gone well. Although he had planned to avoid them, he was obliged to meet the Le Rouxs who had delayed their departure because of the baby. He showed no enthusiasm for the arrangements for Samuel Joseph which brought a sparkle to Charlotte's eyes and a spring to her step. Charlotte realised that she would have to tell John that she was planning to escort

Samuel Joseph to L'Ourmarin and that he would not be pleased. She thought that it would be best if she spoke to him away from the house, and so she asked him to come for a ride with her through the town to Water's Edge the morning after his return. As they came to Cole's Point they paused to take in the scene. The boatyard was a frenzy of activity and people were coming and going.

'Papa says that Osmond is particularly excited because he has a large commission from the Royal Navy. He could see the opportunity for making a small fortune. He is to refit two ships that were damaged in high seas coming around Cape Point. The Navy wants to use the ships to transport provisions and weapons to St Helena, which is preparing to house its famous prisoner Napoleon Bonaparte.'

'You have to admire Osmond you know,' John remarked, as they continued on their way. 'He's certainly been successful.'

'Yes, he has,' agreed Charlotte,' but that doesn't make me like him any better. I think that he's grasping and avaricious. Everything that he does is directed towards his own selfish advancement. Even his marriage to Widow Roussouw's daughter was expedient. Do you really think that he would have married her if she had not come from a wealthy family?'

'I don't know him well, of course. But perhaps you're being a trifle harsh Charlotte. Many great people owe their success to recognising and grasping opportunities when they are presented.'

'That's different. What I dislike about Osmond is the way he takes advantage of people's misfortune to feather his own nest. Papa doesn't like him either, but he gives him work because there is actually nobody else in Simon's Town. If there were, you can be sure that Osmond would find some way of getting rid of them.'

'Nevertheless he's good at his job. He's a fine ship's carpenter. His work compares favourably with the shipwrights of Liverpool and Plymouth.'

By now their horses were picking their way down the rough track leading to Seaforth Beach. Charlotte spoke ruminatively. 'I suppose things are never really clear cut, are they? People are not black or white; but many shades of grey.'

'I assume that you're speaking metaphorically, Charlotte, because there are certainly distinctions between the black and white people as far as I can see, but I suppose you've got a point. Humans are a complex mix: good and evil; love and hate within us all.'

'It's the love part that we have to focus on,' said Charlotte. 'It's love that connects us all.'

'That's true, Charlotte. You know that I love you. Nothing has changed as far as I am concerned, but I sense that you are distant.'

They had reached the grassy bank of Water's Edge and, as she dismounted, Charlotte realised that this was the moment to speak to John of what was uppermost in her mind. They tethered their horses to some convenient shrubs and Charlotte led the way down to the boulder where she had spent many hours in silent thought over the past few months.

'I'm sorry if I've seemed distant,' she said as they sat down on the rock worn smooth by the constant buffeting of the waves. 'It's true that I've been preoccupied with the deaths of Sam and Ellen and the welfare of little Samuel Joseph.'

She looked out at the familiar scene. The sea was like moulded glass which rose and fell, gentle motion with scarcely a ripple on the surface, heaving shoulders of water. Every now and then a wave broke and withdrew, leaving shallow pools of water in the depressions in the rocks. The terns gathered in a massive flock on a rocky outcrop, social birds, revelling in their own company. Two cormorants, dignified and aloof in their splendid isolation, sat apart on a separate rock. Suddenly, for no discernible reason, the terns took flight, sailing around in a great cloud only to return again to gather on the same resting place.

'John, there's something I have to tell you.'

'Yes?' He turned to her and smiled.

'I'm going to travel to L'Ourmarin with the Le Rouxs.'

The smile faded from John's face as though it had been washed away by a wave.

'That's not necessary.'

'It may not be necessary but I have to.'

'Why do you have to?'
'I have to see that Samuel Joseph is well settled.'
'You're being ridiculous, Charlotte!'
'I'm not being ridiculous. Ellen was my friend as well as being my maid. It's the least I can do for her.'
'You don't need to go traipsing around the countryside with a black bastard!'
'John! I can't believe that you've just said that. Charlotte was genuinely shocked. 'And in any case he's not black,' she said as she stood up from the rock.
'I'm sorry, Charlotte.' John stood up too. 'I didn't mean that. It's just that I want you here. I missed you so much in Cape Town and I want to tell you all about my plans for the future after we're married.'
'Oh, John, I'm sorry too.' Charlotte was keen to restore harmony between them. 'But please try to understand that I have to do this for Ellen. It's not that I don't want to spend time with you.' She added as a second thought, 'Why don't you come too?'
'I'm not the slightest bit interested in associating with French peasants!' John's colour was rising again. 'I've spent too much of my life fighting them. They killed my parents, don't forget, and my brother! In fact, I don't know how you can stomach spending time with them at all!'
'It's different, John. The Le Rouxs are Huguenots. They have nothing to do with Napoleon and the Revolutionary Wars. Their family left France a hundred years before the Revolution even started. They don't even speak French! In fact you're half French yourself!'
'No, I'm not! I'm an Englishman. I rejected all notion of French identity as soon as I realised what those barbaric people did to my family! The le Rouxs are still Frogs as far as I'm concerned and I don't want you to go!'
'Well, I'm going,' said Charlotte.
'You're in love with him, aren't you?'
Charlotte's heart lurched. Was it so apparent?
'In love with him? Who? What are you talking about, John?'

'That French oaf who's been looking at you with calf eyes all the time.'

'Paul? You mean Paul? It's you who's being ridiculous now, John. It's not even worth discussing. I'm in love with you and engaged to you remember?' She laughed and looked up at him and continued in a more serious tone, 'But he's not an oaf. He's kind and supportive and he's done us a vast favour by making arrangements for the care of Ellen's baby in a safe environment.'

'I don't know how you can be so concerned about the illegitimate child of a working-class whore and a black slave who is being taken away, thank God, by people who are our life-long enemies!'

Charlotte was horrified at John's words. She looked at him as though she was seeing him for the first time, turned away and ran back across the beach, and leaped onto Amber's back.

'Charlotte! Come back! I'm sorry!'

'So am I!' shouted Charlotte as she galloped away from him and back to Admiralty House.

CHAPTER TWENTY-SEVEN

A Significant Journey

The white, flat-roofed houses of Simon's Town shimmered in the morning sun. It was late spring and the flowers were in riotous colour. The weather was warm and a light breeze rustled the leaves in the trees. The le Rouxs' ox-wagon stood in the dusty road outside Admiralty House. All the barrels and bottles of wine had found their way to their destination and now the wagon was about to embark on the return journey to the Franschhoek Valley with a different burden: a human one. The wagon had been refurbished to accommodate a small baby with all the requisite food, bedding and clothing. Samuel Joseph was to be taken to his new home. Charlotte had engaged a young Malay girl, Andrina, a freed slave, to act as nursemaid.

Since their disagreement at Water's Edge, relations between John and Charlotte had been strained. They had not discussed the matter again, partly because neither of them wanted to, and partly because the time had been taken up with the preparations for the departure of the le Rouxs.

On the last evening there was a farewell dinner for the le Rouxs in the small dining room.

'How do you like this Palamino, Edward?' asked Etienne, holding a glass of golden liquid up to the light of the candelabra. 'It's a new cultivar for us.'

'Delicious,' Edward said. 'It's like a sherry in texture.'

'We have combined our French heritage in viticulture with the good growing conditions that we have in the Franschhoek Valley. Our vines are grown on the terraced vineyards on the slopes of the Groot Drakenstein.'

'That's the mountain range behind your house, isn't it?' Charlotte commented.

'That's right, and the clear mountain water is good for our grapes.'

'Well, I hope that there are several bottles of this in the cellar. But speaking of wine, we'll need to order some for the wedding in December,' Edward said, looking at Charlotte and John.

Charlotte nodded but John spoke: 'I don't think that we'll need to bother the le Rouxs with providing wine for the wedding, sir. It's a devilishly long journey from L'Ourmarin to Simon's Town, and there's some good wine being produced in the Constantia Valley just now. I heard in Cape Town last week that some of it has even been exported to England.'

Charlotte flushed at this obvious rebuff, but Etienne merely smiled and said, 'As you wish, but if you would like some of our wine, as a wedding gift of course, just let me know and I'll make sure that you have it in plenty of time. Is it going to be a big celebration?'

'No,' said Charlotte. 'We don't know many people here in the Cape yet, but there will be the naval officers and their wives from Simon's Town and one or two of Papa's contacts from Cape Town. Papa is giving us a ball as he did to celebrate our engagement. That was a great success, wasn't, it John?'

John smiled in agreement, and Charlotte's heart was warmed by the change in his expression and the memory of that happy evening before the tragedies.

'The ceremony will be in St George's Church,' Edward said. 'It's a charming venue. It's situated in the sail loft which is the upper floor of the mast house in the Dockyard. It's still used for sailmaking during the week, but on Sundays it's used as a church.'

'Isn't that complicated?' Etienne asked. 'I can't imagine using my wine cellar for a church. There would be so much equipment to move.'

'It's actually quite easy,' said Edward. 'The sails are furled at weekends and the masts, which are heavy to move, are housed on the lower level. During the week the altar is curtained off and the pews are moved against the walls to allow space for the sailmakers to do their work.'

'It's been built recently,' John added. 'It was Edward's idea and is specifically designed to be able to house the main mast of a hundred-gun ship, so it's one hundred and twenty feet long.'

'All very suitable for a naval wedding, I'd say,' Edward said with a smile.

'Even though the groom plans to leave the Navy,' Charlotte interposed, but then, catching her father's eye, she said, 'Father's right. It's a lovely spot next to the bay and it's big enough to accommodate all those whom we wish to come.'

'The naval chaplain will conduct the ceremony. He's an old friend, Captain Jarvis. We've sailed together many times,' Edward said.

'I'm not going to have any attendants,' Charlotte continued, 'because I don't have any particular friends here and I want the ceremony to be as simple as possible. But I hope that you and your family will be able to come, sir,' she said to Etienne.

'We're looking forward to it, aren't we, Paul?' said Etienne as he looked at his son. 'I'll try to persuade Marie to come as well, although she doesn't enjoy these long journeys.'

Now the morning after that last dinner party Charlotte was sticking to her original plan despite John's objections, and was going to L'Ourmarin. She had chosen to ride with Paul and Etienne although her father had reservations about her taking such a long trip on horseback.

'It's a difficult journey, particularly over the mountains into the Franschhoek Valley,' he said.

'Papa, I've done it before with you, as you know. And it's far more difficult for the wagon travelling over the mountain pass.'

'Yes, that's true. Somerset is, I believe, planning to improve the road.'

'Anyway, Papa, I'll be perfectly all right. I have Andrina as a chaperone. You know how I love riding, and I shall be quite safe with Paul and Etienne, who understand the land and the ways of the people around here better than we do.'

Edward had to admit the truth of this. He himself would have liked to accompany them, but he had pressing business in Simon's Town. The latest despatches informed him that arrangements were being made to transport Napoleon to St Helena and there was much preparatory work to be done before that happened.

'Why don't you go, John?' Edward turned to his nephew.

'Thank you, sir. But I need to go back to Cape Town to complete the preliminary arrangements for the land that I've applied for,' he said brusquely.

'You could travel with us as far as Cape Town,' Charlotte suggested.

'Thank you, but no. Champion needs to be reshoed before I take him on a long ride.' And he turned and marched off to the stables. Charlotte watched him go with a mixture of sadness and anger. Still, there was nothing that she could do at the moment to redeem the situation, which would just have to wait until she returned from L'Ourmarin.

Edward stood outside the gates of Admiralty House and watched as the party set off: the heavy, lumbering ox-wagon drawn by the slow-moving, steady beasts, and the three riders on horseback. They were to travel back the way they had come, following the coast road around through Visch Hoek and Kalk Bay to Muizenberg and across country through Tokai and Wynberg to Cape Town. From there it would be a lengthy although comparatively easy trek until they reached the Helshoogte Mountain about which Edward had spoken.

As they left Simon's Town behind them Charlotte's spirits were high. What had seemed a dismal prospect for tiny Samuel Joseph was now transformed into a future of hope and light. There was a new understanding between her and Paul as well. There had always been an undeniable physical attraction between them, but now there was a harmony of being that she had not known before. They both cared about the same things. It was strange that she felt she did not have to be grateful to Paul for what he had done. She knew that he did not expect it either. They both knew that the decision had been the right one and the ease with which it had been agreed by the various people involved confirmed this.

Paul was in a buoyant frame of mind as well, although he had to admit that Charlotte's determination to accompany them on the journey was a little unconventional.

'I'm afraid that this adventurous spirit of yours will not meet with the approval of the devout ladies of the Franschhoek Valley,' he teased.

'Well, don't expect me to conform. I haven't been brought up to be your typical lady of the manor. Beside, there's a certain breed of Englishwoman who has always been adventurous. Lady Anne Barnard is a case in point. She travelled extensively through these regions about twenty years ago, I'm told.'

'Ah, yes. I've heard about that. She went right around False Bay as far as Hangklip, which is the promontory more or less facing Cape Point from the other side of False Bay. But she was in the company of her husband.'

'Well, I suppose you'll just have to perform that role,' laughed Charlotte, blushing as she spoke, as she realised the full implications of what she had said.

CHAPTER TWENTY-EIGHT

An Unforeseen Conflict

Charlotte stood at the front door of L'Ourmarin and surveyed the expanse of well-tended estate, the gardens and the ornamental lake, backed up by the grandeur of the mountains. Man had tamed part of the land but one was always aware of a force beyond. She thought back on the recent events. It had been a hard ride with Paul and his father from Simon's Bay to Cape Town where they had spent the night. The journey from Cape Town to L'Ourmarin had been dusty and tiring and difficult over the Helshoogte Mountain, but she was amazed by the skill with which Moses managed the wagon with its precious cargo over the rough track.

Their arrival at L'Ourmarin had gone smoothly. The arrangements for little Samuel Joseph had fallen into place as if a providential hand had taken over. Moses and Heloise were overjoyed with the baby. For them it was an answer to a prayer. Charlotte could imagine the boy growing up here, straight and strong in this fine, beautiful country. It would be a healthy life and he would be given opportunities that would be impossible in Simon's Town. She would be going back to Admiralty House soon, but secure in the knowledge that he would be safe. And it would be a reason to remain in touch with Paul. She smiled to herself.

Charlotte was deep in this reflection when she felt, rather than saw, Paul's presence.

'Juffrouw.'
'Yes.'
She turned.
'Would you care to walk with me around the lake?'
'I'd be delighted.'

Paul offered her his arm and together they walked down to the water. For a while they strolled in companionable silence.

'Do you remember your first visit here?'
'Yes, of course.'

'How could I forget?' she said to herself. She remembered well the moonlight walk and the kiss and her revelation of her engagement to John.

'I want to apologise again for embarrassing you like that.'

'Oh, please don't. It is I who should do the apologising. I should have told you from the beginning that I was engaged.'

'I'm glad that we have been able to remain friends, because we think the same way. You are very different from the ladies around here.'

'Yes, so I've gathered,' Charlotte said.

They paused by the edge of the lake.

'There's something I need to speak to you about, juffrouw.'

'Yes?' She looked up at him. A quiver of excitement bubbled up through her being.

'Paul!' a voice rang out.
'Ja, Moeder.'
'Your father needs you at the stables.'

'Excuse me, juffrouw.' He bowed to her. 'Let us continue our conversation later.'

Charlotte, left adrift in the garden, decided to walk over to the wine cellar to ask Moses about Samuel Joseph. She loved to hear the latest news of her nephew, but of course it was not seemly for her to spend too much time in the cellar manager's cottage, which was near the slave lodge. The day was already getting warm and she was pleased to enter the cool of the wine cellar with its pungent aromas. She walked along the passage past the great wooden casks of wine looking for some sign of

Moses. Suddenly she became aware of a shadow at the entrance of the wine cellar.

'Juffrouw Lacey!'

'Yes?' Charlotte turned to see the angular shape of Marie le Roux outlined against the light of the door. She stepped down into the cellar where Charlotte stood at the point where the passage opened out into the room with the vats.

'May I speak with you?'

'Yes, of course. What is it?'

'I think you know very well what it is, juffrouw.'

'I assure you I do not.'

'I have been watching you with my son.'

'Indeed, Mevrouw le Roux! Whatever for?'

'Because I know about your scheme.'

'I have no scheme madam, other than the business about which you know well, and thank you for making it possible for Samuel Joseph to find a new home.'

'But I know the reason behind all of this, juffrouw.'

Charlotte felt a cold tremor inside. Could Marie have found out the truth about her relationship with Samuel Joseph? Her mind raced. Nobody knew that she and Ellen were sisters except for her father and Agnes back in England. Even Ellen had never known, and Agnes didn't know about Samuel Joseph's existence. Edward had written to Gabriel and Agnes telling them the sad news of Ellen's death, but had decided that it was not necessary for them to know any details of Sam or the baby.

'Don't pretend with me, juffrouw. I know your type of woman well. You English have no sense of propriety.'

'Why, madam, what do you mean?'

'Riding around the countryside in this shameless manner like a woman of the town. You may think that you are gaining favour with my son with your flirtatious ways but you will not succeed!'

'Succeed in what, madam?'

'In winning his heart. Just because he has helped you to find a solution to your problem, do not think that you can win him to your side!'

'Why would I want to do that, madam? I am engaged to be married, you know, to Sir John du Rand, lieutenant in the Royal Navy.' Charlotte drew herself up as she suddenly felt defenceless in an alien environment.

'That may be the case, but I notice that he never comes here with you, because that would get in the way of your manipulations, wouldn't it?'

'Manipulations, madam? That is a harsh criticism, and I really don't know what you mean.'

'You fancy yourself as mistress of this estate, which Paul will inherit one day. But I will not let it happen!'

'Nothing could be further from my mind, madam. You could not be more wrong. If you must know, we have a family estate in England which I will inherit, and where I can live whenever I wish.'

'I think that that is not enough for you, juffrouw. The English like to have more than one home, but you will never lay your hands on this one. And you need to know that my son is engaged to be married to Susanna Cloete. She comes from good French Huguenot stock and her family owns a wine estate in the Constantia Valley as well as their estate in the Franschhoek Valley. It's a most suitable, excellent match and we are all delighted,' Marie said, her voice ringing with triumph.

Charlotte felt disappointment fall like a lead weight. 'How silly,' she said to herself. 'Whatever made you think that anything different could happen? This is probably what Paul wanted to tell me before his mother called him.' But aloud she said, 'Allow me to congratulate you, madam. I can see that you are very pleased.'

'Of course we are,' Marie said with a tight smile of victory. 'We are planning that the wedding will take place very soon.'

'My fiancé and I are getting married in December,' Charlotte said, determined to keep matters at the level of courteous formality. 'My father and I are hoping that you and Mijnheer le Roux and your family will be able to come.'

'Alas, I don't think that that will be possible, juffrouw. We shall be far too busy on the estate at that time.' And with that Marie le Roux turned and walked back towards the house.

Charlotte was nonplussed. Marie's hostility shocked her, but she had to admit that she felt as though a flame had been snuffed out in her life. Despite herself she had had secret hopes that could never now be realised. She felt a sudden surge of anger too towards Paul. Why had he not told her himself?

Her mind preoccupied, she wandered aimlessly along the passages between the huge vats of wine when she was suddenly conscious that she was not alone.

'Juffrouw!'

'Yes?' She looked up to see Paul, who had entered the wine cellar.

'I'm sorry to have deserted you like that. My father wanted my opinion on a horse that he intends to buy.'

'Do not be concerned about that, sir,' Charlotte said with icy formality. 'I'm sure that your family's needs are foremost.'

'What are you talking about, juffrouw?' Paul said, surprised by her change of tone. 'You're being a little dramatic, don't you think?'

'I think that perhaps it's you who has the dramatic talent, sir, and have been keeping your secret well hidden.'

'Secret? What secret?' Paul looked genuinely puzzled. 'What are you talking about, juffrouw?' he repeated.

'Your forthcoming marriage! Not that it's any concern of mine, but you might have mentioned your engagement to my father and me while we were all in Simon's Town together.'

'I didn't mention it because it hasn't happened yet,' Paul replied. 'Who has told you this?'

'Your mother, of course!'

'Ah, Moeder!' A smile of realisation spread across Paul's features. 'She is very keen on this proposal.'

'Are you trying to say that it's not true?'

Paul leant against one of the massive wine barrels and folded his arms over his chest as he said, 'No, it's not true yet, but it probably will be. There has been an understanding for many years that we would get married. Susanna's mother and mine are long-standing friends and they have been plotting this betrothal since we were in our cradles.'

'But do you love her?' Charlotte asked.

Paul laughed. 'Marriage is a very practical arrangement for us in the Huguenot community. But yes, I do love her. She is my dear friend. We were playmates in childhood and our marriage is an understood thing in our families although we are not formally engaged yet.'

'And when do you expect that that will take place?' Charlotte asked more tartly than she would have wished.

'Probably at Christmas time when the families are together.'

Charlotte turned away to hide the tears which were pricking her eyelids.

'Why didn't you tell me?' she said.

'There didn't seem to be the opportunity when we were in Simon's Town or on the journey here. It's not yet the time to make a public announcement and I wanted to tell you myself. That's why I asked you to come and walk with me this morning but my mother called me away before I had a chance to do that. It seems that she got there before me. I would have much preferred you to hear from me because we are good friends, aren't we, juffrouw?' he said, walking up to her.

Charlotte turned and held out her hand. 'Allow me, as your good friend, to be the first to congratulate you, sir. I trust that you will be very happy.'

Paul paused before he took her hand and held it to his lips. 'Thank you, juffrouw. I hope that you will be very happy too.'

Again there was a pause as they looked into each other's eyes.

'Another time, another place, perhaps, Charlotte.'

CHAPTER TWENTY-NINE

Decisions

'He must be well on his way by now,' John said shaking his brandy balloon and sniffing the pungent bouquet.

'Yes, I should think he is,' Edward replied. John and Edward were comfortably ensconced in the Admiral's study after dinner the day after the departure of Charlotte and the le Rouxs. It was not a large room, but it was elegantly furnished with armchairs upholstered in crimson and cream striped fabric. Long, matching drapes hung at the windows and leather-bound books stood on the highly polished desk. A pair of crossed sabres hung over the mantelpiece.

'Sir George Cockburn, Governor of St Helena, was due to leave England with Napoleon on board HMS *Northumberland* on the fifteenth of October. If the weather is fine and the winds are favourable they should reach St Helena within two months.'

'The island will be thick with soldiers by now, judging from the number of transport ships that have docked here laden with troops on their way to the island.'

Edward laughed as he poured another measure of brandy into his glass. 'They're making sure that he doesn't escape this time. The memories of how he slipped through his captors' fingers are very vivid. Three regiments have been sent to Jamestown, the capital of St Helena.'

'That must mean that the population of the island has virtually doubled.'

Edward nodded in agreement. 'It will be too much for the island's resources. And that means that they will have to import all their food and other materials from the nearest point, which means the Cape. Simon's Town is the closest base where there are facilities for ship repairs and an arsenal. There is likely to be a lot of traffic between Simon's Town and St Helena.'

'What effect is it likely to have on you personally?' John asked sipping his brandy.

'The responsibility is huge,' Edward said. 'Ultimately I'm the guardian of Bonaparte. I'm planning to have a continuous patrol around the island to prevent any possibility of his escape.'

'That man has assumed supernatural proportions in the minds of most people. I hear that an outpost has even been established on Tristan da Cunha.'

'Yes, that's quite true, and, as you know, the garrison at the Cape is being strengthened. The Navy will organise its own supplies of course, but private individuals will have to make their own arrangements. I expect the East India Company will be active, but private traders will take advantage of the situation as well.'

'The civilians are bound to depend on the Navy for transport of their supplies, which will be routed through Simon's Town.'

'I see that John Osmond is already taking advantage of this opportunity,' Edward commented. 'He's renting out, at vast expense, a storehouse to the Navy to store goods that have come in from Cape Town en route to St Helena. He managed to acquire most of Endres's property which he had lusted after – Kirsten's House and the Buffelsfontein farm on Cape Point. He regards the acquisition of Buffelsfontein as an estate for hunting, shooting and fishing as being particularly suitable to his position as "King John". All this he manages to achieve while keeping on the right side of the authorities.'

'It seems that the world is full of commoners who want to take on royal or imperial titles,' John said. 'Napoleon is a case in point. But at the same time you have to admire Osmond's adroitness, don't you? He's the wealthiest man in Simon's Town and he's done it all on his own.'

'His marriage to the wealthy Widow Rousseau's daughter certainly helped, and he's fathered a fine flock of children to inherit his name and wealth.'

'Frankly I don't like the man. His pretensions to living in the aristocratic style are nauseating. His purchase of Mount Curtis the year before last, which the locals refer to as "The Palace", says it all. He'll be demanding that we bow and scrape to him soon,' said John dryly.

'He's likely to become drunk with power if he continues the way he is. He's well on the way to buying up half of Simon's Town.'

'He's certainly astute when it comes to property,' John said 'I'm told that he sold his own house to the Navy for the accommodation of the victualling department, and then bought Mount Curtis at an auction a month later for half the price he had received for his own home. Standing up on the hill as it does overlooking Admiralty House and Simon's Bay it has the air of an English manor house.'

'Somerset can't stand him of course,' Edward said. 'He doesn't succeed with him nearly as well as he did with Caledon and Cradock. Somerset regards him as an upstart and the despot of Simon's Town. Speaking of Somerset, how did you get on in your interview with him?'

'Extremely well. But, as you will probably be pleased to hear, I have decided against the eastern frontier. I think that it's not going to be quite as I imagined – pretty rough, pioneering conditions. Not that I'm afraid of that,' John hastened to add. 'It's just that another opportunity has come up. Somerset mentioned to me that the estate "Wittebomen" in the Constantia Valley is up for sale and I'm thinking of making an offer on it.'

Edward's relief was reflected in the softening of the lines on his face. 'Well, needless to say I would be delighted to have you and Charlotte near at hand, and I'm sure that she'll be pleased to hear this when she gets back from L'Ourmarin. I happen to know Wittebomen. It's a beautiful property – a wine estate. But if you'll forgive my curiosity John, what do you know about viticulture?'

John laughed. 'Not much, Uncle. Except that I know a capital wine when I find one,' said John, holding his glass up to the candlelight as he spoke. 'But seriously, I don't view that as an insurmountable problem. The estate has a manager and there is a competent wine-maker, and they're both keen to stay on. I believe that money, good management, and, of course, an interest, which I certainly have got, are enough to ensure a promising future.'

'It's a good time to get into the wine industry,' Edward said. 'The government at home has decided to reduce customs duties on wine imported from the Cape to a third of that charged on wines imported from Europe. So it augurs well for a prosperous venture.'

'That's what I'm hoping, Uncle. The timing seems just right.'

'So you've definitely decided against the Navy?'

John paused and looked steadily at his uncle. 'Yes, I'm afraid so, Uncle. I'm determined to buy my way out. As you can see I've quite fallen in love with this wonderful new country, and I've decided to invest everything in it.'

'You could do worse,' Edward smiled. 'Here's to your future success as a wine estate owner in the Cape!' And he raised his glass to his nephew.

CHAPTER THIRTY

From Franschhoek to Cape Town

Charlotte left L'Ourmarin at the first opportunity after her encounter with Marie le Roux. The atmosphere, a sharp contrast to her first visit, was strained and stiff. She avoided looking at Paul, who was often busy with duties on the estate, so they met only occasionally at meal times when the conversation was at best stilted and formal. Guy and his sister Marie-Louise seldom had anything to offer. Etienne, who seemed oblivious to any tension, was the only one who kept conversation alive.

It was to him that Charlotte went to find out how she might get an escort to Simon's Town as soon as possible. Etienne was inspecting the vines on the lower slopes of the Groot Drakenstein when Charlotte ran up to him.

'Good morning, sir.'

'Ah, Juffrouw Lacey. Good morning, how are you this fine day?'

'Well, sir, and I can see that you are too,' Charlotte said.

Etienne laughed. 'Indeed I regard myself as being a very fortunate man. Look at this wonderful place that God has given me,' he said, raising his arms to enfold the view of the purple mountains and the trails of orderly green vines chasing up the foothills. 'Can you imagine anything more spectacular?'

'I can see your point, sir,' Charlotte said, as she followed his gaze, although, was it her imagination or did those mountains now seem cold and forbidding? Beautiful as they were, they also hemmed in the inhabitants of this valley where she now felt like an outsider. She longed to get back to those whom she loved and trusted – her family, her father and John.

'Yes, sir, you certainly do live in a beautiful place,' she agreed. 'But talking of home, it's time that I went back to mine.'

'You know, juffrouw, that you're welcome to stay as long as you wish.'

'Thank you,' Charlotte said, 'but my father and my fiancé both want me to come home,' and, as she spoke, an image of John's anger when he heard of her visit to L'Ourmarin swam into her vision. 'And there's nothing more for me to do now. Samuel Joseph is happily settled and doesn't need me at the moment.'

'So you're looking for an escort?' ventured Etienne. Charlotte nodded.

'Next week I'm taking a delivery of wine to the Castle in Cape Town but I'm not sure that I'll be able to continue to Simon's Town.'

'That would be wonderful, sir. And you don't need to worry about the journey to Simon's Town. My father or John will meet me in Cape Town.'

'Good,' Etienne said. 'Then it's all settled. We'll send a rider to your father today with a letter.'

'Thank you, sir,' Charlotte said, and her heart lifted in a way that it hadn't since her arrival at L'Ourmarin with Samuel Joseph and Paul and his father when life had seemed so full of promise.

* * *

Within a few days Charlotte received a letter from her father delivered by the postboy saying how delighted he was that she was coming home. Unfortunately he would not be able to meet her, but John would travel to Cape Town on the Saturday to bring her back to Simon's Town the following day. He had arranged that she should stay for the intervening few days with his friends the Lansdownes who lived in a house in Strand Street.

* * *

When Charlotte arrived in Cape Town on the Wednesday evening, dirty and dishevelled, Clarissa Lansdowne met her at the door.

'Lovely to see you, Charlotte, but I wasn't expecting you until tomorrow.'

'No, I know,' Charlotte said, hugely relieved to hear the familiar intonation of an English voice. 'We left a day earlier than expected and made very good time.'

'Well, come in, my dear. You must be tired,' Clarissa said, taking her by the arm and leading her into the spacious hall. 'Where is your luggage?'

'It's on the wagon over there,' Charlotte said pointing behind her where Etienne was directing a slave to carry Charlotte's trunk to the house. He turned and bowed as he saw Clarissa and walked over to the two women.

'May I present Mijnheer le Roux,' Charlotte said.

'How do you do, sir?' Clarissa said sweetly. 'Won't you come in and share a dish of tea with us?'

'Thank you, no,' Etienne said. 'I have to deliver this cargo of wine to the Castle this evening.'

'Thank you for escorting me,' Charlotte said.

'It's a pleasure, juffrouw. Tot siens,' Etienne said as he climbed onto his horse and with a wave disappeared down Strand Street.

'We're going to a reception at Government House tonight,' Clarissa said, closing the front door behind them. 'Would you like to come?'

'I don't know,' Charlotte replied. 'I'm filthy and travel-stained.' Then she checked herself. What she needed most was a change of scene and company. 'Actually, I would love to come,' she said. 'Thank you. All I need to do is wash and change out of my travelling clothes. Do you think I could have a bath?'

'Yes, of course. I'll get Edna to prepare one for you,' Clarissa said as she led the way upstairs.

'That would be wonderful,' Charlotte said.

'I've put you in this room which overlooks Table Bay,' Clarissa said as she opened the shutters.

The sun was setting over the bay and, seeing the tall ships riding at anchor, Charlotte realised how much she had missed the sea and how pleased she was to get back to familiar territory.

* * *

At seven o'clock exactly Charlotte, Clarissa and her husband William stepped into the carriage which was to drive them up to Government House. The journey took them down Strand Street where a number of fine new buildings had been constructed. They turned right into the Heerengracht and passed the Grand Parade on the left. There was little traffic about, so when they reached the corner of the Kaisergracht a tall figure in a blue Royal Navy jacket was immediately apparent. The closer they approached, the more familiar the figure became, and recognition hit Charlotte like a whip.

'That's John!' she exclaimed.

'Is it indeed?' Clarissa said. 'Stop the carriage William. He can join us for the evening.'

'But what's he doing here?' Charlotte said. 'He's supposed to be in Simon's Town. Papa's message stated expressly that John would only be able to travel up on Saturday.'

'Probably on business,' William said laconically.

'I suppose so,' Charlotte said but she felt a disturbing unease as she saw John pause at a handsome front door which was opened by a black footman who ushered him in.

'Do you know who lives there?' Charlotte asked.

'Actually I do,' Clarissa admitted. 'The Crawfords. They've not long been here with their daughter Caroline. He's a retired naval officer.'

'That explains the connection then,' Charlotte said. 'I expect Papa knows them too.'

'I should think so,' Clarissa responded. 'The navy officers' world is a small place, particularly in the Cape Colony.'

'John doesn't know that I'm here,' Charlotte said. 'He's expecting me back on Saturday. I thought that I would surprise him by sending him a message in Simon's Town tomorrow.'

'It seems that you are the one to get the surprise,' laughed Clarissa.

CHAPTER THIRTY-ONE

An Unexpected Meeting

The next day Charlotte sent a note around to the Beaufort Hotel in Plein Street where she knew John usually stayed in Cape Town. The slave returned with a reply:

Dearest Charlotte,
  What a wonderful surprise. Longing to see you. Will wait on you this afternoon, if that is convenient with Clarissa.
  All my love,
  John.

At four o'clock that afternoon John was ushered into Clarissa's elegant drawing room with its view of Table Bay. Charlotte and Clarissa both rose from their chairs as he entered.

'Good afternoon, Sir John. Welcome to our home,' Clarissa said.

'Oh, come now Clarissa, you don't have to be so formal with me. We've met several times at social occasions in Cape Town.'

'Oh, have you?' Charlotte said with raised eyebrows. 'I didn't know that you had such an active social life in Cape Town, John.'

'Well, I couldn't just sit around, could I,' John said, 'while I was going through all that eastern frontier land business? But you don't know, Charlotte – I've been keeping it as a surprise – I've bought a wine estate in the Constantia Valley. It's called

Wittebomen because of the white bark of the trees in the area.'

'Indeed!' Charlotte said. 'This is a surprise! So you've given up your idea of the eastern frontier?'

'Yes. I thought you'd be pleased?'

'Oh I am,' Charlotte said. 'I think that the Constantia Valley is a much better choice than the eastern frontier but that doesn't explain what you were doing at that house in the Heerengracht yesterday evening.'

John started. His confident air was shaken for a second like a bud on a branch caught suddenly in the wind.

'The Crawfords' house,' prompted Clarissa. 'We saw you in the Heerengracht on the way to the reception at Government House last night.'

'Yes,' Charlotte said, 'we were about to stop to offer you a lift but you went inside. What were you doing?'

John recovered his composure and laughed. 'Don't make it sound so dramatic Charlotte. I was visiting Captain Crawford. He's an old friend and I served under him several times at sea. I had been invited to dine with him and his family.'

'But Papa said that you wouldn't be able to come to Cape Town until Saturday,' Charlotte said.

'That was the original plan,' John replied. 'As I've said, I've had several things to do in connection with the purchase of Wittebomen – inspecting the house and grounds, carrying out surveys, and of course arranging payment, so I decided to come up a few days before meeting you. But explain why you're here so early,' he said, turning the focus of the conversation onto Charlotte. 'Your father said that you would be arriving at the end of the week and asked me to chaperone you back to Simon's Town on Sunday.'

'We left earlier than expected,' Charlotte said, 'and there wasn't time to send you a message. I was going to send a rider to Simon's Town today to surprise you and I thought perhaps you could come up on Friday and we could travel home together.'

'That's a splendid idea and as I've finished my business now, what's to stop us travelling back to Simon's Town tomorrow?'

John said with his charming smile back in place as he walked towards her and took her hand.

'I'd like that,' Charlotte said. 'I've hardly unpacked but I won't need to if we go home tomorrow.'

'I thought you might like to see Wittebomen on the way back to Simon's Town. It's somewhat out of the way, but we can send the luggage on ahead by wagon and ride down to the Constantia Valley. Then you will be able to see what your new home looks like.'

* * *

John had had the foresight to bring Charlotte's horse Amber with him and so the next day they set off early from the Lansdownes' house in Strand Street. They rode through the town where there was very little activity other than a few Malays who were setting up their stalls in the market place. They soon left the city behind them, nestling under Table Mountain, and descended into the Constantia Valley.

'Wittebomen is very close to Groot Constantia,' John said.

'Groot Constantia is an old estate isn't it?' Charlotte said.

'Yes, it was established in the seventeenth century by Simon van der Stel, who allegedly named it after his wife Constance.'

'So I've heard,' Charlotte said.

'It's a thriving estate, but I think Wittebomen, which lies alongside it, has the potential to be just as successful. It was founded more recently and hasn't been properly developed. It's been waiting for me,' John said, flashing his brilliant smile at Charlotte.

By now they had reached the entrance gates to Wittebomen. They rode down a fine avenue of trees which met overhead like the nave of a cathedral and then through park-like meadowland until they arrived at the house. It was a simple thatched Dutch gabled farmhouse with traditional outbuildings and a jonkershuis. It crouched under oak trees and was surrounded by a garden bursting with blossom and an orchard full of peach, pear, plum and apricot trees.

'Someone has loved this place and tended it with care,' Charlotte said.

'Yes, it was owned by an Englishman, William Duckitt, which accounts for the flower gardens. It's unusual to have the English owning property here. Most of the landowners are Dutch.'

They ambled around the property on their horses. In front of the house was a stretch of green lawn.

'What a lovely place for children to play,' Charlotte said.

'Yes, and you'll like this, Charlotte. It's a tree summerhouse,' John said, getting down from his horse and leading the way to a gigantic oak tree that had a wooden summerhouse built into its leafy branches. 'Follow me. Come and look at it.'

Charlotte dismounted and followed John up a rustic ladder attached to the trunk of the tree and into the summerhouse. It was circular and had a wooden half wall surrounding it so that the upper part of the building was open to the elements. As Charlotte emerged from the ladder she had a view of the gardens, the main house, the jonkershuis and the vineyards and the mountains beyond. The interior walls were lined with a wooden bench and there was a round wooden table in the middle.

'This is delightful,' Charlotte said with a laugh as she sat down on one of the wooden benches. 'You could seat six or eight people here. It's a lovely place to have a summer party. You feel as though you are part of the tree itself, very secluded and yet with a fine view of everything that is going on on the estate.'

'Well, do you think you'll like living here,' John said, taking Charlotte's hand, '"Mrs du Rand"?'

'Oh, don't say that,' Charlotte said. 'You're tempting fate. It might bring us bad luck.'

John laughed out loud at this. 'You're being fanciful, Charlotte,' he said.

CHAPTER THIRTY-TWO

The Homecoming

Charlotte arrived back in Simon's Town with John in the late afternoon. Edward, who was waiting outside the main entrance to Admiralty House as they trotted through the toll gate, was delighted to see her. Charlotte slid off her horse and into his arms.

'Papa, how very happy I am to see you again!'

'I've been expecting you for the last hour,' Edward said wheeling his daughter around in an unaccustomed display of emotion. 'I've missed you Charlotte. The house seemed very empty without you,' he said, putting his arm around her. They walked through the entrance hall and into his study while John led the horses over to the stables across the road.

'And I've missed you, Papa. It wasn't the same at L'Ourmarin without you. Marie le Roux was really quite hostile. She seems to think that I've set my cap at her son.'

'And have you, Charlotte?' Edward asked. The expression in his voice and eyes was humorous with a serious undertone. 'You and Paul seem to get on very well.'

'Papa, how can you say that, even in jest?' Charlotte said, pulling away from him. 'I'm engaged to John, for goodness sake, and you know how fond I am of him.' She would not meet her father's eyes as she took a handkerchief from her reticule and sat down on one of the fine leather chairs.

'Because it's possible to be in love with more than one person at the same time,' Edward said.

Charlotte understood the significance of his words. She continued: 'Paul and I are very good friends. I'm eternally grateful to him for what he has done for Samuel Joseph, and for Ellen, but he's engaged anyway, Papa, to Susanna Cloete.'

Edward turned from the cabinet where he had been pouring out a glass of muscatel. 'Well, that's news,' he said. 'I wonder why Etienne didn't say anything about it when they were staying with us?'

'I asked Paul about that, but he said that the appropriate moment didn't arise. Apparently their betrothal has been an understood thing in the families for years.'

'I can understand that,' Edward said. 'The Huguenot people keep to themselves.'

'I certainly felt excluded from the family on this visit,' Charlotte said. 'I wondered why Marie had agreed to the plan with Samuel Joseph.'

'People are a mixture of dark and light,' Edward said. 'Her Christian principles will dictate that she does her duty by the poor and homeless, and remember that the Huguenots were forced to flee from their homes in Europe. But at the same time that does not make her like you. As an independent, free-thinking Englishwoman you are a contradiction of her sense of propriety.'

'I'm sure that you're right. That explains her behaviour towards me to some extent, but not her vicious accusation that I have been trying to ensnare her son into marriage.'

'Perhaps she senses that her son has tender feelings for you, and she wants to nip those in the bud before they grow into something stronger?'

'I haven't thought about it like that,' said Charlotte, 'but whatever the truth of the matter she has certainly succeeded in getting me out of the way. But,' she continued, changing the subject, 'it's good to be home. How has John been?'

'Actually, he's not been here very much. He seems to have been in Cape Town most of the time since you've been away. The purchase of Wittebomen has taken up a great deal of his time. He must have told you by now about his change of plan. He wanted it to be a secret until he saw you again. What do you think?'

'I couldn't be happier, Papa. It's a lovely estate. John took me to have a look at it today on the way back from Cape Town, and it's not too far from Simon's Town so I'll be able to see you often. Have you been there?'

'Yes, actually I saw it before John did. It was owned by an Englishman and I visited it with a couple of my naval friends on a visit to Cape Town. They produce some good wine. The wine that we're drinking comes from there, doesn't it John?' Edward said to his nephew who, by this time had joined them from the stables.

'Indeed it does, sir. I brought it back from my last visit. Need to sample the produce of my own estate, don't I?' laughed John as he accepted a glass of wine from Edward. 'Well, Charlotte, how do you fancy being the mistress of a lucrative wine estate?'

'That seems to be my lot in life,' Charlotte said, thinking of the irony of Marie le Roux's accusation. 'There will be a great deal to learn, I'm sure, but I'm always willing to accept a challenge.'

'Indeed you are Charlie. Let's drink to that,' John said, raising his glass.

'Meanwhile there are a few things to do here in preparation for the wedding,' Edward said. 'The invitations have gone out, St George's Church is booked and my old friend Reverend Jarvis has agreed to conduct the ceremony. There's only the women's side to sort out – dresses, flowers, food and so forth.'

'I'm going to wear Mama's dress,' Charlotte said.

'Are you?' Edward said with a start. 'But it's at Everhurst. You'll never get it here in time. The wedding is only two weeks away.'

'Actually it's here,' Charlotte said.

'You mean that you brought it over from England last December?'

'Yes,' Charlotte said, remembering with a pang how Ellen had packed it carefully away in tissue in one of the trunks for its journey out to the Cape. 'You never know when a wedding dress will come in useful, do you?' Charlotte laughed, her eyes twinkling at John.

CHAPTER THIRTY-THREE

The Wedding

St George's Church, as Edward had told Etienne, occupied the upper floor of the mast house in Simon's Town Dockyard. During the week its functional purpose was as a sail loft, but on Sundays it was used as a church. On this particular Saturday it had taken on its ecclesiastical role for the wedding of John du Rand and Charlotte Lacey.

The entrance to the building was through large wooden double doors which led to a narrow metal stairway which climbed up to the second storey. The room was long and wide, and at the back of it and at one side lay the evidence of the weekday activities – furled-up sails, twine and sail maker's tools. On the other side of the room deep sash windows faced the Dockyard and naval storehouses with glimpses of the bay. The morning sunlight streamed through the windows and lit the great banks of flowers which were arranged at either side of the altar. It was a small congregation. Naval officers with their families were ranked on one side, and on the other were a few friends from Cape Town, including the Lansdownes. The le Rouxs were conspicuous by their absence.

John stood at the front of the church waiting. As the pianist began to play he turned to look. At the other end of the aisle Charlotte stood with her father. Admiral Lacey was resplendent in his full naval dress uniform, proud, dignified and impressive.

Charlotte looked ethereal in white silk and lace, her hand resting lightly on the fore-arm of her father. As she moved forward, poised and expectant, she felt a sudden pang of sadness as she remembered Ellen, loving, loyal Ellen, who should have been here to share the moment with her. Ellen, who should be enjoying her own promise of life, had been so cruelly cut off. But there was little Samuel Joseph at L'Ourmarin. Charlotte would do all she could to ensure that he had every opportunity to enjoy a fulfilled life. Life was full of tragedy as well as sublime happiness, Charlotte knew that now. Joy, it seemed, was a fragile thing, hung on a slender thread which must, at all costs, be nurtured.

'If anyone knows any reason why these two should not be joined together in holy matrimony, let him speak now or forever hold his peace,' intoned the naval chaplain, Reverend Jarvis.

'Yes, I do!' A young female voice reverberated around the sail loft.

The congregation turned as one, to see a young woman, several months pregnant, who stood at the top of the spiral staircase. The silence was palpable.

'Caroline, for God's sake, what are you doing here?' John shouted.

'I've come to see the father of my child. It is I who should be kneeling before the altar with him because I'm carrying his baby.'

Charlotte felt sick. She looked at John. The colour was drained from his normally ruddy cheeks.

Suddenly all those incidents which had caused her misgiving flashed into her inward eye. Everything around seemed to have moved into slow motion. Admiral Lacey stepped forward and his resonant voice echoed throughout the sail loft.

'Go away, Caroline. This is not the time for dramatics. We'll talk to you later.'

'I'm afraid, sir,' Reverend Jarvis said, moving forward and speaking firmly but respectfully, 'that the rituals of the church have to be honoured. We cannot continue with the marriage at this point.'

Charlotte looked from Edward to John, the two men whom she

had loved and trusted all of her life. The moment seemed timeless and she felt as though she were an observer looking on at a strange pantomime in which she herself played a central role. What was real? Who could she trust? She gathered up her skirts, ran down the aisle, pushed past the woman at the door and clattered down the metal stairs of the sail loft. The brilliant sunshine was clouded over and the southeaster was blowing fiercely. She ran through the Dockyard without conscious thought, around boats, anchors and coils of rope. She ran out onto the road, to the amazement of passers-by. Her aim was to get to Water's Edge – the sanctuary that had become dear to her – the place where she could be at peace.

CHAPTER THIRTY-FOUR

Confrontation

The next day Charlotte was at the breakfast table in the room overlooking the terrace. She was in a state of shock, unable to eat anything. The image of the young pregnant woman at the entrance to the church was seared into her brain. She stared mindlessly out at the beautiful garden which still looked the same, tamed and tended in contrast to her own turbulent feelings. Suddenly her attention was distracted by a tap on the door. She looked up to see John standing uncertainly on the threshold. Charlotte stood up, anger surging through her body like jets of steaming water from an underground geyser.

'I'm amazed that you have the audacity to come and see me!'

'It's not what you think, Charlotte.'

'Indeed! What am I supposed to think? Are you trying to deny that you are the father of Caroline's unborn child?'

John paused and looked away.

'No, I can't do that but I want to explain...' he said as he took a step into the room.

'Explain what? Your infidelity? How long has this deceitful, miserable affair been going on, John?'

'Don't make it sound so sordid, Charlotte.'

'Well, it's sordid to me. It's obvious that you have been deceiving me for months ...' Charlotte's voice broke. 'How could you, John? When you had told me how much you loved me and we had all those plans.'

John did not reply.

'Do me the honour of telling me the truth,' Charlotte said, looking into those hazel eyes that she had come to love so well.

John smiled the charming smile that showed his perfect teeth.

'Now, Charlotte, have I ever lied to you?'

'You have concealed the truth which is the same thing. Can you tell me in all honesty that you did not have an affair with Caroline?'

'Hardly an affair, Charlotte.'

'Did you make love to her?'

'Well, it was nothing significant. A dalliance.'

'A dalliance that has had considerable repercussions, it seems.'

'It's true that I met Caroline about the time when you and your father went to L'Ourmarin. You'll remember that that's when I first went to Cape Town to apply for land on the eastern frontier. I met Captain Crawford unexpectedly in the street one day and he invited me to dine with him. I'd served under him at sea and we'd always got on well, so I was pleased to accept his invitation. It was at the dinner that I met Caroline.'

'How convenient for you.' Charlotte's tone dripped with bitter irony. 'So did the liaison begin right then?'

'You're being unfair, Charlotte. I'm not the insatiable philanderer that you seem to think I am. But Caroline was young, pretty and completely infatuated with me. I think as much as anything she was in love with the romantic idea of a Royal Naval officer. I seemed to represent glamour, nobility, heroism…'

'Spare me all the disgraceful details,' Charlotte said. 'This doesn't explain why you had to make love to her. You did, didn't you?'

John was looking out onto the garden and paused before he spoke.

'Yes, I did. One night at a party at Somerset's house. I'd had a little too much to drink and succumbed to Caroline's charms.'

'Don't make yourself sound like the victim of the piece,'

Charlotte said. 'Have the courage to take responsibility for your actions.'

John ignored this comment and grabbed her hand.

'Listen, Charlotte, it doesn't have to make a difference to us. We can still get married.'

'Do you really think that?' Charlotte said, searching the face that she knew so well of a man whom she no longer knew.

'Of course, Charlotte. You should never have run away from the church, you know. That just made it seem that Caroline's story is true.'

'Oh, so I'm to blame now? That's a clever twist, John,' she said as she pulled her hand back.

'No, Charlotte, you've got it wrong. We have the kind of love that really matters, that will grow for all our lives. We're a family after all – the du Rands and the Laceys – old stock, French and English. Our families have stood the test of time.'

Charlotte turned away from him to look out of the window. 'That all sounds so sensible, so smug, John, but I don't believe it any more. I trusted you and you have betrayed that trust. I can't pretend that it all just didn't happen and marry you now.'

John's expression slipped. A sharp glint appeared in his eyes.

'Then what, dear Charlotte, do you intend to do? Your chances of marriage are finished. No-one in Simon's Town of any rank and standing will want anything to do with you, because of the scandal.'

'But what scandal? You are the one that had the affair – couldn't control your passions. It's your actions that have provoked this!'

'It's not quite so simple, my dear,' John said, walking over to the fireplace, where he stood with folded arms looking down at her. 'Simon's Town society is agog with the story of your involvement with the coloured community and a small baby...'

'How would people know about that? In any event Ellen was my s...' Charlotte stopped, horrified by the fact that she had nearly given the secret away. But John had guessed.

'Your sister!' John threw back his head and laughed. 'Why, respectable old Uncle Edward had more red blood in him than I suspected! It seems that we share some strong family traits after all! He must have had a romp in the hay with Agnes – a good-looking woman I have to say.'

'You forget yourself, sir,' Charlotte said in a voice charged with icy contempt. 'My father is an honourable man, and nothing on God's earth would persuade me to marry someone who treats people in the cavalier fashion that you do.'

'So what will you do, little Charlotte? You won't have me. Simon's Town won't have you and, from what I hear, London society won't have you either.'

'I don't know what I'll do,' Charlotte said, walking from the breakfast room and on to the terrace, 'but I'll manage somehow.' And she stalked off towards the glistening waters of Simon's Bay.

CHAPTER THIRTY-FIVE

Reflections

Early the next day, before any of the staff were up and about Charlotte went across to the stables. She saddled Amber and rode down to the one place where she was always able to find peace: Water's Edge. She tethered Amber to a shrub and walked down to her favourite rock.

The sun had just risen over the horizon now and lay adrift it seemed, clearly delineated and yet soft in the translucent morning air. On the far side of False Bay the outline of the Hottentots Holland Mountains was softened by drifts of falling cloud. As the sun rose higher it caught the water so that it shimmered and glistened like crystal. The waters of the bay were still, with only a ripple now and then as a fish jumped from the shallows or a bird swooped down to collect its early breakfast. Noah's Ark appeared to be floating on the mirror-like surface of the sea. On its flat table-top the cormorants gathered, their black feathers gleaming in the early morning light. Every now and then a flock of them would take off, in strict linear formation, flying low over the water to some destination known only to themselves. This deliberate movement emphasised the calm. On the lower, flatter rocks close to the shore scrambled the terns, a flurry of white reflecting the pearly colours of the morning.

Charlotte sat on her rock looking out over the tranquil scene. The sun warmed her skin and the pungent smell of the seaweed stung her nostrils. To her right and behind her rose the craggy peaks of the Simonsberg against which wafted cotton wool puffs of cloud. A lone dark cormorant stood sentinel on a rock in front of her, looking as though it was ensuring that everything was in order. The gentle, rhythmic swell of the waters near the shore eased her tormented being. The shock of Caroline's appearance at the wedding had been bad enough, but the subsequent conversation with John had struck her to the marrow. She found it incredible that he could have expected that she would still marry him after the revelation of his affair with Caroline but his subsequent callous words were even worse somehow. Emerging through her confused emotions was the realisation that she was relieved that she was no longer formally committed to him. Sooner or later this side of his nature would have shown.

It was just over a year since she had arrived in Simon's Bay with Ellen. She thought back over the events. So much had happened this year: so much suffering; so much pain. She had fallen in love, she had to admit, with two men and had been bitterly disappointed in both of them. She had lost two people who were very dear to her: Ellen and Sam. In fact it was in this very cove that she had discovered Sam. She shuddered at the memory of that awful moment.

Absorbing the peace of the scene into the innermost fibre of her being, Charlotte found it hard to understand the violence and bloodlust among men. Why were they all so keen to fight? What had it ever brought but tragedy? She thought of her cousin Charles, that handsome upright youth, John's brother, elder son of her father's sister Cassandra, who had been snuffed out at Trafalgar. It was all very well for her father and his naval friends to speak with pride of his courage and say that his death was ennobled by the fact that he had died for his country. To her it seemed a futile waste of life. Cassandra too and her husband had died a horrific death in Paris in the wake of the French Revolution. What was the point? Charlotte felt almost guilty in harbouring these thoughts. But really, how could one justify the sudden loss, the cutting off of youth with all the promise of life ahead? How did one begin to fill the empty space left behind? One couldn't, actually, and that was that.

Yet despite all the pain, suffering and tragedy, Water's Edge remained the same. The sun still rose over the mountains on the far side of False Bay and set over the rough terrain behind her. The tides still rose and fell. The birds still continued with their age-old pattern of flight, feeding and rest. The rhythms of nature were not disturbed. Did this indicate a lack of care, the indifference of the natural world to the plight of man? She could not accept that when she felt so much at home with the environment. No – life went on, indeed it had to go on. Birth, decay and death were the natural order of things. And in this inexorable rhythm lay man's hope and salvation. Death, after all, was not the end. It was merely a stage in the passage of life.

Suddenly she became aware of the sound of a horse quietly harrumphing and stomping. She looked up to see her father dismounting from Champion on the grassy slope behind her.

'Elsie told me that you would probably be here,' he said, holding out his arms.

When she saw her father something was released inside Charlotte. She was not alone in this dark world of disappointment. She got up, ran and flung herself into her father's arms. All the pain of the past few weeks exploded in great shuddering sobs as she held onto her father. As Edward's arms encircled his daughter he felt overpowering, protective love for her.

'Come,' he said as he lifted her onto his horse. 'Let's go home.' Father and daughter moved as one on the sturdy back of Champion while Amber followed behind on a loose rein.

CHAPTER THIRTY-SIX

Caroline

John du Rand married Caroline Crawford quietly in the Crawfords' house in the Heerengracht in Cape Town early in January 1816. It was a rushed affair with very little in the way of celebration. There had been a difficult meeting between John, Edward and Arthur Crawford, Caroline's father. He was a stocky man, of medium height, with a broad face and high cheek bones which were burnished by the sun. His legs were planted firmly on the ground in the manner of one who has kept his purchase on deck in many stormy seas. This experience with his daughter was one which threatened to upset the equilibrium of his being in other ways.

Caroline's parents were mainly concerned about the scandal. Having a pregnant daughter mooning around the house was an embarrassment, although they had forbidden her to go out and about, cooking up a story that she was delicate, suffering from the recurrence of a childhood illness which required her to stay quietly at home. However, a real live baby in the house could not be concealed, and they wanted her to be respectably married as soon as possible. They were shocked when they found out that Caroline had managed to escape from their home early on the Saturday of John and Charlotte's wedding day, and had bribed a junior groom in her father's stable to saddle up her horse and accompany her on the long and in parts treacherous ride to

Simon's Town. They would not have planned it this way but, in fact, it precipitated events and provided a solution that was not ideal but at least acceptable and would preserve their position in Cape Town society.

'Caroline has a dowry of course,' Arthur said, standing with his back to the fireplace in their house in the Heerengracht, 'five thousand pounds which should help you in setting up your new home in Wittebomen.'

'I appreciate that, sir,' John said.

'It's not the way in which we would have liked to have our daughter married, but at least she's marrying an officer in His Majesty's Navy.'

'Not for much longer,' Edward said wryly. 'But nevertheless he can still wear his dress uniform for the wedding.'

'Caroline herself has always wanted a big wedding with all the frills and trappings that women like,' Arthur said, wiping his florid forehead with his handkerchief, 'but this obviously will have to be a muted affair.'

'Under the circumstances it's the best thing to do,' said Edward, whose composure had been undermined. He loved both John and Charlotte and he had been deeply contented when they had decided to marry. Now all that had imploded like the squashed top of a newly boiled egg. 'We can't totally avoid the scandal, but John is doing the honourable thing in marrying the mother of his unborn child who should be entitled to all the privileges of his or her birth.'

'It'll be a seven day wonder,' Arthur said. 'The ladies of Cape Town will soon find something else to gossip about.'

John, who had been standing at the window looking down the Heerengracht, was lost in thought. He was not really keen to marry Caroline, beautiful though she was. In his way he still loved Charlotte, but that marriage, as he had discovered, was no longer a possibility. Two things were certain: he didn't want to go back to sea and he did want to continue with the purchase of Wittebomen. He had spoken the truth to Charlotte when he had told her at Cape Point that he wanted to start a new life on the land. He turned to face the older men, his handsome features downcast.

'You're right, Uncle Edward, and you too sir,' he said to Arthur. 'Needless to say I'm ashamed of what I've done and I know that it's a disappointment to you both. All I can do is apologise and say how grateful I am that you have been so civilised about it all. I appreciate your support and I will do my very best to make Caroline happy and be a good father to my child.'

Edward put his hand on his nephew's shoulder.

'It's not the first time that something like this has happened and it's certainly not the last. I know that you will make the best of things.'

'For obvious reasons, the sooner the wedding takes place, the better,' Arthur said. 'Reverend Jarvis has agreed to conduct the ceremony at home and we'll have a small reception for close family and friends.'

CHAPTER THIRTY-SEVEN

Finding a Purpose

For weeks Charlotte felt numb. Like an automaton she carried out her routine duties around the house: checking the linen cupboard, organising the daily meals with Elsie and supervising the gardeners. Her father, thinking that a change of scene would help her to recover her former zest for life, suggested that she accompany him on an official trip to Cape Town. The Lansdownes were pleased to welcome them to their house on Strand Street where Charlotte had stayed on her return from L'Ourmarin in November the previous year. She had spent such a short time in the city on that occasion that she had observed very little. This time she was at leisure to take it all in.

Cape Town was vibrant and cosmopolitan with a heterogeneous, largely itinerant population. It was a place of contrasts, from the elegant Government House near the top of the town bordered by the Company Gardens, originally established by the Dutch East India Company, to the slums near the Castle on the foreshore. She travelled around the city in a sedan chair carried by household slaves on streets with no paving stones, and in the late summer sun the canals by the side of the roads gave off an odour which turned her stomach. The shoreline was polluted by the offal deposited from the shambles and the fish market at the bottom of the town. Rotting carcases of whales on the beach added to the stench. Market Square was a riot of colour, movement and noise.

Malay traders in their conical hats hawked fruit and vegetables while pigs and stray dogs ran amok and visiting farmers drove their wagons through the town to deliver their produce. Slaves congregated on the portico of the Burger Senate House on one side of Market Square. Although English and Dutch men, in their top hats which marked out their status, wandered around the market, there was an absence of women and Charlotte did not feel at ease herself to wander around the stalls.

Although Charlotte was accustomed to socialising with Royal Navy officers in their brilliant blue jackets, she was astonished at the number of motley sailors from all over the world who walked through the Heerengracht and frequented the taverns, particularly those close to the docks. Hundreds of British soldiers from the artillery companies and the cavalry regiment were a dominant presence, and the firing of the noonday canon from Signal Hill became a familiar sound. The Parade Ground which had been established by the Dutch in the seventeenth century for the drilling of their troops, served as a general market during the week where everything from wheat to timber and poultry was sold. On a Sunday evening it was a favourite place for people of all classes to stroll to the accompaniment of a military band. Fashionable ladies and gentlemen also paraded through the Company Gardens outside Government House.

The Governor, Lord Charles Somerset, was the leader of a small, upper-class, quintessentially English society which easily accommodated Charlotte and her father in its pursuits. She attended a three-day race meeting at Green Point on the outskirts of the city with a ball to crown the event. She went to the theatre in Riebeeck Square and was invited to banquets and dances at Government House, where she met the enigmatic English doctor James Barry with his high-heeled boots and padded jacket whom Somerset had appointed physician to the Government household. The English had introduced their passion for the hunt from their first arrival in the Cape, and Charlotte, an able horsewoman, participated in a hunt over the Cape Flats where the quarry was not the accustomed English fox but a jackal, the scavenger dog of Africa.

She could not avoid seeing John who, because of the close-knit English upper-class society, was often invited to the same social events, but she chose not to speak to him. Caroline, who was now heavily pregnant, stayed indoors out of the public eye. Apart from this, Charlotte tired of the endless social round, the inconsequential chatter, the obsession with fashion and the latest gossip in the narrow English community. She had never actually enjoyed it, even in London, and now after the events of the last year when she had encountered the stark realities of life and death, these social occasions seemed unbearably trivial, and she was pleased to return with her father to Simon's Town. She thought of what she might do to make her life more meaningful.

* * *

She broached the subject with her father one night after dinner as they were sitting on the veranda of Admiralty House having coffee in the moonlight.

'Papa, I've been thinking that I might start a school in Simon's Town,' Charlotte said as she poured coffee for them.

Edward turned a quizzical look on his daughter.

'A school? But you don't know anything about running a school.'

'Neither does John know anything about running a vineyard, but he's going ahead with that venture.'

'But he's a ma...' Edward checked himself as he saw the expression in Charlotte's eye. 'Come and sit down and tell me more about your idea,' he said, patting the wicker chair next to him.

Charlotte sat down with her coffee cup and began. 'I suppose I've become more aware of the plight of the coloured people since I've known Sam and Elsie and Christina and Johannes and their family. There's really no provision for the education of the children of slaves and freed slaves.'

'There was never any need for them to have an education,' Edward remarked.

'Yes, but that's changing now. The slave trade has been abolished throughout the Empire, and more and more slaves in the colony are buying their freedom. But if they're really going to advance they need to be educated. If Sam had been able to read and write he would have been able to find other work, and he would have probably been alive today, as would Ellen.'

'There's no point in speculating about that,' Edward said. 'What's done is done and you can't undo it.'

'Yes, I know, Papa, but we can learn lessons and make a difference for other Sams and Ellens.'

'Well, what's your idea?'

'I thought I'd start a school initially for the children of people who work for us.'

'Who would you employ to teach?'

'I thought I'd do that.'

'But you're too busy with running the house.'

'Not really. It doesn't take lot of my time. It's supervising rather than actual work for me. Elsie's in charge of the kitchens and has the coloured girls dancing to her tune. Silas has got the garden under control. He just likes me to visit occasionally to approve what he has done.'

'And what about social duties? I rely on you as a hostess.'

'I can still do that, Papa, because most of the entertainments are in the evening, and if they're not, if we have to go away for a few days, then I'll close the school. Children have to have holidays, you know. But in any event, I'll probably train someone to be an assistant.'

Edward looked unconvinced. 'But you've had no training as a teacher. What would you teach?'

'On the contrary, I've had excellent training to be a teacher. I had that governess at Everhurst, Miss Price, who taught Ellen and me to read and write. She also taught us basic arithmetic. I've learned all my history and geography from you.'

Edward knew his daughter well enough to know that when she had made up her mind about something she was not easily dissuaded. He tried another tack.

'Where do you think that you would hold this school?'

'I've found two places, actually. The Anglican Church has acquired a building in the High Street which Reverend Jarvis said we could use. Or else there is the old tack room next to the kitchens now that the stables are across the road. It would have to be cleaned out, of course, and we'd have to get some desks and benches but that has the advantage of being close to home.'

Edward sighed.

'Very well, Charlotte. Let's give it a trial. I think though, that it would be better for you to hold your little school within the environs of Admiralty House. I don't like the idea of your marching through the town every day.'

'I think I'd prefer that, Papa – at the beginning anyway, especially as we're going to be looking after the children of those who work for us in the first instance.'

'When do you think that you're going to start this venture?'

'The sooner the better. The end of January?'

Edward picked up his coffee cup, and nodded his head.

CHAPTER THIRTY-EIGHT

Restoration

The little school was a success from the beginning. Charlotte had the old tack room painted and several benches and small tables installed. She acquired individual slate boards for the children to write on. She had brought some of her favourite children's books from England and she borrowed others from friends and acquaintances in Simon's Town and Cape Town.

Every morning she donned a plain pinafore over her working dress and greeted her young charges. There was James's daughter Aletta, Elsie's two nieces whose father worked in the Dockyard, and Christina's young daughter Maria. Christina and Johannes had returned to their cottage on the hill above Simon's Town. Cape Town had not been a success for them. Although Johannes had got a job working for one of the fishing fleets, they had not settled in the city, which they found harsh and unwelcoming. Christina had thought that a new environment would ease the pain of the loss of Jacobus, but the wound was a gaping hole that was merely plastered over. Charlotte had kept in touch with them and had helped them to pay for the boat which they had borrowed and which had been lost on that tragic night. Through the Admiral's recommendation Johannes had got a job in Osmond's boatyard, and they were pleased to be back in Simon's Town among friends and family that they knew. They felt safe in the close-knit Muslim community which they had known all of their lives.

The children were bright-eyed and eager to learn. Charlotte found that she looked forward every morning to greeting these shining young faces like newly-washed plums. Most of them had some idea of number learned from their parents: how long did the rope of a fishing boat have to be to tie it securely to its moorings? How many shoes did a horse wear out in a year? How many pennies did you need to buy a haunch of beef from the market?

She read to them from *Tales from Mother Goose* – Cinderella, Beauty and the Beast and Little Red Riding Hood.

'What's a wolf, juffrouw?'

'It's somewhat like a jackal, but larger. It doesn't live in Africa.'

'A jackal took one of the lambs from my uncle's farm,' Aletta said. The other children shook their heads in sympathy. They knew about jackals.

'I'm glad we don't have any wolves here,' Maria said. 'I often take a basket of food to my ouma who lives up near Seaforth and there's a tree there where a wolf could hide and jump out and eat my ouma and me too.'

Charlotte's mouth twitched as she suppressed a laugh. 'Well, you don't have to worry about being eaten by a wolf in Simon's Town, but you must be careful not to talk to strangers when you walk alone,' she said.

She taught the children to read and write and took them for walks along the beach near the Admiral's jetty, where they collected shells and sea treasures which they brought back to draw and make jewellery and ornaments from. She taught them English folk songs and they taught her plaintive Malay folk songs that they had learnt from their parents and grandparents.

Charlotte was happier than she had been for a long time occupied in this way. It was a predictable world in which the same pattern was repeated every day: the children arrived at the same time; they had regular lessons; they themselves were always cheerful and she got caught up in their curiosity and enthusiasm about things. But more than that, Charlotte found that you could depend on books and children. They were what they appeared to be. It was a world apart from the universe of emotions which she had found as untrustworthy as the quicksand at the Silwermyn River. The two men in her life had seemed to promise so much, but their appearance, particularly John's, had been specious, and she had been thrown off balance and was no longer sure of her bearings. She laughed a lot nowadays, and the sound of the children's voices rang out from across the courtyard. Edward was pleased to see her looking so content. The old house was injected with a new vitality and Elsie frequently baked biscuits and cakes for the children. It was a calm and happy time.

One morning they had news about Samuel Joseph. Etienne sent a letter to Edward with his delivery of wine.

Dear Edward

Here is the wine that you ordered: 16 barrels of red for the ships; and for your cellar 30 bottles of Chenin Blanc; 30 bottles of Hanepoort and 30 bottles of muscatel. I trust that they are to your liking.

You will be pleased to know that Paul and Susanna's wedding took place on 15 January. It was a happy occasion. They have gone to manage Susanna's father's estate in Constantia. We shall miss them but that is the way with the young is it not? They have to lead their own lives. I am pleased that Paul is continuing with the tradition of wine-making which has been part of our family heritage for generations.

Samuel Joseph is thriving with Moses and Heloise. He is growing quickly into a fine boy.

Please give our regards to Charlotte. I trust that her wedding to John took place with all due celebration and that they are now happily settled at Wittebomen. They will be neighbours of Paul and Susanna. I expect that they will meet.

I look forward to another visit from you in the not too distant future.

Yours sincerely
Etienne

'So they don't know about John and me,' Charlotte said as she handed the letter back to her father.

'I must confess that I have been remiss, Charlotte. I should have written. There was so much else to think about at the time that I just didn't do it.'

'Well, I certainly don't feel like writing,' Charlotte said. 'That part of my life is closed forever.'

CHAPTER THIRTY-NINE

A Visit to Water's Edge

Some weeks had passed since the weddings of John and Caroline and Paul and Susanna which, Charlotte calculated, must have taken place at much the same time. She immersed herself in the school which was growing in numbers. Other fisher-folk sent their children when Marie told them how much fun she was having and how she was able to read. They knew that being able to read and write was a key to getting on in the world.

In the long summer days Charlotte took the children on expeditions. Once they walked to the top of Red Hill to look down on the little settlement hugging the shore and the Dockyard, the tall ships resting in the Bay and beyond them the misty Hottentots Holland Mountain range. They visited the Dockyard to observe at first hand the boats being laden with goods going out to the anchored ships which were preparing to take soldiers and supplies to St Helena where, Charlotte told the children, the notorious French military leader, Napoleon Bonaparte, was in exile.

One day she decided to take them further afield. James had been commissioned by Elsie to take the cart to Groendam to collect some haunches of beef.

'That's a fine opportunity for an outing for the children,' Charlotte said to her father when she heard of the planned expedition. 'We'll go to Water's Edge which is quieter and cleaner than the beaches near the town, and I'll get Elsie to pack up a picnic lunch for us.'

And so it was that Charlotte and the children were happily engaged in collecting shells on the beach at Water's Edge.

'Juffrouw, here's a pretty one,' Maria bubbled, running up with a perlemoen shell which reflected the colours of the sea and sky.

'Come, look here in this rock pool,' Aletta called. 'There's hundreds of fish.'

'There are hundreds of fish,' Charlotte corrected. 'Now we're going to draw what we have found. Here are your drawing books and pencils. Find yourselves somewhere to sit and sketch your treasures.'

The children settled themselves like small birds on rocks and the grassy knolls at the edge of the beach. As Charlotte walked around and tended to each of them in turn, praising and correcting, she felt a deep contentment. The early autumn sun warmed her shoulders and the gentle lapping of the waves on the beach was soothing.

As the sun reached its peak in the sky Charlotte called the children together under the shade of some fynbos which grew near the edge of the beach. As they feasted on chicken, bread and fruit washed down with Elsie's home-made lemonade the children's carefree laughter rang around the cove.

'Can we come here again, juffrouw?'

'This is a lekker place.'

'We'll see,' Charlotte said. 'It's a long way to walk for ordinary lessons. We'd better pack up now because James will be back with the wagon soon.'

They bundled the remains of the lunch into the large hamper and made their way up to the main road into Simon's Town where James collected them. It was a happy party of singing, laughing children which rumbled back through the town to Admiralty House. At the stables the children jumped off the wagon and Charlotte waved them good-bye as James carried the hamper into the house.

'Hello, Elsie. Where's Papa? I want to tell him that we're home safely.'

'He's in his study, ma'am. The post rider came this morning with the mail.'

'I wonder if there's anything for me?' Charlotte said. She ran to her father's study, tapping lightly on the door.

'Come in, Charlotte.' Edward rose from his chair to greet his daughter. 'I thought that it would be you. Have you had a good day?'

'Yes indeed, Papa. The children loved Water's Edge and have asked to go again, but I hear that the post boy has been. Is there any mail for me?'

'As a matter of fact there is,' Edward said, picking up an envelope from the desk and handing it to her.

'It's John's handwriting and seal,' she said, breaking it open. Her fingers trembled as she opened the pages. What did he have to say to her after their last angry confrontation in December?

Dear Charlotte

I hope that you will forgive my liberty in writing to you after our last painful meeting. You made it very clear when you were in Cape Town last month that you didn't want to have anything to do with me. That is understandable and I'm sure that on one level you do not want to see me again. However, we are family and have known each other for all of our lives and I desperately want to heal the breach.

As your father may have told you, Caroline was safely delivered of a son on the 15th March. We have called him Charles Edward after my brother and Uncle Edward. He is a fine little fellow and I have to say that I am immensely proud to be a father. As you are my closest relatives I would like him to grow up regarding you as an aunt and with this in mind I want to ask your forgiveness for my appalling treatment of you and ask you if would come with Uncle Edward to Wittebomen for Charles Edward's christening next month. Caroline joins me in pressing the invitation to you both to visit us in our home.

Your affectionate cousin
John.

Charlotte had sat down while reading the letter. Now she looked across at her father.

'John wants us to come to Wittebomen for his son's christening.'

'Yes, I know. He wrote me a letter too,' Edward said, holding it up. 'What do you want to do?'

'Will you go?'

'Yes, I feel that I must. I supported him in the wedding and I can't withdraw my support now. But it will be more difficult for you. You don't have to go.'

Charlotte got up and walked over to the window. The keeper was opening the toll gate to allow a horse and rider to pass through.

'This is a critical decision, isn't it?' she said, turning to face her father again. 'I feel more comfortable now than I've ever felt before and I don't want to destroy that calm. But this is not just about me. It's about others as well – people who have been part of my life as far back as I can remember and about new people who are just coming into it. You have to embrace life, don't you, even though sometimes it's difficult and you really just want things to go on as they were before?'

'And so?' said Edward, walking over to his daughter.

'I'll go.'

'You're a brave young woman,' he said.

CHAPTER FORTY

A Strange Meeting

'Are you sure you want to do this Charlotte?' said Edward. They were in the carriage on the way to Wittebomen for the christening of John and Caroline's son.

'Yes, Papa. It'll be hard. I haven't talked to John since he tried to persuade me that I should marry him despite that ghastly scene in the church. But, as I said before, he's family after all, this child is your great-nephew, and I'm afraid that you're not likely to have a grandson.'

'I wouldn't be too sure about that,' Edward said. 'You're only twenty-one and you're very attractive. You've years ahead of you for marriage and child-bearing.'

'It's not very likely now, is it, Papa? As John pointed out to me rather forcibly I've burned my marriage boats in London and Cape Town, and my known connection with the coloured people doesn't help either.'

Edward was silent. In his heart he had to acknowledge the truth of all that she said.

'Don't worry, Papa. I'm quite resigned to being a schoolmistress. In fact I'm more content now than I have been for years.'

'We won't be here forever,' Edward said. 'Sooner or later I'll be recalled to England.'

'Well then, I'll go back to Everhurst, but there's no point in worrying about that now. Look we must be nearly there.'

They had drawn up at the gates of Wittebomen where a gatekeeper nodded them through, and the carriage rolled down the long oak-framed avenue to the homestead nestling under the trees.

John met them on the steps of his home. As he stood in front of the fine Cape Dutch building the setting sun brushed his handsome features and Charlotte felt a pang. All this might have been hers – marriage to a promising wine estate owner, children and social respectability. But she refused to waste time on what might have been.

John shook hands with her father and then moved tentatively towards her. She held out her hand to him. He grasped it and held it to his lips, searching her eyes. Charlotte thought how restrained this meeting was compared to their reunion in Simon's Town the previous January when she had fancied herself in love with him.

'Congratulations, John, on the birth of your son,' she said with as much cheerfulness as she could. 'You must be very proud.'

'Yes, well … come in …come in,' he said as he led the way into the voorkamer where Caroline was waiting, attired elegantly in green silk.

'Welcome to our home,' she said.

Charlotte had been prepared to dislike Caroline, and the memory of her appearance at the church was of a malignant harpy, but when she saw her standing in the voorkamer at Wittebomen she was struck by how young she really was, barely eighteen, she judged. Now that the bump of pregnancy was gone you could see that she had a slight frame, but she held her head high and her eyes were challenging. Charlotte felt a sudden rush of sympathy for her. Did she realise what she was doing in marrying a man whom she barely knew? Charlotte knew that this moment was crucial in defining the nature of their future relationship and that it was her responsibility to take the lead, so she put out her hand in an overture of friendship as she walked up to the younger woman.

'Congratulations on the safe arrival of your son,' she said. 'Papa and I are delighted with the new addition to the family. May we see him?'

Caroline's face relaxed visibly, and Charlotte realised that Caroline must have been dreading this meeting as much as she had.

'Yes, of course,' she said. 'He's asleep in the nursery but come, let's go and take a peek.'

CHAPTER FORTY-ONE

A New Direction

Charlotte found Wittebomen delightful. She took to riding out every morning around the estate, and sometimes John would accompany her. He was genuinely enthusiastic about his new life as a wine estate owner and was pleased to share his plans and excitement with her. He seemed eager to forget about the past and to focus on the present which Charlotte, on her part, was also willing to do. She and John had always been good friends and shared confidences with each other during their childhood at Everhurst.

One morning they tethered their horses and walked through the vineyard together.

'Look at this grape, Charlotte,' John said, plucking a bunch off the vine. 'It's a Hanepoort and it's doing really well. We're going to harvest it here for the first time this year. Van Riebeeck called them Spaanse Druiwen or Spanish grapes, but we think they were French rather than Spanish, known as Muscat d' Alexandrie.'

'What will you do with the wine you produce?' Charlotte asked. 'Is there enough local demand for it?'

'No! Export is the thing, Charlotte. Since the war there has been little wine exported from France to England and the British government has reduced the tax on wine imported from the Cape by a third, which gives us a huge advantage compared to European producers. The market is wide open, and since I'm on good terms with Somerset it's all in my favour,' he said as he opened his arms to embrace the scene before him.

Charlotte could not help but share in his happiness. This was the John she had known and fallen in love with – enthusiastic, keen to take on new enterprises – a contagious energy.

'Why, that's wonderful John. You'll be well on the way to making your fortune!'

'Yes, perhaps, Charlotte, but more importantly, I feel as though I have come home. You remember when we had that conversation at Cape Point last January I told you that I wanted to put down roots? Well, that's what I'm doing. I'm only sorry that you are not…by my side…' his voice trailed off.

'Don't say that, or even think it, John. You've made a commitment now and you've got a wife and beautiful son.'

'But she's not the woman that I am in love with.' As John spoke these words he took Charlotte's hand and looked into her eyes.

For a moment those old feelings of passion and longing arose, recalled from far away in her being, but they were soon supplanted by the knowledge of the pain, deceit and embarrassment over the last year. She drew her hand away and said gently but firmly, 'Don't allow these thoughts any purchase in your mind, John. It's not possible for us. And even if you weren't married to Caroline I couldn't take you back after all that has happened between us. I don't trust you any more,' she said quietly. 'Your job now is to provide for Caroline and Charles Edward.'

'You're right, of course,' John said. 'But there's something else I want to ask you. I've been thinking about it for a long time. I thought about writing to you but I felt that I wanted to talk to you face to face.'

Charlotte looked up at John who was gazing over the trails of lush vines. Then he turned to her.

'Caroline and I would like you to do us the honour of being godmother to Charles Edward.'

'Godmother! Me? Are you sure?' Charlotte was genuinely surprised. 'How does Caroline feel about this? She and I were rivals for your affections in her eyes weren't we? I shouldn't think that she would want me hovering about in your lives forever.'

'Well, actually it was her idea. She admires you, Charlotte, for the way in which you have conducted yourself in this affair. If it comes to rivalry I suppose she's the winner, as she scooped your husband from right under your nose.'

Charlotte felt a flicker of anger as she remembered the dramatic scene at St George's Church on her wedding day.

'That's true, but I would have thought that she would never want to see me again.'

John laughed. 'Well, there's no chance of that. You and Uncle Edward are all my family, and if I hadn't been so foolish we would be married right now. Just because we're not married that doesn't alter that fact of us being one family, and I want to endorse that by your being godmother to Charlie.'

'But how does Caroline feel?' Charlotte repeated.

'As I said, she admires you, not only for your response to our marriage but generally in the way that you defy convention. You don't allow yourself to be boxed in by what society wants. You insist on riding from Simon's Town to Cape Town when other ladies expect to travel by coach. You blatantly support the coloured people, and despite all opposition you have succeeded in opening up a school for their children in Simon's Town. These are not the things that a gently-reared young English woman generally does.'

'I don't know about that,' Charlotte said. 'There's a tradition of Englishwomen who defy convention. I'm just being true to myself though. I learned early on that society doesn't really care about me. It's a monster that demands obeisance and if you don't comply it spits you out.'

'Exactly. Caroline understands that too. She has something of your spirit, you know. Her riding to Simon's Town to confront me on our wedding day is a prime example of that. She was taking a huge risk.'

'Desperate times call for desperate measures,' Charlotte said quietly.

'It could have gone either way,' John continued, 'and if you had agreed to continue with the marriage her reputation would have been ruined. But society has a short memory, and as she is now married to me, she is respectable and society has forgiven her.'

'But she loves you too, John. You can see it by the way she looks at you.'

'Yes, she does, but I'm afraid that I can't return her love in the same way.'

'Perhaps you will in the fullness of time,' Charlotte said. 'Be kind to her, John.'

'Yes, of course I will. She's the mother of my son, after all. But Charlotte, you still haven't answered the question. Will you be godmother to Charles Edward?'

'Yes, of course I will,' Charlotte said, echoing his words with a smile. 'It will be an honour.'

John grinned and held out his hand as he answered her while they walked back towards the horses. 'Come on. I want to show you our new wine cellar.'

Charlotte walked with him back through the corridor of vines and they mounted their horses together. John led the way towards the wine cellar which reminded her poignantly of Samuel Joseph and L'Ourmarin. She thought of how they were all connected. John, as little as he would want to admit it, was Ellen's cousin, and therefore Charles Edward and Samuel Joseph were second cousins. They were all family, and, as she had said to her father when they arrived at Wittebomen – that was what mattered.

CHAPTER FORTY-TWO

Another Farewell

There was still no English church in Cape Town, so Reverend Jarvis conducted the baptism ceremony in the voorkamer at Wittebomen. As Charlotte held the baby at the makeshift font, she felt a fierce pang for another small boy who had never, in all of the chaos surrounding his birth, had a baptism. She wondered if Moses and Heloise had organised a naming ceremony for him. Etienne, she knew from experience, held evening Bible readings for the entire household at L'Ourmarin. She must let that go now, she realised. Samuel Joseph had his own family. But still there was an invisible cord which linked her to him through Ellen – all of which must be forever a secret known only to her father and herself and John.

After the service John and Caroline hosted a garden party on the lush lawn in front of the manor house. Many men in naval uniform and others in smart tailcoats and women in diaphanous gowns swirled around under the oak trees. A particular point of interest was the summerhouse built into the branches of the oak tree. John leapt up into this now to address his guests.

'I'd like to welcome you all here today on this very auspicious occasion. It's a time of new beginnings – a new baby, a new estate and a new wine. I invite you all to sample the fruit of the latest cultivar, our very own Semillon,' he said, holding the glass up to the light. 'I ask you first to join me in a toast to my son and heir Charles Edward du Rand, named after my brother and my uncle,' he said, gesturing towards Edward. After the mumblings of 'Charles Edward' were fading away, John called out again. 'And now please join me in another toast. We're living in an exciting time in Europe. Napoleon is defeated at last, securely incarcerated at Longwood on St Helena. It's a new age of freedom for the common man; freedom from the tyrant in Europe and Africa too. The English are victorious at last. Let's drink to this new English colony!'

There was a general hubbub as people raised their glasses and the voices joined in unison: 'To the new English colony!'

There was a movement among the group and a tall fair man stood forward. He opened his mouth to speak, then thought better of it and turned away, but not before Charlotte had recognised him. It was Paul. She had not seen him since that last painful meeting at L'Ourmarin. He detached himself from the group and walked over to where a young woman sat under the shade of an oak tree. As he approached she stood up and it was obvious that she was pregnant. 'That must be Susanna,' thought Charlotte. 'What on earth are they doing here?' Then she remembered Etienne's letter to her father. Paul and Susanna had got married in January and were to live on Susanna's father's wine estate in Constantia.

Charlotte hesitated. Had Paul seen her? Was he deliberately ignoring her? Should she speak to him or pretend that she hadn't seen him? She thought of their past history and her sense of betrayal and acute disappointment when she learned of his betrothal to Susanna, and of his mother's cold spurning of her. On one level she wanted to put all that behind her, but then she remembered Paul's actions in helping with Samuel Joseph. She realised that she was aching to hear news of her nephew, so she walked over toward the oak tree where the young couple were gathering their things, obviously preparing to leave.

'Mijnheer le Roux!' Charlotte's voice carried clearly across the lawn. He looked up surprised; then his face broke into a smile and he walked towards her in the sunlight.

'Juffrouw Lacey!' he said. 'How very happy I am to see you! I thought that you might be here.'

'John didn't mention your coming to me,' Charlotte said.

'Well, he probably didn't realise that it was me. The invitation was sent to Susanna's parents, the Cloetes, who are back on their estate in the Franschhoek Valley, so they asked us to come in their place. It's important to be good neighbours, is it not?'

'But if you thought that Papa and I might be here, why didn't you visit us before now?' Charlotte said. 'We've been here nearly a fortnight already.'

'Sometimes it is better to let things be,' Paul said. 'We don't want to stir up unhappy memories.'

'I don't see it like that,' Charlotte said. 'We always enjoyed each other's company before that unpleasant interlude with your mother, and I don't see why we can't continue to be friends. Our fathers are in regular contact. That's how I knew that you had moved to the Constantia Valley.'

By now they had reached the shade of the tree and Charlotte saw his companion: tall, dark and sloe-eyed. 'She couldn't be more different from me,' Charlotte thought to herself.

'You must be Mevrouw le Roux,' she said, extending her hand.

'Ah juffrouw, I am forgetting my manners. Please allow me to introduce to you my wife – Susanna. Susanna, this is Juffrouw Charlotte Lacey.'

Susanna extended her hand with a little curtsey.

'I'm happy to meet you, Juffrouw Lacey. I'm afraid that I do not speak English very well.'

'I'm sure that it is better than my Dutch,' Charlotte said. 'You're not leaving now, are you?'

'My wife is tired, juffrouw. As you can see, she is in a delicate condition.'

'I understand,' Charlotte said. 'But surely that is not a reason for your departure? The party is only just beginning.'

Paul paused. 'To be honest, juffrouw, we feel uncomfortable here in this very English party. We cannot celebrate the English colony with you.'

'Oh, please don't go!' Charlotte said. 'There's so much I want to ask you. How are your parents? Where exactly are you living? How's Samuel Joseph?'

'My parents are well, thank you,' Paul said, 'and as far as I know Samuel Joseph is too. We are living on Buitenverwagting estate which Susanna's father bought from Gideon Roussouw. It is not very far from here, just a short journey by coach or on horseback. Susanna is going back to the Franschhoek Valley for the birth of the baby. She wants to be with her mother and sisters for her confinement.'

'Of course that's understandable,' Charlotte said. 'But I'd like to have an opportunity to talk to you, to find out more about what has been happening in your lives. Could you come to dine while Papa and I are here?'

'I think not, juffrouw. We are leaving for the valley in a couple of days. It is a long and difficult journey, as you know. We shall travel by carriage as far as Meerlust but from there on Susanna will have to go on the wagon with the luggage as the pass over the Helshoogte Mountains is too rough for carriages. It is even difficult for ox wagons.'

'Would it not be better to go by horseback all the way?' Charlotte suggested.

Paul looked solicitously at his young wife. 'Susanna does not enjoy riding at the best of times, and we think that it is safer for the baby that she travels by wagon. In any case we do not want to take any chances, and we think that the sooner we go the better.'

'Of course,' Charlotte said. 'It is best that your wife gets well settled in before her confinement.'

'That is right, juffrouw,' Paul said, putting on his hat. 'I'm very happy to have seen you. I'm pleased that you are looking so well.'

'Thank you,' Charlotte said. 'I'm glad to have seen you too. Please keep in touch, won't you, and let me know how Samuel Joseph is getting on.'

'I promise that I will do that,' Paul said. 'I will write from L'Ourmarin very soon. But, for now, tot siens, juffrouw.'

'Good-bye, Mijnheer le Roux,' Charlotte said, shaking his hand, 'and Mevrouw le Roux. I wish you everything of the best for the safe arrival of your child.'

'Thank you,' Susanna said, curtseying slightly. 'Good-bye, Juffrouw Lacey.' And she put her hand on her husband's arm as they walked off to where their carriage was waiting for them in the driveway.

Charlotte felt a pang. Was she fated always to see the men that she loved walk off with other women? She remonstrated with herself. She didn't need to have a man to make her feel valued. In fact both Paul and John had, in their separate ways, made her feel much undervalued. Life required one to persevere and, after all, there was much to be grateful for: she had her father and her school back in Simon's Town. Meanwhile this was a special day in her family, and she turned with a determined step back to the party.

CHAPTER FORTY-THREE

An Eventful Return

The remainder of the time at Wittebomen was uneventful. Charlotte was keen to go shopping in the metropolis of Cape Town, as there were no shops to speak of in Simon's Town, and she wanted to buy materials and equipment for her school. The shops were very different from the shops which she knew in England. There were no custom-built shop-fronts, but goods were sold through the open ground-floor windows of the two-storied flat-roofed houses of Cape Town. She avoided the colourful market in the middle of town, and bought paints, paper, pencils, paintbrushes and slates from an inconspicuous retail shop that Clarissa Lansdowne recommended. Laden with packages, she made her way back to John's carriage, and as they rattled back to Constantia Charlotte found that she was longing to get back to Simon's Town and her charges. After the christening there was not in fact much more for them to do, and her father was eager to resume his responsibilities. After breakfast one morning he announced, 'I've had word this morning that a cargo of prize negroes is anchored in Simon's Bay and I need to get back as soon as possible.'

'Prize negroes?' Charlotte said. 'What on earth do you mean?'

'Well, you know that the Royal Navy has been responsible for intercepting ships that contravene the 1807 Act abolishing the slave trade.'

Charlotte nodded.

'The problem is what to do with the wretched cargo once the ships have been seized. It seems that the Navy has brought one of these ships into Simon's Town and is waiting to disgorge the unfortunate captives.'

'But what will happen to them?' Charlotte asked.

'They'll be apprenticed to anyone who is prepared to take them on.'

'Perhaps I could take a few to work here on the estate,' John said. 'Goodness knows good labour is hard to find.'

'They're not skilled, you know, John,' Edward said. 'They're from East Africa and Madagascar, and though they may be used to agricultural work, they won't speak English.'

'Well, they can't be much worse than the locals,' John said. 'Probably just need a bit of discipline, and I'm used to meting that out in the Navy.'

Charlotte caught the glint in John's eye and thought once again how alien his way of thinking was to hers. 'We mustn't forget that these are people,' she said, 'and there are probably women and children among them. They will need succour and support.'

'There you go again, Charlotte,' John said. 'Always championing the underdog. You don't know anything about these creatures. They're not like us. They're primitive and tribal. They don't understand civilised values that we have taken centuries to develop.'

'There's no point in continuing this conversation, is there?' Charlotte said, with heightened colour. 'Let's just agree to disagree. Meanwhile, Papa, I'll go and start packing. When would you like to go home?'

'As soon as possible. Early tomorrow morning?'

'Excellent!' Charlotte said, rising from the table.

* * *

As Charlotte and Edward rode into Simon's Town in the evening of a fine autumn day they could feel a buzz of excitement. People were gathering at the waterfront. Others were hurrying up the street. As they reached the stables of Admiralty House, Maria, Christina and Johannes' eldest daughter, came running up to them.

'Juffrouw Lacey! Juffrouw Lacey! There's a walvis! Come and see!'

'A whale? It's far too early for the whales to visit. They don't usually come before June.'

She looked at her father quizzically. He shook his head.

'Ja, I know juffrouw but it really is a walvis. It's at Water's Edge. It's a kleintjie.'

'Water's Edge?' Charlotte said.

'Ja, juffrouw where you took us for a picnic. It's a baba. I've seen it already. Pa saw it when he was out fishing this morning. It swam up on the beach. I knew you'd want to see it. Elsie said you would be back today and probably about this time. I've been waiting for you.'

'Well, if we're going to go we'd better go as quickly as possible. Four legs can go more quickly than two. Come on and get up on Amber's back.'

Maria stood on the mounting block outside the stables and jumped up onto the saddle behind Charlotte, who wheeled her horse and trotted as quickly as she could through the main street of Simon's Town. The townspeople were out in force, riding, walking, and running, all in the same direction. As they came to the hill going out of the town Charlotte urged Amber to a canter, and they were soon on the track leading down to Water's Edge. They dismounted and joined Christina, whom they saw among the gathering crowd on the beach. There indeed was a young whale, grey, about thirty feet long. Johannes and some other men had managed to wrap some fish netting around it, and now, in two boats, they were attempting to pull it out into the waters of False Bay.

'They must be very careful,' Christina said. 'They don't want the baba to panic. It could hurt itself seriously. But Johannes understands the creatures. He waited until the tide was high so that he could float the baba out and not drag it over the sand.'

'Where are they taking it to?' Charlotte asked.

'They want to take it out to the open sea,' Christina replied. 'It probably got separated from its mother and the rest of the pod and swam by mistake into False Bay.'

'Just like those early mariners who sailed into Cape Falso,' Charlotte said.

Christina smiled. 'Ja. It's a young male. Probably inquisitive and got side-tracked. His mother is almost certainly looking for him now. Mother whales get very attached to their offspring.'

'Just like us,' Charlotte said thinking of John and Charles Edward, and Paul and his unborn child and, of course, Samuel Joseph, whose parents had wanted so much for him but had been cruelly denied that possibility.

'I heard news of Samuel Joseph in Cape Town,' Charlotte said.

Christina turned to Charlotte, her eyes alight with interest.

'Did you, juffrouw? Who? What? Where?'

'I saw Paul le Roux and met his wife at my cousin John's son's christening. I asked particularly after Samuel Joseph and he says that he is growing into a fine boy. He's thriving, in fact.'

'I'm so happy,' Christina said. 'It's a part of Sam kept alive, and I only wish that we could see him again.'

'We will, Christina,' Charlotte said. 'I don't know how or when, but I know we will.'

CHAPTER FORTY-FOUR

The Shadow of Death

The incident of the beached whale was the subject of excited interest in Charlotte's school. Marie gained a new importance because it was her father who had seen it first and had been instrumental in its rescue.

'Pa and the other men took him out into the middle of False Bay and let him go,' Maria said in class the next day.

'Did he find his mother?' Charlotte asked.

'Ja, juffrouw, we think so, because we saw another large walvis and it looked as if they swam off together.'

'How old does your pa think the whale is?'

'He says six to eight months.'

'That means it was born last spring,' Charlotte said, 'probably last September. He would just about have been weaned. Do you know what that is?'

'Ja, juffrouw. It means that he doesn't suckle from his mother any more.'

'That's right. He was probably born right here in this bay and travelled down to the Antarctic to feed in the summer months.'

'Let's hope he doesn't get caught by the whalers now,' Maria said.

'I hope so too,' Charlotte said, 'but it's a bit early for them to be hunting whales. The pods normally come from June to November, as you all know.'

The children nodded their heads. They knew. It was an annual event to have the whale families visit False Bay every year. They used to play games seeing who could count the most.

'My Pa says that there are not as many whales as there used to be,' Maria said. 'He says that the whalers are greedy people and they are killing too many whales and if they carry on soon there won't be any left.'

There was a hush in the normally talkative classroom. They could not imagine a time when the whales would not be swimming into their lives.

'Whales can sing. juffrouw,' Maria volunteered.

'Indeed? Have you heard them?'

'Ja, juffrouw. Once when I was out with Pa in his fishing boat we sailed near a groot klomp of whales and we could hear them sing to each other.'

'Well, it's time for us to sing,' Charlotte said. 'Let's sing a fisherman's song.'

The children's voices rose to the ceiling, pure as larks, and across the courtyard. Elsie, kneading dough in the kitchen, smiled and hummed along with them. Edward, on his way back from the stables, smiled too. He popped his head into the schoolroom door.

'Good morning, Miss Lacey. Good morning children.'

'Good morning, sir,' shouted the children, as they all stopped singing and jumped to their feet.

'Sit down, sit down,' Edward said. 'That's a lovely song you're singing. Please carry on. Miss Lacey, could you come and see me after school?'

'Of course, sir,' Charlotte said, keeping to the formal mode of address which was appropriate in front of the children. 'I'll come at four o'clock, after the children have gone home.'

* * *

At four o'clock Charlotte waved the children goodbye and ran to her father's study. Edward opened the door to her knock. The expression on his face was inscrutable.

'Yes, Papa?'
'We've had some bad news, I'm afraid.'
'What is it, Papa?'
'It's a letter from Etienne. Here, read it for yourself.'

Charlotte took the letter and walked over the deep sash window where the late afternoon sun threw panels of light into the room.

Dear Edward

It is with a heavy heart that I write this letter. A terrible tragedy has befallen us.

Two weeks ago Paul and Susanna travelled back from the Constantia Valley so that Susanna could be with her family for her confinement. They travelled by carriage as far as Meerlust where they outspanned as usual for the night. The pass through the Helshoogte Valley is, as you know, not suitable for carriages, so Paul decided that Susanna should travel on the wagon with their luggage while he would go on horseback.

The first part of the journey was uneventful but there had been heavy rain and the road surface was much more uneven than usual. The storm water had gouged deep gullies and potholes in the road. It's difficult to establish exactly what happened next but it seems that one of the oxen stumbled in a pothole and fell, one wheel of the wagon got stuck in a ditch and broke off and the whole wagon overturned. The wagon driver who was sitting on top of the wagon was thrown clear but Susanna was trapped underneath. When Paul and the wagon driver managed to right the wagon again they found that Susanna was dead. Her neck was broken.

Paul laid her across his saddle and brought her home, but there was nothing that could be done, and the baby was dead.

We are devastated by this turn of events. As if this was not enough, a few days after Susanna's funeral, her father had a heart attack and died too. Under the terms of the will, Buitenverawagting is to be sold, and all the contents, including the slaves, are to be auctioned.

Paul is seriously considering buying the estate. He loves the

Franschhoek Valley, but it reminds him too much of what might have been. I think that it would be good for him to take up the challenge of managing an estate on his own. He plans to travel to Constantia soon to make arrangements.

There is another development as well. The wine cellar manager at Buitenverwagting is elderly and wants to retire. As a freed slave he is able to do that and we think that if Paul is successful in buying the estate, he should take Moses with him to take over management of the cellar. It will give Paul the support that he needs. We will miss him here, of course, but he has been training another young man in the trade, and Guy and I know the business well. It will mean that Heloise and Samuel Joseph will go too.

I'm sorry to be the bearer of such bad news but I thought that you would want to know.

Yours sincerely
Etienne

Charlotte felt as though she had been hit over the head with a sledge hammer. She slumped down on the chair next to her father's desk. Her memory of the beautiful young woman under the oak tree at Charles Edward's christening rose before her.

'I can't believe it,' she said. 'What a dreadful and unexpected end for poor Susanna. Can you imagine how Paul must feel?'

'Yes,' Edward said. 'Marriage, a baby, management of a promising wine estate...'

'All viciously snatched away,' Charlotte finished. 'Buitenverwagting – beyond expectations, yes, but not in the sense that the original owner intended. Life throws up unexpected tragedies. Poor Paul. He must wonder what it all means – what life is all about. What can we do, Papa?'

'Not much from Simon's Town,' Edward replied. 'I'll write to Etienne by return and we'll notify John. As he's such a close neighbour he will be able to offer a helping hand.'

'But will he?' thought Charlotte, remembering John's animosity towards Paul and the tension at Charles Edward's christening.

'I'd like to go to Wittebomen,' Charlotte said, 'and see if I can help in any way.'

Edward looked searchingly at his daughter. 'What do you think that you could do Charlotte?'

'I don't know until I get there,' Charlotte said, standing up. 'Paul has been a good friend to us, especially in the arrangements for Samuel Joseph, so I'd like to see if I can support him in his hour of need.'

'I'd like to come as well,' Edward said. 'I've got too much to see to here to go straight away, but James can escort you and I'll come in a week or so. I'd like to see John and Caroline and my great-nephew again, and then I can bring you home.'

'That sounds like an excellent plan,' Charlotte said.

CHAPTER FORTY-FIVE

A Promise to Help

John was pleased to welcome Charlotte to Wittebomen again, but she felt a little awkward on her own with him and Caroline. She missed her father.

'How very happy I am to see you, Charlotte. How long are you going to stay?' he said as he escorted her into the house.

'Not long this time. I have my schoolchildren to get back to, but I felt I must come and see if I could be of any assistance to Paul.'

'Ah, yes, a shocking business! I never liked the fellow,' he said, looking at Charlotte meaningfully, 'but I wouldn't wish a tragedy like that on anybody, and his wife was with child as well, I believe.'

'Yes, it's a double blow,' Charlotte said. 'I think that he's very courageous to be prepared to start again, and I'd like to help him in any way that I can.'

'And how do you propose to help?'

'I don't know until I talk to him and it's not appropriate for me to visit him alone and unannounced, so I want you to ask him to dine with us.'

'I wouldn't normally be in a hurry to socialise with him,' John said, taking her travelling cloak, which he handed to a black footman, 'although…'

'You invited him to Charles Edward's christening,' Charlotte interrupted.

'I invited the Cloetes, who've been established in this valley for generations. He and Susanna came as their representatives, and it was part of good neighbourliness.'

'So you aren't prepared to be a good neighbour to Paul?' Charlotte said with an edge to her voice.

'Yes, of course I am,' John said, flashing his brilliant, familiar smile. 'This is not the time for churlishness,' he said, meeting Charlotte's eye. 'We'll invite him to dine next week.'

* * *

They sat at dinner at the polished mahogany dining table in the agterkamer at Wittebomen. Although the manor house was built in the traditional Dutch manner with thick white-painted walls, a gable and a thatched roof, John and Caroline had furnished it in the English style. Charlotte reflected that the furniture, much lighter than the heavy oak favoured by the Dutch, contributed an air of elegance.

It was a sombre party despite the fine food and wine, as everyone was making a point of not speaking about Susanna and the accident.

John was the first to speak. 'What do you think of this wine, Mijnheer le Roux?' he said as he looked in his direction. 'It's a new muscatel. We haven't tried this particular cultivar before. I've decanted a little for this evening.'

Paul raised the glass, twirled it, sniffed it, pursed his lips and sipped thoughtfully. 'Not bad,' he said. 'It probably needs to lie a little longer. These Spaanse Druiwen do.'

'Mm.' John was not entirely pleased with this response but took a sip as well. 'I take your point, and have to bow to your superior knowledge and experience.' He resumed his meal before he said, 'Has your offer on Buitenrverwagting been accepted?'

Paul nodded. 'Ja. There were no other prospective buyers, and the executors of Philippe's estate were happy to let me have it at a reasonable price, but all the furniture, farm implements and the slaves of course have to go up for auction.'

Charlotte pricked up her ears at that. 'A slave auction? What do you mean? When will that be?'

'The slaves are part of Philippe's estate, but obviously he has no need of them any more, so they are to be sold. An auction is the best way of selling them.'

'Should get a good price,' John said, taking another sip of wine. 'Slaves are in short supply now that the slave trade has been abolished. I'll probably try to buy a few myself.'

'You wouldn't, John, would you?' Charlotte exclaimed, looking at him with dagger eyes.

John looked away. 'Why not?' he responded. 'Everyone has slaves. The success of our farms depends upon it.'

'But you can't buy people!' Charlotte said. 'That's immoral!'

'That's how it is, Charlotte. My priority is to turn Wittebomen into a thriving wine estate, and I'm going to do everything in my power to make that happen. There's a scarcity of labour in the colony, and the Hottentots aren't keen to work on the farms.'

Paul was silent during this conversation, and Charlotte decided that now was not the time to pursue the issue. She continued eating her meal and then said to Paul, 'When do you plan to have the auction?'

'As soon as possible. Definitely during the next week. The auctioneer mentioned Friday. I need some time to get things organised.'

'Is there anything I can do to help?' Charlotte asked.

Paul considered for a moment.

'Ja, there is,' he said. 'All the household furniture and fittings need to be listed – and the slaves. The British officials have started keeping a register of the slaves but I'd like to have my own list. I don't really trust these officials. Do you think that you could help me with that?'

This was not a task which Charlotte relished, but she had offered to help. She hesitated before she said, 'Yes, I could do that.'

CHAPTER FORTY-SIX

The Slave Auction

A week later, Charlotte rode over to Buitenverwagting. It was her first visit, and as she trotted up the driveway with John's groom she was awed by the panorama of the majestic purple Constantiaberg which stood like a sentinel guarding the estate. The bridleway led them past a green sward framed by thatched white-washed buildings.

'It's like a village green in England,' Charlotte enthused, 'with all of the buildings crouched around it.' The groom took both of the horses as she alighted at the entrance of the manor house where Paul was waiting for her.

'Come in,' he said, 'and have a look at the house, although it's not in the best condition at the moment with all the furniture stacked up ready for sale.'

Charlotte followed him into the house and was surprised by the size of the rooms and the light which seemed to illuminate every corner. There was a feeling of peace about the house which entranced her, but it felt as though it was marking time waiting for life to begin again.

'Where are the servants?' she said.

Paul paused before he replied, 'You mean the slaves? They're outside waiting for the auction.'

'Then we'd better go outside too,' Charlotte said.

They stepped out of the back courtyard of the manor house

and Paul led her to the slave lodge, a rustic whitewashed building with a gable and a thatched roof, which stood at the side of the rectangular green on which she had remarked before. Even as she watched, the mantoor was calling out the names of the slaves who came out of the lodge and stood in a line along one side of the green.

'The mantoor knows their names but he can't write. I'd like you to write down their names and ages and as much information as you can about them – their skills for example,' Paul said as he handed Charlotte a large ledger drawn with columns. 'I've put a table and chair here for you. Are you sure that you are happy about doing this?'

'Of course I am.' Charlotte willed her voice to express a confidence that she didn't really feel. The whole situation was anathema to her, but she had agreed to help and she was not a person to renege on what she had said, so she sat down at the table and prepared to make the entries.

'January!' shouted the mantoor.

'Ja, Baas.' A strapping black youth about thirty years of age stepped forward.

'Ontong.'

A Malay man, about forty, in a conical headdress, raised his head.

'Ja, Baas.'

'Rose.'

'Ja, Baas,' came the low voice of a black woman with downcast eyes. And so it continued until the entire complement of the slave lodge was lined up on the lawn. Charlotte found it difficult to believe that so many human beings could have been confined in an area about the size of an English cottage.

As they waited on the green with the breeze riffling the leaves of the oak trees and the sun casting dappled shadows, Charlotte thought how beauty was often deceptive and hid great ugliness.

There was a stirring and the sound of deliberate footsteps as the auctioneer who was to conduct the sale arrived. A barrel of a man with a voice like the sawing of wood, he took his place at a dais on one side of the green. In front of him were the burgers, men for the most part, Dutch, broad-shouldered and broad-faced with felt hats and leather boots. Since the abolition of the slave trade the value of slaves had risen, and there were many who were eager to replenish their diminishing workforce. Hottentots were generally reluctant workers and with more and more slaves being able to buy their freedom, the supply of labour was often problematic.

'First of all we have this fine specimen of a man.' January was pushed forward by an official. 'Thirty years old, born on the farm Groot Constantia, an excellent labourer, bought by Mijnheer Cloete to work in the vineyards. January is experienced in planting and harvesting. What am I bid for him?'

'One hundred rix dollars.'
'Two hundred.'
'Three hundred.'
'Four hundred.'
'Any advance on four hundred rix dollars?'
Silence.
'Sold to Mijnheer van der Merwe for four hundred rix dollars!'
'Now here's a woman, young, twenty years old – Rose – originally from Madagascar, unpolluted flesh!' His rasp of a voice was greeted with raucous laughter from the predominantly male crowd.

'Who is willing to take this wench?' roared the barrel.
'She looks a bit skinny to me,' muttered a voice. 'Probably not much good in the fields.'
'Might be good in bed though,' shouted another voice.
'What am I bid for her?'
'One hundred rix dollars.'
'Two hundred.'
'Three hundred.'
'Any advance on three hundred?'
Silence.
'Sold to the gentleman in the top hat.'
Charlotte turned to see with a shock that her cousin John had bought the slave woman. She felt revulsion to the inner core of

her being. She remembered their argument about slaves at the dinner table, but to see him actually buying another human being as one might buy a new horse or a cow, considering its physical features and capabilities for work without any consideration of its essential human qualities, was abhorrent to her. She walked over to him and was about to remonstrate with him when her attention was arrested by the sight a small child, a boy of about three who was standing on the dais.

'What am I bid for this lad?' shouted out the auctioneer.

'Not much good for anything! Too young!' came another voice.

'Just be a liability,' said another. 'Another mouth to feed for the next ten years before you can get any work out of him.'

'So what am I bid for this child?' the auctioneer repeated.

There was silence. Then a clear female voice was heard.

'Three rix dollars.'

Everyone turned to see who had spoken. It was the young female slave Rose whom John had just bought.

'Can a slave buy another slave?' someone asked.

The auctioneer looked nonplussed.

'This has never happened to me before, so I'm not sure of the legality of the situation, but do you have the money?'

The young woman produced a screw of cloth from inside her bodice from which she took and held out three shining silver coins.

'Why do you want to buy this child? He will just be dependent on you, and how will you keep him?' the auctioneer said.

'He is my son,' the slave Rose said simply.

Silence again as the implications of the woman's actions penetrated everyone's consciousness.

'You are assuming that your new master will provide for him,' the auctioneer said, looking towards John. Charlotte's heart missed a beat as she waited for John's reaction.

'Of course he can accompany his mother. He can stay with her in the Slave Lodge. Who knows, he may be a valuable asset one day.'

Charlotte was not sure how much she liked that last comment, but she admired the courage of the young slave woman and realised the awful implication if she and her son had been sold to separate families.

'You can be fairly sure that you've made a good investment there. You've got two slaves for the price of one,' she said to John, her words dripping with biting irony as she turned her back on the proceedings and walked over to the stables to find her horse.

* * *

The next day they gathered for lunch in the summerhouse in the oak tree at Wittebomen: John and Caroline, Charlotte and Paul, and Edward who had arrived from Cape Town to escort Charlotte back to Simon's Town.

'You must be glad that the sale is over,' Charlotte said to Paul.

Paul nodded. 'Ja, it's a relief,' he said, leaning back on the wooden seat. 'Thank you for your help. Now I can begin to build my own place.'

'Did you buy any of the farm implements yourself?' John asked.

'Ja, all those in good condition. I should be able to prepare the lands for the next planting.'

'And the slaves? Did you buy any of them after I left?' Charlotte said with a challenge in her voice.

'Ja, I did buy four slaves,' Paul said, answering her challenge as he fixed his blue eyes on her.

'Don't sit in judgement like that, Charlotte,' John said 'These slaves would rather stay at the place that they know, working for someone whom they know is a fair master, than go and work for someone they don't know, who might treat them badly.'

'There's no excuse for slavery,' Charlotte said, standing up.

'Charlotte, sit down,' John said. 'You can't fight every battle over what you perceive are human rights and wrongs.'

'But we don't have to support evil practices.'

'I don't think you understand,' Paul said. 'The slaves are

the backbone of the economy. Without their labour we simply couldn't grow our crops, raise our cattle or produce the wine that you are drinking now,' he said, pointing to the glass of muscatel that Charlotte had in her hand. 'Without them our economy would collapse and then where would we be?'

'There is another alternative,' Charlotte said, putting down her wine glass on the table with a determined thud. 'You could set them free or allow them to work for you out of choice. But would you be prepared to take that risk? Whether you like it or not, that change is going to come sooner or later, and I would have thought that it would be better to be ahead of the legislation.'

She stalked across to the ladder where she turned and looked at Paul.

'I think that I should probably say goodbye. My father and I are planning to return to Simon's Town early tomorrow, aren't we, Papa?' she said, looking at her father. 'So I need to go and start packing. I'll see you gentlemen later.' With that she stepped quickly down the ladder of the summerhouse and walked off towards the house.

CHAPTER FORTY-SEVEN

A Proposal

As Charlotte had told Paul, she and her father had decided to return to Simon's Bay on the day after the luncheon in the tree house. Edward was anxious to get back because a post rider had brought him news that another slave ship had been intercepted. On her part, Charlotte was eager to see her schoolchildren again and resume the harmonious rhythm of her Simon's Town life. She was deeply troubled about the slave auction. She had known of course, that although the slave trade had been abolished, slavery was still practised, and she had seen slaves working in Simon's Town, Cape Town and Franschhoek, but the stark reality of the commercial transactions shot through her like a bullet. She was disappointed when Edward told her that he needed to collect some papers from Governor Somerset in the city and that they would have to leave the following day.

To make the most of the last day in Constantia Charlotte decided to take a farewell ride around the Wittebomen estate. She was not inclined to watch the slaves working in the vineyard, so she turned her horse down the avenue of oaks that led towards the entrance gates. The trees were a russet glow and she savoured the sharp autumn air as she trotted lightly down the avenue. Suddenly the morning quiet was punctured by the sound of galloping hooves and a horse appeared lathered in sweat, its rider urging it on. As he saw her he reigned in his horse so that the animal reared up on its hind legs with a whinny.

'Mijnheer le Roux! What a dramatic entrance! What has happened?' she said, noting his heightened colour and his breathing coming in gasps.

'Juffrouw Lacey! Thank God you haven't left yet!'

'But what is the matter? What are you doing here so early?'

'I hoped that I might catch you before you left. Aren't you leaving today?'

'We were, but as my father has to collect some documents in Cape Town we decided that we would leave early tomorrow.'

It was a few moments before Paul could bring his mount and his heaving chest under control.

'Do you think that we could talk somewhere quiet, just the two of us?' he said.

Charlotte considered. 'Yes, I suppose so,' she said tentatively. 'Would you like to go and sit in the summerhouse? That's private and we won't be disturbed at this time of the day.'

Together they rode to the stables where a groom took over the horses, and Charlotte led the way to the summerhouse nestling in the crook of the giant oak tree where they had had lunch the day before. They climbed the ladder and sat down on the rustic benches.

'Would you like a dish of tea?' Charlotte said, realising even as she said it how banal and inappropriate the offer was.

'No, I don't want tea, thank you. I just want to talk to you.'

Charlotte sat back on the bench and waited while Paul fiddled with his riding crop and seemed to be studying the floor of the summerhouse. After what seemed an interminable silence Charlotte eventually spoke.

'What do you want to talk to me about?'

'I can't bear the thought of you disappearing out of my life again.'

'I'm only going back to Simon's Town. It's not the other side of the world,' said Charlotte in a bantering tone.

'I know, but you're so involved in your life there and I'm so involved in my life here that we might as well be on different planets. I don't know when I'll see you again.'

'Papa and I are bound to be in Cape Town again in the next few months.'

'The next few months is not soon enough, juffrouw. I need to be sure that I see you again soon.'

Charlotte looked at him with a question written over her face.

'I think that I'm in love with you. I think that I have been in love with you since we first met.'

Charlotte was stunned. She looked wonderingly at him, remembering that first magical evening in the moonlight at L'Ourmarin, the painful meeting with his mother in the wine cellar and his subsequent admission that he and Susanna were engaged.

'But you married Susanna! And as your mother told me that was a plan from your cradles.'

'That's what I wanted to talk to you about that day at L'Ourmarin.'

'You told me that what your mother said was true,' Charlotte insisted.

'Please don't mention my mother. I would have broken the engagement for you and I think she realised that. That was why she intervened in the way that she did. I wanted you to know how I felt even though I knew that you were engaged to John, although when we stayed with you in Simon's Town I suspected that things were not as happy as they might have been.'

'You're right there,' Charlotte said, remembering the scene when she had told John that she intended to escort Samuel Joseph to L'Ourmarin.

'When I met you I realised for the first time what a relationship between a man and a woman could be. Not just the playing out of roles but a sincere friendship and a sharing of ideas…'

'But we have very different ideas,' Charlotte interrupted, remembering their last conversation. 'On slaves for example.'

'Ja, juffrouw, I know,' Paul said, standing up and walking over to the railing of the summerhouse from where he could see the slaves toiling in the vineyard. 'I have thought a great deal about what you said and I think that you are right. I know that I have slaves, but can you understand that I have never thought before that there was anything wrong with that? My family has owned slaves in the Cape for over a hundred years. We have three or four generations of some slave families at L'Ourmarin. That's just how it has always been.'

'But surely you must have thought about it, discussed it at some time. What about all that has been written since the Revolution about the rights of man?'

'I think you don't realise how cut off we are in Franschhoek,' Paul said, turning to look at her. 'We get the Gazette from Cape Town occasionally, but that is months behind the news in Europe, and a lot of those books you talk about are just not easily available.'

'But what about the church? Your family goes to church. There must have been sermons on the evils of slavery.'

Paul shook his head. 'Our religion confirms our way of life. The Bible often makes reference to slaves.'

Charlotte looked at Paul and said nothing as he continued with deliberate emphasis on his words. 'I'd like to work out a way of setting my slaves free so that they are independent workers.'

'This is a change of heart since yesterday,' Charlotte said. 'Two days ago you bought four slaves and seemed to be delighted with your purchase.'

'I know, I know, juffrouw, but when you challenged me yesterday, you forced me to think seriously about my actions. I'd like to change things and I'd like you to be by my side to help me do that.'

'What are you trying to say?' Charlotte said, looking at those blue eyes that she had come to know so well in the past.

'Will you marry me?'

Charlotte stood up.

'Indecent haste, Mijnheer le Roux. Your wife has been dead only two months. In fact this is probably just a response to your loss,' she said, remembering the fair Susanna with Paul under these very oak trees three short months ago.

'Ja, I know what it looks like, although as I told you, my ancestors,' he said with a twinkle, 'Pierre and Isabeau, who had lost their spouses on the voyage from the Netherlands had remarried by the time they arrived in Table Bay. The Le Rouxs don't like to be lonely.'

Charlotte did not respond to this attempt at humour. 'But you told me that you loved Susanna. You told me yourself at L'Ourmarin, after your mother did, of course.'

'Please don't keep referring to my mother,' Paul said with a flash of impatience. 'It is true that I did love Susanna and, in a sense I still do, but I love you too in a much more passionate way. Don't you think that it's possible to love two people at the same time?'

Charlotte thought about this and smiled to herself. Paul's words echoed those of her father when she had returned from her last visit to L'Ourmarin. Although she had not admitted it to him, that was exactly how she had felt when she had met Paul but was still engaged to John. She had realised that she loved both men but in different ways. And she had been confused.

'I think that we belong together,' Paul continued. 'We could be helpmeets and strength to each other. We could show the world that the French and English can make a harmonious match.'

'You're not a proper Frenchman, you know. You're more Dutch than French. You've just got a French name. My family is just as French as yours, probably more so. As I think I told you, the Laceys were Normans who came to England with William the Conqueror in 1066, and my cousin John has a French name too, du Rand. His parents were murdered by the mob in Paris.'

'You see, we do have a lot in common,' Paul said. 'I've never met anyone like you and I don't want you to go away. It's like a light going out.'

'Well, I'm not going very far away,' Charlotte said in a softened tone. 'Simon's Town is just a day's ride away. It's much closer to Constantia than the Franschhoek Valley.'

'Yes – that's one of the reasons why I decided to return to Constantia,' said Paul, 'so that I could be closer to you. And I thought that bringing Moses and Heloise and Samuel Joseph would ensure that you would visit.'

Charlotte's eyes lit up as she heard mention of her nephew.

'When are they coming?' she said.

'As soon as things are sorted out here. I'm going to convert the Slave Lodge into a cottage for them, with the green in front which will be a good place for a child to play.'

'So you're serious about freeing your slaves?'

'Ja, I am, juffrouw. That's why I have to ensure that Buitenverwagting is prosperous, that it makes a profit, so that I can pay fair wages and free the slaves that I own. I can't do it all at once, you understand, or I will go bankrupt, which is what many of the Dutch farmers fear with the British moves towards the abolition of slavery.'

Charlotte caught the expression in Paul's eyes. There was no doubting his sincerity.

'I admire your courage,' she said. 'Why don't you come and visit us in Simon's Town and we can talk about it all with no pressures, at peace.'

'I'd like to do that,' Paul said, offering her his hand to help her down the ladder of the summerhouse. 'I hope to be with you and your father at Admiralty House in the next month.'

CHAPTER FORTY-EIGHT

The Slave Ship

On the journey back to Simon's Town Charlotte was preoccupied with the conversation she had had with Paul. Edward, on his part, also had much to think about. The disembarkation of slave ships was a tricky business and usually involved the army which was why he had had to go into Cape Town the previous day to make contact with the military headquarters and collect documentation.

They had travelled some distance beyond Wynberg before Charlotte broke the silence.

'You seem troubled Papa?'

'It's this capture of the slave ship.'

'It's not long since the last one. In fact we were on the journey from Wittebomen after Charles Edward's christening.'

'Yes, our Navy is being very conscientious in capturing slave ships,' Edward said dryly. 'This one is Portuguese. I've given orders that they remain at anchor, but that can't be for too long. There is precious little room on board in any case and their supplies will be running low. It's a matter of urgency to sort matters out as soon as possible.'

'What will happen to the slaves?' Charlotte asked, thinking that slavery seemed to dominate her consciousness at every turn.

'We'll bring them in on the lighters and keep them in a holding area until they can be apprenticed.'

'Do you think that that will take long?'

'No. As you know from the slave auction there is a dearth of available labour, and people will be clamouring to get hold of one of the unfortunates. In fact, several officials from Cape Town and farmers from the outlying areas are coming to Simon's Town in the hopes of acquiring labour.'

'You're not going to have another auction, are you?' Charlotte said shuddering.

'No, of course not, Charlotte. These men and women will be indentured labour. They will be apprenticed to whoever takes them on.'

'At least they'll be free,' Charlotte said, thinking once again of the nightmare slave auction at Buitenverwagting.

'Yes, theoretically that's true,' agreed Edward, 'but I'm not sure that their living conditions will be very different from those of the slaves. They'll be living alongside them after all.'

'Why don't you take on one, Papa?'

'Me?' Edward was taken aback.

'Well, us. Me if you like. That would mean a home for at least one of them.'

Edward considered for a while, looking out of the carriage window as they came in sight of the shimmering blue of Muizenberg Bay.

'I would never have thought of taking on one myself,' Edward said, 'but with you it's different. You've already taken the slave cause to heart and this would be a logical extension of that. Perhaps you could find a replacement for Ellen.'

'I shall never find a replacement for Ellen,' Charlotte said, her voice shaded with sadness, 'but I could do with a lady's companion. I'd like to try to find a young woman whom I can train and educate.'

'There's only one problem that I can foresee,' Edward said. 'We won't be in the Cape forever. In fact, my tour of duty ends in just over a year's time.'

Charlotte was silent. Then, 'I'm not sure that I'm going to go back to England, Papa.'

Edward's eyes were saucers. 'What? You can't stay here on your own, you know.'

'I don't intend to be alone, Papa.'

'What do you mean?'

As Charlotte didn't reply he continued, 'I suppose you're thinking that you've got John and Caroline here, but it wouldn't be wise to live in their pockets. I'm sure that you wouldn't like that anyway.'

'No, I certainly wouldn't like that,' Charlotte said with emphasis.

'You don't mean to say that you'd live on your own?'

'Well, there's no reason why I couldn't live on my own in either Simon's Town or Cape Town. There are several Dutch widows who do just that. And if I were to make that decision I'd take the staff that we know and trust from Admiralty House – Elsie, James, perhaps Christina would like a job – but that's why I'd like a lady's maid.' She paused as Edward continued to focus all his attention on her.

'But I think that I might not be alone for long.'

'Why?'

'Paul wants to marry me.'

'Paul!' Edward's jaw dropped like a plumb line. He fell back against the padded carriage seat. 'Charlotte, you never fail to surprise me! The last time I saw you and Paul together you were remonstrating with him about his purchase of slaves. And now, within two days you are entertaining his proposal of marriage!'

Charlotte smiled and nodded her head. 'I know that it sounds implausible but Paul has changed his views on slavery,' she said.

'Just like that? I wonder who or what would make him change his mind?' said Edward, leaning forward again and looking at his daughter.

Charlotte shrugged her shoulders.

'And he's recently widowed. You don't want to be a replacement wife do you? You know what these Dutch are like. One vrouw dies and they find another as soon as possible to manage their houses, provide their food and produce their children.'

Charlotte burst out laughing at this. 'No, it's not like that at all, Papa. Paul and I liked each other from when we first met at L'Ourmarin. You must remember that.'

Edward did. He remembered the handsome young man who was so keen to take his daughter on a moonlight walk, and Charlotte's heightened colour when he asked her. He had thought then that there might be some spark between them, but he had pushed that thought out of his mind. She had been engaged to John and their marriage had seemed a settled thing.

'Yes, of course I do, Charlotte. You got on very well from the beginning, and he was a saviour in finding a home for Samuel Joseph.'

'Yes, I'll be eternally grateful to him for that.'

'But that doesn't mean that you have to marry him, Charlotte!'

'No, I know that, Papa, and I'd never marry anyone out of gratitude or because I've helped him to see the error of his ways. But I've always found Paul very attractive and, as you say, we became firm friends. It was a shock when I discovered that he was engaged to Susanna, but, after all, I was formally engaged as well. You can love two people at the same time, you know,' she said thinking of her conversation with Paul the previous day at Wittebomen. 'You said so yourself once.'

Edward nodded his head. Of course he knew. He had loved both Elizabeth and Agnes.

'I think that I said that to you when you told me about Marie le Roux's accusation that you were trying to ensnare her son. I know what it is like to be in love with two women, but Agnes could never have been seriously considered as a suitable wife, while both John and Paul would have been suitable husbands for you.'

'Although each of them married someone else,' Charlotte said. 'I have to remember that.'

'Well, what do you expect to do? You're not going to do anything in a hurry, are you?'

'No, Papa. Don't worry about that. But yesterday, when you were in Cape Town, Paul came to see me to declare his feelings and ask if he may pay his respects and come and visit us in Simon's Town.'

'He's welcome at any time. He knows that.'

'Yes, but how would you feel if he asked your permission to marry me? Would you agree?'

Edward laughed. 'You've never accepted my choice of a prospective husband for you in the past. You're old enough to know your own mind, Charlotte. You refused enough offers in London, didn't you? And you know that it has always been my dearest wish for you to be happily married and settled, although I thought that that would be in England, not too far away from me in Everhurst. I hope that you don't plan to move to the Franschhoek Valley. I can't imagine you living there. You would feel cut off from everything you know and love in the country – John and Charles Edward, your school, the sea, even the friends you've made in Cape Town.'

'No,' Charlotte laughed, 'and it's too early to talk about that anyway, Papa. Paul hasn't even proposed formally yet, but, to put your mind at rest on that score, he has decided to settle in Constantia. He has bought Buitenverwagting, as you know, but he's not going to be an absentee landlord like his father-in-law, and he has decided to try to develop the farm on his own. He likes the prospect of making a new start but, apart from that, I think he knows that I could never live in the Franschhoek Valley. I would be suffocated by those humourless Calvinistic farmers, besides which Marie le Roux would find it difficult enough to accept me as a daughter-in-law, but to have me living in the jonkershuis would be intolerable,' she said, thinking of the sharp-nosed, sharp-tongued Marie with her blackbird eyes.

'So what's the next step?' Edward asked sinking back again into the cushions of the carriage seat and thinking that although he was called upon to make weighty decisions every day it was a relief to have a daughter who could make her own.

'Well, I have to make up my mind, and then his intention is to speak to you, Papa.'

Edward raised his eyebrows.

'Well, he may be a French Dutchman or a Dutch Frenchman, whichever you prefer, but he still knows how to do things properly, and if I decide to accept his offer he wants to come and ask you formally for permission to marry me.'

'As I said before, he's welcome at any time, but when do you think he will come?'

'I think we'll probably see him in Simon's Town in the next month,' Charlotte said. 'There is much to organise at Buitenverwagting. He's converting the slave lodge into a house for Moses and Heloise and Samuel Joseph. He also has to arrange matters for the running of the house and farm. As you know, everything was sold at the auction, and although he bought a few pieces of furniture and implements he still has to acquire quite a lot of equipment before the beginning of the new season.'

'A new season indeed,' Edward said.

CHAPTER FORTY-NINE

A New Strand in the Tapestry

Charlotte and Edward slipped back into the rhythm of their Simon's Town world. Edward's immediate task was to make arrangements for the apprenticing of the prize negroes on the *Sao Joachim* which had been captured by the Royal Navy.

'I have been in contact with the Collector of Customs who arranges for the distribution of prize negroes,' he said to Charlotte at breakfast one morning. 'The slaves from the *Sao Joachim* are being kept in a temporary camp in the Dockyard. I told him that you are looking for a lady's maid, and he has found a young woman whom he thinks may be suitable. You could, if you like, go down and look at her today.'

Charlotte put her cup down on the table before she answered her father. 'Yes, Papa, I'd like to do that.'

'Do you want me to come with you?'

'No, I don't think so. This is something that I need to do by myself. I'll go down after lunch when I've settled the children to work at school. I'll ask James to keep an eye on them.'

'Very well. I'll tell Mr Edmunds to expect you,' Edward said, getting up from the table to return to his study.

* * *

At two o'clock that afternoon, after leaving the children under the supervision of James, Charlotte mounted Amber and rode down to the Dockyard gates. A sentry on duty at the gate directed her to a building on one side of the Navy yard which had a veranda in the front. As she approached, Mr Edmunds, a portly civil servant, welcomed her.

'Good afternoon, Miss Lacey. Your father told me that you would be visiting us. I hope that you will be pleased with my choice,' he said as he gestured towards a figure on the veranda.

A girl of about eighteen, with skin the colour of milky coffee, and a shining fall of ebony hair, stood with her head bowed on the veranda. As Charlotte watched she raised her head, a buck peering through the bush, and liquid eyes caught hers in a snatch of recognition.

'I'll take her!' Charlotte said to Mr Edmunds. She raised her hand to the young woman.

'Come with me,' she said, beckoning, aware that the girl did not understand English. 'Come,' Charlotte encouraged, pointing to the rough steps that led down from the veranda.

Like a frightened foal the girl stepped down to the ground where Charlotte took her hand.

'Follow me,' Charlotte said, leading her to the tree where she had tethered Amber. 'Climb up behind me,' she said, signalling with her hands as she climbed into the saddle herself. The girl hesitated then sprang up behind Charlotte. She felt intuitively that here was someone she could trust.

'This is most irregular. There are papers to be signed,' Mr Edmunds shouted.

'My father will see to that,' Charlotte said, aware that she was taking full advantage of the privilege of being the Admiral's daughter. Turning Amber towards the Dockyard gates, she waved to the sentry and trotted down the main street back to Admiralty House.

Their arrival caused a stir of excitement at the house. James was the first on hand to take her horse. The schoolchildren swarmed out of the schoolroom like curious kittens and Elsie, flour-white hands waving in the air, ran out of the kitchen as quickly as her bulk would allow.

'Ag, ma'am, what a mooi meisie!'

The girl shrank from the attention.

'Yes,' Charlotte said, 'but she's had a difficult time, Elsie. Just think about it. She's been on a slave ship in those cramped, dark quarters. She's been thrown off the ship onto foreign shores and been bundled together with others waiting for who knows what.'

'Ag, but she's thin. We need to feed her up,' Elsie said, waddling towards the kitchen.

'Not just yet, Elsie,' Charlotte laughed. 'Let's take her to her room first.'

'Which room for her, ma'am?'

'Ellen's room,' Charlotte said firmly.

Elsie nodded. She was surprised but she understood. The room had been empty since Ellen's death. 'Where's her things ma'am?'

'She hasn't got any,' Charlotte said looking the slight figure up and down. 'She will have been taken just as she is from the jungle in Madagascar and hurled in with others irrespective of sex, age or colour. The officials called her a prize negro but, as you see, she is clearly not a negro. She's got silky hair and a slight figure.'

'Nee, ma'am. She's more like us Malays that live here in Simon's Town.'

'You're right,' Charlotte said, 'but let's get her settled in. You arrange a bath for her, Elsie, and I'll give her some of Ellen's old clothes.'

Charlotte led the young woman to Ellen's old room, which was on the ground floor of the house near the kitchens with a view onto the gardens. The girl cowered in a corner: fear and bewilderment were written all over her face. Charlotte knew that she should just let her be. She motioned to the bed and the wardrobe where Ellen's clothes still hung. She smiled and said, 'This is for you. Elsie will bring you some food and drink,' miming the words as she said them, and left the girl.

* * *

A little later in the day Charlotte took a stroll around the garden and decided to go down to the Admiral's jetty. The harbour was teeming with craft. There was the *Sao Joachim*, the Portuguese slave trader, riding at anchor; there were several square-rigged tall ships, some engaged in ferrying personnel and provisions to St Helena; and smaller fishing boats heading out for an evening's catch. She breathed a contented sigh. She loved this scene of maritime activity. The smell of the salt air and the rhythm of the waves washed over her spirit like a balm. She had faced these waters many times in the last two years when her life was a fallen pack of cards and they had never failed to calm her.

She thought about Paul as she gazed on the water. She would hate to leave this bay which had burrowed into her being, but Paul's words rang persistently in her ears. 'I think that we belong together. We could be helpmeets and strengths to each other. Will you marry me?' She knew too that she would be marrying not only a man but into a family and that family loyalties ran deep, even if Paul was living in Constantia. Charlotte knew that she would never be acceptable to Marie le Roux and her ilk.

'And now what?' she said to the water. 'Do I accept Paul's offer of marriage? Do I stay here with Papa who needs me as a hostess and a support in these difficult times with Napoleon across the water and the frequent capturing of slave ships, and eventually go back to England? Do I stay here with my schoolchildren where I really feel I'm making a difference, and become a maiden aunt to Charles Edward and any other children whom John and Caroline may have?' A year ago when, engaged to John, she was weighing up her feelings about the two men in her life, the problem had seemed difficult, and it was no easier now, even though there wasn't another man involved, as Charlotte's life had become more entwined with those of other people.

There was a rustle and the crunch of gravel. She turned to see that the young woman whom she had taken on as an apprentice had braved the alien environment and had followed her down onto the beach. The two women looked at each other. There was an undeniable connection and Charlotte realised that another strand had threaded itself into the tapestry of her life. Here was a woman, younger than she, with nothing. She had left behind country, family and friends, and here she was stepping forward with courage to the person who offered her light. Charlotte knew in that moment, with certainty, that she would do the same. She loved Paul and she would go that way even though it meant marrying into a family whose culture and beliefs were very different from her own.

Charlotte smiled and walked over. She spoke and gestured to herself at the same time. 'My name is Charlotte. Char - lotte. What's your name?' she said, pointing to the girl.

The girl spoke for the first time. 'Vileelagani,' she said.

'Vileelagani,' Charlotte repeated.

She put her hand out to the girl who stepped beside her, and together they watched the tall ships lose their colour to inky blackness against the apricot sky.

CHAPTER FIFTY

Father and Daughter

Once Charlotte had made up her mind she longed for Paul's visit. Time seemed to move very slowly but in the meantime life demanded her attention. She and her father took to sitting in the evenings together on the veranda of Admiralty House if the weather was fine or next to the fire in the drawing room if it were not. It was during one of these evenings that she told her father of her decision.

'I'm sure you've thought of every aspect,' Edward said, 'that you might be here alone with me back in England at Everhurst and the long voyage that separates us.'

'Yes, I have, Papa, and I would dearly love to have you near at hand. But I have to follow my heart in this. I know it is the right thing to do.'

'You thought it was the right thing to do to marry John a year ago,' Edward reminded her gently.

Charlotte watched a log of wood crumble to ash in the fireplace. 'That's true, Papa. I was in love with John. He had been my romantic hero since I was a little girl. He was so handsome and brave, climbing the highest trees, riding the most spirited stallion, and then when he went away to sea as a midshipman under Lord Nelson he became a hero in my eyes. I couldn't imagine anything more glamorous than marrying an officer in His Majesty's Royal Navy. But I didn't really know him, Papa. Not as a man. We'd played together as children, but from the time he went away to sea at fourteen I never really knew him anymore. And I think he changed.'

'In what way, Charlotte?'

'He became harder. Is that what the Navy does to you when you're away at sea with only men around you? Do you have to crush all your natural feelings in order to fight your enemy who is probably just the same as you?'

'There's much in what you say, Charlotte. I remember one encounter when we captured a French ship and I was a leader of the boarding party. I fought with and overcame an officer of about my age. I didn't kill him though. When the heat of the battle had calmed down we spoke. I have some French, as you know, from school, and also from Cassandra marrying Pierre. It was then that I realised that his situation was much the same as mine. His family had a home in Normandy. As a second son he was sent to be an officer in the French Navy. He was a career sailor like me, not a follower of Napoleon. He had a wife and small child back in France and he was longing to get back to them.'

'But John seemed to get entrenched in his views on class and slaves and authority and women. There were so many things that I couldn't talk to him about like Ellen and Sam and Samuel Joseph that he didn't understand.'

'Would you have gone through with the marriage if that incident hadn't occurred in the Dockyard Church?'

'Yes, I would have,' Charlotte said. 'I think you know that. I had reservations but I would have ignored them, thinking that marriage would solve everything.'

'But a baby can't be ignored, can it?'

'No, it can't. And I admire Caroline for her actions. It was really a very brave thing to do and it could have gone horribly wrong for her.'

'John could have denied everything, couldn't he?'

'Yes, he could,' Charlotte said, remembering how John had come to plead with her the day after the wedding at Water's Edge. 'At least he had the decency to go through with the marriage to Caroline.'

'Yes, there was a whiff of scandal at the time, but the Crawfords managed to keep the whole affair quiet and the wedding took place discreetly.'

'Perhaps it's just as well for Caroline's sake that there aren't any Anglican churches in Cape Town, apart ironically from the Dockyard Church here in Simon's Town, and they would hardly be likely to choose that.'

'And now they're settled and respectable,' Edward laughed. 'But we're not talking about John. We're talking about you.'

'Yes, I know, Papa. With the wisdom of hindsight Caroline did me a huge favour in forcing John to marry her, but I want to marry Paul because I love him. I thought initially that he had been dishonest with me but I understand the reasons now. He's been a loyal friend and his support over Samuel Joseph has been inestimable.'

'I suspect that one of the reasons that persuade you to marry Paul is that Samuel Joseph will be at Buitenverwagting too.'

'You know me too well, Father. I do feel as though there will be a spark of family there from the beginning, although it has to be a closely guarded secret. And I believe in family, you know.'

'Yes, Charlotte. Family gives us roots and identity – a haven from the world. That's why I was so pleased when you were to marry John.'

'But he's still family, Papa. We've always been more like brother and sister and now that will continue.'

'So when does Paul arrive?'

'The latest letter says that if all goes according to plan he'll arrive this coming Sunday.'

'In that case we'd better tell Elsie to produce the fatted calf,' Edward said, leaning back in his chair and taking another sip of wine.

EPILOGUE

December 1816

The sun streamed through the windows of the Dockyard Church, illumining the young man and woman who knelt before the naval chaplain.

The gathering was not large. After the last experience in the Dockyard Church, Charlotte wanted a quiet ceremony. John had travelled over from Wittebomen although Caroline, who was with child again, had chosen to stay at home. Charlotte couldn't help but feel relieved by her decision. Her presence would have conjured up images from the last time when she had stood before the altar of the makeshift church. Paul's father, Etienne, had made the journey from L'Ourmarin together with Guy and Marie-Louise and her husband. His mother, Marie, had pleaded indisposition and did not come. Charlotte wondered if this was an excuse and whether Marie was making a statement about the marriage, but decided that overall it was a good thing. She didn't want any dark shadow to cross this day.

As Charlotte and Paul got up to sign the register a choir of Charlotte's school children stood and sang a song. As the young couple walked out hand in hand into the sunshine of the Dockyard the children laughed and clapped their hands. Elsie, in her best bright floral dress, wept copiously. A number of naval officers and midshipmen formed a guard of honour through which Charlotte and Paul walked into the sunshine to begin their new life together. They had decided to walk from the church to the party at Admiralty House. The people of Simon's Town lined the road. Moses and Heloise were in the crowd holding an eighteenth-month-old boy child with tawny hair and emerald eyes. 'Samuel Joseph,' whispered Charlotte as she picked him up and hugged him. Maria, Christina and Johannes smiled and clapped.

The party which was held in Admiralty House afterwards was long remembered. Charlotte insisted that all her friends in Simon's Town were invited. Naval officers and their wives had to be included as well. Never had there been such a party, which included the old and the young, the stuffy English officers and the raucous fishermen from the bay.

'Richard!' shrieked Kitty Clarendon. 'I don't think that I want to stay! These people are de trop at a society wedding!'

'Suit yourself, Kitty!' said her husband, who was beating his foot in time to the Malay music and eyeing up Vileelagani who was afire in a brilliant red dress. Charlotte had requested a Malay band with their guitars, whistles and drums.

Elsie had outdone herself with the food. There was waterblommetjie stew, bobotie, Malay curries, and, for the English palate, roast beef and potatoes. There were baskets of fruit and mountains of shivering jelly. The wine flowed freely – Semillon. Muscatel, Chenin Blanc and Palamino from the Constantia and Franschhoek Valleys.

Towards the end of the party Charlotte and Paul walked down to the Admiral's jetty hand-in-hand. In comparison with the energy and colour of the party, this world was still. Their feet crunched on the gravel and the water slapped the uprights of the jetty. In the distance they could hear the rhythm of the party band.

'This is where I first arrived in the Cape nearly two years ago,' Charlotte said. 'It seems like another lifetime. I knew nothing of you then.'

'No,' Paul said. 'You've come from the sea and I've come from the land, although a long time ago my ancestors came from over the sea as well.'

'I suppose,' Charlotte said, 'we're both heirs of wind and water.'

BIBLIOGRAPHY

Bickford-Smith Vivian, van Heyningen Elizabeth and Worden Nigel *Cape Town: the making of a City*. David Philip Cape Town 1998

Brock B B and Brock B G in collaboration with Willis H C *Historical Simon's Town* A A Balkema Cape Town 1976

Bryer Lynne and Theron Francois *The Huguenot Heritage. The story of the Huguenots at the Cape* Chameleon Press South Africa 1987

Burman Jose *The False Bay Story* Human and Rousseau Cape Town 1977

Burman Jose *In the footsteps of Lady Anne Barnard* Human and Rousseau Cape Town 1990

Dane Philippa and Wallace Sydney-Anne *The Great Houses of Constantia* Don Nelson Cape Town 1981

Danziger Christopher *Lord Charles Somerset* Looking at South African History Series Macdonald South Africa 1978

Dommisse Boet and Westby-Nunn Tony *Simon's Town An illustrated historical perspective* Westby-Nunn Publishers 2002

Dommisse Boet *Admiralty House Simon's Town* 2005

Fruits of the Vine Website *Cultivating in Good Hope* August 2010

Goodwin Peter *Men o' War The Illustrated Story of Life in Nelson's Navy* Carlton Books in association with the National Martime Museum, London 2003

Le Roux Tania and Malan Alet *The Huguenot Contribution to the Cape Wine Industry* History Series no 12 Huguenot Memorial Museum Franschhoek 2001

Loos Jackie *Echoes of Slavery Voices from South Africa's Past* David Philip Cape Town 2004

Loos Jackie sundry articles on Cape Town and slavery in South Africa during the early nineteenth century, many of which were published in the Cape Argos

Malherbe J E *The History of Franschhoek* History Series no 1 Huguenot Memorial Museum Franschhoek 1996

Malherbe J E *Pierre Joubert and His Family* Ancestor Series no 1 Huguenot Memorial Museum Franschhoek 1997

Phillipps K C *Jane Austen's English* Andre Deutsch London 1970

Rivett-Carnac Dorothy E *Thus Came the English in 1820* Howard Timmins Cape Town 1961

Simons Phillida Brooke *A Concise Guide to Cape Dutch Houses* C Struik Pty Ltd, Cape Town 1987

Simon's Town Historical Society Biennial Bulletins

Simon's Town Museum Archival Records

Tredgold Arderne *Bay between the Mountains* Human and Roussouw Cape Town 1985